717.

BOOKS BY
FREDERICK BUECHNER

The Return of Ansel Gibbs
(1958)

The Seasons' Difference
(1952)

A Long Day's Dying
(1950)

THESE ARE BORZOI BOOKS
PUBLISHED IN NEW YORK BY
ALFRED A. KNOPF

THE
RETURN
OF
ANSEL GIBBS

FREDERICK BUECHNER

THE
RETURN
OF
ANSEL GIBBS

ALFRED A. KNOPF: NEW YORK

1 9 5 8

L. C. Catalog card number: 57–10302
© Frederick Buechner, 1957

THIS IS A BORZOI BOOK,
PUBLISHED BY ALFRED A. KNOPF, INC.

FIRST EDITION

FOR

JUDITH

THE
RETURN
OF
ANSEL GIBBS

C H A P T E R

I

"THEY SAY that after two years I have lost touch," Ansel Gibbs said, looking not at the reporters who questioned him, but beyond them to the huge pane of blue sky where from time to time a plane climbed, slow and silver, into the bright day. "And out of touch with what, I have wondered? The state of the world? I wish I were. A man is seldom out of touch with the sickness in his own belly. They also tell me I'm unequipped to deal with tragic issues since by good fortune I've never had to deal with them personally. You will have to take my word for it that no good fortune is ever that good." But they were not to quote him, he added, his zestful, autumn-colored face for the first time smiling, and thus he both said and in effect unsaid what they had come to hear. This was his way, some might have held: rarely seeming to follow any single course, but, wherever possible, replacing a plus with a plus-or-minus, making of that little mathematical cross of Lorraine a kind of heraldic emblem.

By air he had arrived that early January afternoon to be

met by Porter Hoye, whose great face was clenched like a fist at what he felt to be the gravity of the occasion, and by his only child, Anne or Annie, Annie, as he had greeted her, repeating her name and holding her at arm's length for a moment, as though some sudden sadness rather than his triumphant return had reunited them. And triumphant it was, for if on one hand the newspapers printed the derogatory remarks of Senator Farwell, on the other their editorial views were for the most part sanguine, and one of them went so far as to quote:

> *Beat loud the tabourine, let the trumpet blow*
> *That this great soldier may his welcome know*

this great and civilized soldier for whom even the trumpets of the new year seemed to be blaring a welcome. Immediately upon returning, he received the press in an office at La Guardia field, Hoye at his side, Anne seated behind them.

Of course, he was aware that there was opposition to his appointment from here and there in the Senate, he told them, but as far as he knew there was no formal or organized resistance. Had he read Senator Farwell's speech? "Every man has his hobby," Gibbs said, "and mine is paying close attention to all personal attacks."

It was Senator Farwell who had resurrected an anecdote that had been current during the war. He told it in such a way as to suggest its having happened specifically to Gibbs; and although when pressed later, he admitted that there was no proving this, and although Gibbs and his supporters totally denied it, it persisted as at least a myth, as something which might very well have happened, which poetically if not historically had its own accuracy and made its own point. According to the Senator, who was speaking before the Senate Foreign Relations Committee, the event had taken place during those dark days of the Second World War in the winter of 1944. Gibbs, who was then with the War Shipping Administration in Washington, was supposed to have dropped into the Mayflower bar one late afternoon and to have been approached there by a young Air Force lieutenant. Seeing Gibbs, a man then in his late forties, wearing civilian clothes in a room crowded with uniforms, the young officer was said to have gone over to him and asked: "Well, my friend, and what are you doing to save civilization?" Gibbs's answer, as the Senator handed it down, was simply: "I am civilization."

This alleged pronouncement by Gibbs became a kind of rallying point both for those who fought his return to public life and for those who fervently applauded it. The former held that it represented the very crux of the matter. Not only was he possessed of megalomania enough to have made the impossible statement in the first place, a megalomania not uncharacteristic for a man of inherited wealth and social position, but in the pejorative sense of the word "civilization"—in the sense, that was, of "civilizedness"—there was an unintentional truth in what he had said. Was this urbane, detached, and moneyed man a likely one to appoint to a Cabinet post at a time of poverty, violence, and fanaticism? As for his supporters, they denied, of course, that he had ever said such a thing and proceeded then to say it for him. As much as any other single man, they suggested, Ansel Gibbs indeed was civilization, was among the rarest treasures that his era had yet produced: a living proof that idealism could still flourish in out-of-the-way corners of the political scene. In the end, it came to matter little whether the encounter at the Mayflower ever had taken place, to matter only what construction you gave to the statement which he had or had not made there.

Yes, he was glad to be back, Gibbs told his questioners, sitting at a desk in the airport office with the winter sun glittering from his glasses, though glad, too, to have been away—away for two years on a ranch he had in Montana, where he supervised the testing out of various theories of forest conservation. But he made no attempt to describe those years, those forests, and there was no echo of them in his expression as he rose to his feet and, in answer to no question, but rapidly, drily, to bring matters to a close, made a last statement. He would be going to Washington in a few days, a week, whenever his appointment was confirmed, and in the meanwhile he would remain in New York with his daughter and Miss von Louwe, a cousin of his late wife who had served as Anne's foster mother and from time to time as his official hostess. He believed that there were to be no public engagements in the interim—Porter Hoye confirmed this with a nod—but he would be busy enough setting his private affairs in order. He remained standing there a few more minutes, first alone, then with Anne beside him, while the photographers flashed their cameras at him. At last, amid a scattering of applause from the reporters, they left the room and followed the two policemen, who cleared a way through the little crowd that had gathered to watch him pass by. He walked, as always, in an oddly tentative manner as if suspicious of even the most substantial floor, his glance dead ahead, head erect, so that he could make his way past such public gaze as this with the same apparent unconcern as across an empty room. In all, he was impressive in appearance, and there was a keenness and vigor about him despite the whole chart of his disorders, real and rumored, such as a silver plate in his skull with a flap of toupee to cover the scar, a brace at his back, and some vascular disturbance, an intermittent numbness of the hands and feet which necessitated hydrotherapy and a careful diet. Louise von Louwe once told Robin Tripp—there was nothing that young man did not for a while try to discover about Gibbs—that, of course, he was a handsome enough man, dear Ansel, but just imagine him at night, undoing all the straps and buckles, putting half of himself away in a dresser drawer, and then scuttling, tiny and shivering, to bed! But if that or anything like it was true, it served only to accentuate the morning miracle of reassembly, for the world found Gibbs as reassuring in his physical presence as in the attainments of his statesmanship. Hoye had gone ahead and was waiting in front of the terminal to drive them back to the city. Several more photographs were taken at the car, Gibbs waved good-by with his hat, and

then they were off, Hoye at the wheel, driving slowly along
Flushing Bay toward the twin steel towers and mighty
concrete abutments of the Triborough Bridge.

Throughout the press conference there had been an air
of preoccupation about Gibbs, and not until they were on
their way did he give evidence of having returned in any
sense more complete than could be proved by the pictures
that had been taken of him, the words which he had spoken
and which the reporters had been then requested not to
use, the footprints that he had left in the melting snow on
the way to Hoye's car. In the back seat there was a large,
flat package which Anne insisted that he open immediately—a present from her, she said, patting his knee—and
he did so to discover that it was the framed original of a
cartoon that had been run in a number of papers following
the Farwell speech. It consisted of a single diagonal line
which ran up from left to right in depiction of the evolu-
tion of mankind. At the bottom was sketched one of the
mysterious, little one-cell organisms, then the swimming
things, the creeping, climbing, flying things, the mammals,
monkeys, apes, until finally, way up in the top right-hand
corner, you came to a spindly little caricature of Gibbs,
out of whose mouth issued a cloud bearing the words: "I
am civilization." Directly below him, because of the way
the diagram was drawn, there was nothing but three or
four inches of empty newsprint so that the effect was of an
enormous ladder leaning out precariously toward a wall
which did not exist.

"Where on earth did you get hold of it?" Gibbs asked,

and as he smiled down at his caricature, he looked not unlike it—the imperious, blunt nose and heavy chin might
well have been worn down by the rushing winds of history,
the puffy eyes as serene as though, having come from so far
and seen so much, they were no longer prey to surprise.
Yet at Anne's answer: "Tripp bullied it out of somebody,"
there was a coming to life if not a startling of those eyes, a
sudden turning away from the picture to her.

"Which Tripp?"

"The Tripp."

Gibbs leaned deeply back in his seat at her reply, his
fingers immobile on the cool glass of the picture propped on
his knees.

"Rudy's son," Hoye said from the front. There was no
need for the remark as explanation, and he offered it as
definition only because he was incapable of leaving anything undefined.

"Yes, yes," Gibbs acknowledged, "young Tripp, the
famous Tripp. I hadn't realized you were friends, Anne,"
and before he turned aside to the window from whatever
she was to say, in the rear-view mirror he saw her exchange
with Hoye the briefest flicker of a glance not of complicity
but merely of recognition that a deed had been done which
might better not have been, that a name had been named.
Gibbs was touched by their concern and located himself
by it, for the first time saw himself as having returned not
only officially, but specifically to them—to Hoye, all prepared to throw everything aside as in the past and once
again to follow him wherever his appointment might lead;

to Anne, a girl escaping her girlhood for she herself did not know quite what. For good works among the East Harlem poor under the guidance of old Kuykendall; for the ponderous carrousel that was the world of Louise von Louwe; for the attentions perhaps of Robin Tripp, Rudy's son. "Thank you," he said, tapping the framed cartoon. "I'm delighted to have it. And thank the boy." From the car window he looked down at the river below them, at the white arc of bridge slowly climbing toward the winter sky. He closed his eyes.

"The evolutionary ladder with Gibbs at the top. First-rate. And just last week, you know, I saw a foal born. So you could say we came face to face—man *par excellence* and beast." Gibbs had described the scene before, and the words came easily, letting his mind stray elsewhere, as he told them how he and the farmer had stood on a slope of pasture in the cool, bright sun and watched the foal deliver itself, wrenching, wrenching out of the sac, breaking the cord, and then struggling for close to an hour to rise to its almost useless legs until, when at last it did, trembling and erect there, the color of honey in the morning light, with the mare still down, her sides heaving, there had seemed such a valiance and triumph to the act that "So help me," Gibbs said, "I found my eyes suddenly filled with tears, and the old fellow with me must have thought I'd lost my mind. Was I all right over there, he wanted to know. Well, and I most assuredly was not." Whereupon, curiously and abruptly, what he had been thinking—wordlessly, as slow as clouds feathering and billowing in a still sky—and what he had been saying came together, and it was of Rudy Tripp's death that he had spoken as well as of the foal's birth.

"Dear Gussy!" Hoye sadly roared. "We've taken the wrong ramp down."

"So much the better," Anne leaned forward, talking to him. "We'll go through East Harlem and wave at Kuykendall sorting Christmas cards. Everybody thinks the poor love second-hand Christmas cards more than anything. We get piles of them every day."

And if there was a valiance and triumph to one, Gibbs thought as they rolled down the spiral ramp, perhaps there was a valiance and triumph to the other. Rudy Tripp's death had been of Rudy's own choosing. He had risen from bed one Saturday morning and had gone out into the back yard and shot himself. Sylvia was still in bed when the shot went off, and she was there again when at last Gibbs virtually forced a meeting with her six months later. She had been sitting propped up among pillows in a ribbony, pink bedjacket with her face all cold-creamed and her hands pressed to her ears as she had sunk back deeper and deeper into her pillows and ribbons and cried out, half in desperation, half in anger: "I can't hear you, Ansel. I can't hear what you're saying. I can't hear!" Couldn't hear, that was, because—with her eyes screwed shut and tossing her head from side to side *no, no*—she positively refused to hear, Gibbs's attempt to explain somehow what he had done, what he was now in her behalf prepared to do. He had been forced to dismiss Rudy because the man had been clearly on the point of nervous collapse. He had been keyed up, not himself, talking too much, boastfully, indiscreetly, to the point at which even those who loved him most, and there were many of them, Gibbs certainly of their number, had noticed it. And in having him notified of his dismissal, Gibbs had, of course, made it clear that his salary would be continued for six months, a year, whatever was necessary. Rudy had understood that. But "Oh, Ansel," Sylvia had said, her voice suddenly quiet, trembling with reproach, "you should have told him all that yourself, not just had some hireling do it. It was the last, terrible straw. His oldest friend. He never survived it." And then, as Gibbs had tried to protest further that it had seemed the less painful way for both of them, that he had had no way of knowing the extremity of his friend's condition, she had continued with: "I can't hear you, Ansel. I won't listen to any more. It's over and done with." And there she was, getting ready to put out the light, trying not to frown for wrinkles' sake, so what a time to start tormenting her. "You had no right to come," at which he had turned to leave her altogether and would certainly have done so if at the sight of his sudden dispassion she had not begun to cry and thus held him there for a few moments longer. She must at least let him send to her and her son the salary that would have been Rudy's, he had said, but she would not, and with her hands at her temples she had drawn the skin of her forehead tight so that there would be no wrinkles as the tears went trickling down. This had been fifteen years ago, and remembering it now, Gibbs glanced down again at the cartoon on his knees. Hoye had stopped for a red light, and at the curb a group of men stood warming their hands over an ash-can fire.

"The civilized human animal," Gibbs said, "unlike his simpler precursors, never merely swims or creeps or climbs, but manages somehow to do them all at once."

"Civilized human animal," Anne said, "and midwife to foals."

"It didn't know where to find its mother's milk," Gibbs said. "The general area, yes, but not exactly. So I grabbed it behind its damp ears and tried to show it. But I'm happy to say it was horse enough to balk at that."

"The farmer should have milked it first, you know," interjected Hoye. "The first drops have blood in them."

Gibbs reached out and patted his shoulder.

"Look, there it is." Anne pointed to the window. "*Pronto viene Jesús Cristo.*"

"Kuykendall?" Gibbs looked at the building that she indicated, a low tenement with the sign that she had quoted nailed above the door.

"Yes. I've told him how rude it sounds. Come *pronto*. Like Tonto to the Lone Ranger."

"*Pronto* isn't rude in Spanish," Hoye said. "It just means quick."

" 'Come quick, *Jesús Cristo*' then. Do you like that?"

"I'm sure Kuykendall would," Gibbs said. The old man would like it because it was direct and faintly scandalous. As a professor of Old Testament History at Harvard some thirty years before, he had scandalized Gibbs with his performances on the lecture platform or, more accurately, off it, for he would stride up and down the whole length of the room as he chanted the war songs, the taunt songs, the dirges of Israel. With his stiff, awkward body, his knees bent, his arms scarecrowed far to either side, he had acted it all out, had been Adam trembling in the garden of his lost innocence, Moses on Sinai, Jahweh creating the heavens and the earth; and when, with his head uptilted, his eyes staring in wonder, he had said: "Let there be light!" the young Gibbs had for an instant expected that there would be, that there could not help but be, whole new-created torrents of it. Yet if it was the extraordinary ardor and drama of Kuykendall that had originally caught Gibbs up as never in college had he been caught up before, it was Kuykendall's sober erudition—his uncompromising insistence upon the necessity of exposing the Bible to all the modern instruments of literary and historical criticism; his refusal ever to sacrifice scholarly integrity for the sake of sentimental piety—that had encouraged Gibbs to seek him out as a friend and to go to him more than to anyone else with the problems and ambiguities of his young life. When one day shortly before graduation Gibbs had told Kuykendall that he was considering entering the ministry, Kuykendall had scandalized him again. Kuykendall's voice had become almost scathing. "How comfy!" he had said, in parody hunching his shoulders, clasping his hands to his breast bone, delicately lowering his eyes. "The Ladies' Friendly. Bible class. Little pills of pious wisdom flipped out to the faithful every Sunday," and with his

long fingers he had flipped them one by one as he spoke.
"No, Gibbs! The Lord God of Israel is a God Who acts in
human history, creating and destroying, speaking His
Word to the particular man at the particular time—in the
year that King Uzziah died, when Abraham was ninety-
nine years old—not soliloquizing piously on truth and
beauty. Oh, I don't mean to confound piety, of course. Of
course. But hold on to whatever it is that's brought you
here today, Gibbs—and it may be purely pathological, always remember that—and take it not into the ministry but
into the world. Because you know the world, Ansel. That's
what I love you for."

"Sorting second-hand Christmas cards, Annie?" Gibbs
said. "That's what the old fellow's up to these days?"

"That's part of it," she said. "He wants very much to
see you while you're here."

"Which makes him one of about seventy-five I could
mention offhand," Hoye said. "The Senate committee
hasn't scheduled your hearing yet, but it can't be more
than a few days away. I hope you won't try to spread
yourself too thin, Ansel. You said yourself there'd be no
speaking."

"And you're prepared to hold me to it," Gibbs said.
Hoye had turned to him anxiously for a moment, his small
features huddled together at the center of a broad expanse
of cheek and balding brow, a caricature of the globe as a
great, headaching head. The source of his anxiety was as
plain as lines of latitude and longitude; not that Gibbs had
possibly decided to speak after all, but that he had done so

without informing him. "Well, you don't have to worry,"
Gibbs said. "I'm being appointed, not elected. I don't have
to campaign, and until the committee hearing I'll hold my
tongue." Hoye's gloved hands visibly relaxed their grip on
the upper part of the wheel. "I'll maintain a resonant,
public silence," Gibbs continued. Yet how implausible, it
seemed to him, for what was he, he wondered, if not a
language, a way of speaking, and for him to say nothing
was in effect, perhaps, to be nothing. His very life, he
thought, might be described as simply the turn of a phrase,
a phrase turning in and out among such lives as Rudy
Tripp's, Kuykendall's, Porter's, and Anne's, and as little
affected by them as a word by the ear of the listener. Yet if
he went to see Kuykendall, the old gentleman would be
forced to admit that he had indeed entered the world, had
even taken some part in shaping it. "But I'm on trial," he
said, "even if I don't choose to speak in my own defense.
Even if a favorable verdict is more or less assured, in the
meanwhile I'm on trial, and I know it. Not so much for
what I've done, of course, as for what I am. . . ." A voice,
a word, a photograph, a footprint in the melting snow. But
more than that, he thought, and tapped his foot on the car
floor, feeling it unresisting and firm beneath him, beneath
that the unresisting earth, and beside him his daughter—
he reached out and took her hand—the daughter of Corinne, his wife, who in dying had left behind her, like any
well-bred guest, no more than could be easily sent after her
in the way of occasional reminiscence. Holding Anne's
hand by the wrist, he raised it, then let it fall again. He

He must ask her more about this young Tripp. There are those who say that I murdered his father, he would tell her. Rudy flourished in an age of charming people, but he had been the most charming of them all. Everybody had loved him, though no one, apparently, enough to save him. Not he himself, Gibbs thought, not even Sylvia, beside whom, that night when at last he had forced his way in to see her, there had lain a hand mirror around whose frame was painted a scarlet ribbon linking little painted gold medallions that bore, a word apiece, the legend *Il faut souffrir pour être belle*. Gibbs would tell his daughter about that, too, he resolved; that, if anything, the reverse was closer to the truth. *Il faut être belle pour souffrir*. Not anybody could suffer, he would tell her. It might even be that you had to be beautiful to begin with, even as she was, Anne, and he looked at her smiling a little puzzledly at him, her hand on the seat between them where he had let it fall. Like his, her face seemed somehow windswept, blown smooth and keen, but finer-featured, not a beauty to catch a stranger's eye, but sufficient someday perhaps to suffer with.

"Of course, the verdict will be favorable," she said, "and in the meanwhile . . ."

"I'll see Kuykendall, for one," he said.

"And Tripp, too? He's dying to see you."

"I'm honored. But why?"

"I don't know why. I suppose just because you're you. Or to make sure for himself that you are."

"That I'm genuinely me," Gibbs said. "I suppose that's

it. That's what the world wants of public men—that we keep reaffirming our identities, keep proving who we are. The private man always needs to be reminded who exactly the public man is in order to help him remember who exactly he is himself. Nobody wants us to change, not even for the worse. And for the most part we don't. Those reporters at La Guardia knew in essence perfectly well how I was going to answer their questions. I spoke what I believed, you understand, but only on the subjects they wanted me to speak on. The ones on which they knew that I would prove myself to be myself all over again."

"You haven't proved it to me," Anne said. "Not once since you got off that plane. No, really, I mean it," she went on, above his quick laugh, laughing slightly herself. "You really haven't. I don't know who you are today at all."

"Well, my dear, then it's just because today I'm not dead sure myself. When you first get back from anywhere, you know, it's hard. When a man travels—through the air on wings, over the land on wheels—he becomes a kind of thing, an object in transit, and as for who he is apart from that . . . a man forgets, Annie," Gibbs said, "simply for the time being forgets."

"Then maybe seeing Tripp again would help you remember," she said, and he watched how all in an instant the current of her glance shut off, her fading half-smile alone remaining to brave out the consequences, whatever they might be, of her blunder.

"Believe me, just the mention of his name already has,"

Gibbs said, his voice quiet against the sound of traffic, the rising sigh of gears, alarum of horns, coming through the window Hoye had opened to signal from. Already the winter dusk had begun, the air of the city cold and gray, faintly bitter-smelling, people hurrying home. From somewhere a whistle blew. "You know that his father and I were very close friends. He shot himself—years ago now— and some people, friends of his, of mine, thought that to a degree I was responsible. You knew all this?"

She nodded. "Yes," she said. "Though never from Tripp. I don't know who. Aunt Louise or somebody."

"So if the boy wants to see me now, whatever his reasons, of course I'll see him. And tell him that. Whenever he wants. You arrange it. God knows, I should have done something about it long before this."

"And do you know why?" Anne asked. "I don't know what you're thinking, and I don't want to. I never do— what anybody's thinking. But the reason you ought to see him is so you can know for yourself you haven't ruined his life—if that's what you're thinking—because Tripp's *life* is . . ." her voice became high and almost incredulous. "I honestly think he's the happiest person I've ever known."

"When we were in college together, his father and I," Gibbs said, "Dr. Kuykendall once made a remark that neither of us ever forgot. He was talking to us about our futures, what was to become of us once we'd grown up, you know, and what he said was—you never knew what he was going to say—'I'd invest in Gibbs, but I'd bet on Tripp.' I don't think we were either one of us ever sure who was supposed to have come out on top by the comparison. Neither, probably. I don't know what Dr. Kuykendall would say now."

"Certainly that his investment had paid off anyway. So what with the other, he'd just about break even."

"And what would it be with young Tripp?" Gibbs asked. "Bet or investment?"

Anne did not answer immediately, but glanced outside where the street lights had gone on, and with them the lights on the Christmas trees down the center of Park Avenue. She worried the thin thread of gold bracelet on her wrist.

"Bet," she said at last. "Because you invest in what's safe, don't you? Fairly safe, anyway. And being happy somehow isn't. It's lucky. So I'd bet on his luck . . . oh, and on his *beaux yeux*, I suppose. Not really so *beaux:* queer little gray eyes, and when he smiles, his whole face simply goes to pieces, especially his chin. But you know. You must have watched his program. You can just see the luck in him."

"As a matter of fact, I never have," Gibbs said. "Watched his program. Because I never see television. But it's a great success, I understand."

"Good heavens, yes."

"And he sings, is it?"

"Not so much any more. But sometimes. He has an awful voice really—a kind of whispery, hoarse tenor—and he doesn't sing songs, just whatever comes into his head at the time. How he once saw Greta Garbo in Central Park, for instance. What he had for supper the night before, the weather report, a little girl he overheard on a street corner. Almost anything, and he accompanies himself on a guitar, just strums chords. Plunkety-plunk, 'and she said, "Every time Muriel kisses her grandmother, she gets a dollar." ' Plunk. That was the little girl. But he's gotten much more serious lately. He interviews people mostly."

"Little girls? Grandmothers?"

"Famous people. *Personalities*. Lord, I hate that expression. As if only famous people had them. But anyway, yes, he's very successful. So do see him."

"I will," Gibbs said. "You arrange it. Is that satisfactory with you, Porter?"

"I beg your pardon?"

Either he had not been listening to their conversation or wished it at least to appear that he had not, but in any event Gibbs was obliged to repeat the question, his tone serious now where earlier it had been amused, and seriously Hoye answered it. If Ansel wanted to see Rudy's son, of course it was satisfactory with him, Hoye said, his small eyes hurrying on anxiously ahead of his words and into apprehensions which he probably could not himself have altogether explained. Perhaps it was simply that Gibbs had described himself as being on trial, and in a sense, granting the metaphor, Hoye would admit this: Gibbs was on trial before the Senate, the issue being whether or not he was qualified for the position of honor and high trust to which he had been called. But this was not a trial that caused Hoye any very great concern, for its outcome would rest

on facts that investigation by serious men could not help
but eventually verify, he felt—the facts of Gibbs's years of
conscientious public service, of his successful law practice
which again and again he had given up at considerable
financial sacrifice. Let his detractors inveigh against him
as an impersonal, coldly competent, over-educated do-
gooder or whatever they liked. Let them caricature him as
they chose. These were the merest fancies; and whether
you agreed or disagreed with them, you could not make
them otherwise, could not hope to raze with them the im-
pregnable fortress of fact. Indeed, it was Porter Hoye's
conviction that if, in general, you stood by the facts, you
were standing on solid, even holy, ground. Yet here was
Gibbs idly straying from it, speaking not merely of the
tragic death of an old friend, a fact, but of the shadowy
possibility of his own involvement in it; not merely of the
birth of a colt, but of whatever had watered his eyes at the
sight of it; not merely of Henry Kuykendall, but of an
obscure remark that the old man had made thirty years
before. On the eve of trial, you prepared yourself to be
tried. You assembled the facts. You kept your eye peeled
and your mouth closed. You did not lose yourself in shadows. Good God, Hoye thought, you did not for an instant
lose track of what was at stake, both for your own sake and
and for the sake of those who stood to win or lose by you.
And as a taxi pulled out unexpectedly in front of him, he
pressed long and heavily on the horn, taking pleasure not
only in the strident noise itself, but also in the wonderful
predictability of it: you pressed the horn, and it sounded.

A fact. Whereupon, with a single, sharp cut of the wheel, he drew up to the curb in front of Louise von Louwe's house and braked abruptly so that Gibbs and Anne were jolted slightly forward in their seats. "We made it," he said, and turned around to look at them, his gaze unblinking, his little pshaw of mouth drawn tight.

On a side street in the upper sixties between Madison and Fifth avenues, the house rose five stories high between a modern apartment building and a much turreted and crenelated chateau which blocked all but its uppermost windows from a view of the Park. Its classical entablature was supported by a pair of caryatids which still wore patches here and there of gray, leftover snow, and within seconds of Hoye's ringing the bell, the heavy front door of wrought iron and glass opened, and a white-coated butler came out followed closely by Miss von Louwe herself. With her gray hair in an untidy bun, a fur cape askew on her shoulders, she waited on the threshold to receive them, watching Gibbs as, step by step, he climbed the short stone stairs toward her. Like a great rock at a harbor's edge, unmoving but vastly accessible, allowing the little waves to lap against its heavy skirt, she pressed Gibbs to her full bosom, kissing him on both cheeks, and somehow managed almost simultaneously both to embrace Anne and to shake Hoye by the hand. "Ah, Ansel, how wonderful!" she exclaimed. "Porter dear. And now we are all going to be famous again. Such a happy bother. And, Annie . . ." this over Gibbs's shoulder, for she had not yet released him, "he's already called three times this afternoon. I

can't think what you've done to the poor boy. You must all
come in out of the cold. It makes my nose run. The bags,
the bags . . ." which the butler picked up and carried
after them into the house, where all was warm, light, soft.
On a table in the hall Gibbs set down the caricature of
himself which Anne had given him, only to have Louise
von Louwe snatch it up, look at it with her quick, dark
eyes, and say: "It is never all happiness, is it? They shoot
at kings. But, of course, to say such a thing is to ask them
to shoot."

"Which I never did," Gibbs said with a laugh.

"Then you must soon," she answered, leading them into
the living-room, stout and heavy-footed, talking rapidly.
"It's a good remark. Classic almost. And it's true. You *are*
civilization, Ansel, and that is why I am so glad to have
you under my roof again if only for a few days. Maybe
you'll even be able to civilize this house, though I doubt it.
Only the other day Annie said to me, 'You spend your life
in this house killing time.' And I said to her: 'Kill or be
killed,' which is also a good remark. But she was right. I
need you here as does she. She does not kill time, perhaps,
but kills this poor young man instead. She will tell you
herself later. Now you must see our Christmas tree. I've
kept it up for you. Then a little drink before dinner. I
know you are tired. Porter," she concluded, "will you turn
off the lights, please?"

In this room which Hoye knew with its wood fire burning, its stout, mahogany furniture; with this woman whom
he knew, whose will he had drawn up, whose investments

he supervised; in this familiar, comforting place which in detail he knew, his anxieties were forgotten, his spirits restored, and, *"Enchanté!"* he boomed out in answer to her —his atrocious French a persisting joke between them— and switched off the lights. So there they stood, the four of them, in darkness broken only by the low fire and the lights of the Christmas tree, red, yellow, green, glittering against the tinsel and sparkling the tinfoil stars so that the room seemed all strewn with tiny flakes of color reflected bright in the dark, curved arms of the chairs, in the silver and glass.

C H A P T E R

II

Not long after Anne had met Tripp for the first time, during the summer preceding her father's return, they had been together at a dinner party in the city one August evening when the heat had been such—like breathing warm olive oil, Tripp had said—that it was suggested they all drive out to Long Island and go swimming. This, despite the fact that it was already after midnight, they decided to do, arriving at the beach nearly two hours later with their original enthusiasm for the project somewhat diminished by the long drive, but still determined to see it through. With the moon set and the stars hidden behind clouds, the night was so deeply dark that it was with an almost complete absence of self-consciousness that they undressed and ran down the slope of sand into the dark ocean, where trails of phosphorus followed in their wakes and the night air rang like a room with their voices. Then suddenly it was cold, and drying themselves as best they could, they put on their clothes again and would have started back for the city if Tripp had not noticed on the

horizon the first faint pennant of dawn so that there was no
longer any choice, they agreed, but that they stay to
watch the sun come up. So they sat huddled together
against a dune and gazed out at it in silence until all at
once, as the sky began to flood the color of roses or the inside of shells, someone said that this was Tripp's birthday,
and Anne glanced down at where he leaned with his head
on her shoulder, eyes closed, his cock's comb of red hair
tangled and damp, and kissed him lightly on the cheek,
only then with a start to exclaim that, look, while no one
was watching, like a flower sprung up overnight, his face,
which at dinner had been as smooth as anyone's, had
grown a dusty red stubble of beard. It was as if she had
seen a miracle, her voice cracking with surprise in the stillness of the morning, and she looked down at his sleeping
face beside her with such real astonishment that for a
moment or so it was for all the others, too, as if something
miraculous had happened indeed, and only then were they
struck by the absurdity of it, laughing at her—come on
now, Annie, after *all!*—to the point where in giddy embarrassment she leapt up from the sand and ran down to the
water's edge where, gathering up her skirt in a knot at her
knees, she stood to her ankles in the shallow water and
kicked little glittering sprays of it toward them. Rubbing
his eyes, scratching his head, and yawning, Tripp parodied
waking, gazed about him in mock bewilderment, and it was
not until weeks later that he told Anne that he had not
been asleep at all when for his birthday she had kissed him,
but had felt her kiss and heard her cry of surprise and all in

an instant knew precisely then that he was in love with her.

And what was she to do? He had told her this late one evening as they were walking back from the studio where she had gone to watch his telecast, and he had suddenly gripped her by the arm, stopping her, and said that from that moment on the beach he had loved her, said it with his sharp face grave and intent before it suddenly broke in two with his helpless smile at Heaven only knew what— the joke of loving at all, of loving her, this tall, thin girl, of telling her that he did on the dark city street. He kissed her then, on her lips, on her throat, and she dropped her purse with the result that *damn* was her first word, not spoken as response to him, but almost becoming so as she stooped down with him to gather up her scattered belongings and thought that oh Lord but this year was already complicated enough with her job under Kuykendall, who said always that he had let her father slip through his fingers and must tighten his grip on her; with Aunt Louise, who told her that it was all very well to do good works among the poor, but that she must move about more freely among her own kind and meet people. *People*, Louise von Louwe would say, tapping all ten fingers on the arms of her chair. And that was the last thing that Anne wanted, want- ing rather to be left alone, to be allowed time to prepare for people if people there had eventually to be at all. Mother- less almost from birth, and, in effect, fatherless with Gibbs again and again away, she had constantly been shuttled around to Aunt Louise, to the Montana ranch, to nurses and schools, and there seemed to her never to have been time enough to prepare for anything, so that whatever happened caught her unawares, she felt, found her ludicrously off guard even as now she was, crouching there on the sidewalk, picking up her lipstick, comb, letters, a pack of stale cigarettes. Her unpreparedness did not cause her any self-pity as the orphaned victim of an unsettled childhood, but instead a kind of embarrassment as at being taller than most of the young men whom Aunt Louise had from time to time summoned for her. And now Tripp had said that he loved her, and if her *damn* had blossomed to include people in general, it included him, too, unless, of course, she returned his love. With this suddenly in mind, she looked at him there crouching beside her and with something like panic knew that perhaps she did. She said only: "I can't get *up*. My knees have come unhinged or something," so he helped her to her feet, and, leaning against a store window full of Halloween pumpkins and candy corn, she said: "At least I understand now this 'It's so sudden' business because it is—suddener than anything else. There ought to be some signal about an hour ahead of time. This way's so unfair. I just don't *know*," she said— although her hands, held in his, seemed close to knowing— "whether I do or I don't. Love you. But if you make me say one or the other, right now, I'll say I don't."

He said nothing further himself except, lifting her hands in his and clapping them together twice: "Why, take your time then, for Pete's sake! And now I'm going to send you home," as, with surprising haste, he did, hailing a cab, thrusting her into it, then streaking off on foot himself without so much as a wave good-by, so that driving away in the dark she thought that she had angered him and would never see him again.

But she did, of course; saw him often afterwards that autumn and into the winter. Yet never once did he speak to her directly again of his love; and if she could have conceived of him as being capable of making mistakes at all, she would have seen this as one of them, for moments came when she felt that if only he would speak some further word or give some second sign, she would scatter all her hesitations in the wildness of fleeing to him. But he did not speak, and she felt that somehow it was not a mistake, and for that very reason her hesitations grew. A number of times she sat in the glass-enclosed control room of the television studio and watched him perform, to all appearances unconscious of the cameras lunging out like engines of destruction toward him, the blare of incandescent light, his face damp with perspiration and powdered pale to soften the glare. Perched on the edge of a table, leaning against a wall, or sometimes moving erratically from place to place, he managed in general to put the people whom he interviewed at such ease that their consequent candor and the incongruity of the subjects that they were drawn into discussing led many of his followers to believe with some delight that he was consciously making fools of them. But the interviewed themselves rarely did, and a marine general, who had spent most of his time talking about the care and feeding of dachshunds, sent on several days later, accompanied by a note of warm appreciation, a plump, red

bitch which Anne kept for a week until Louise von Louwe
protested that her house was menagerie enough as it was
and Tripp had to take it back. He presented it eventually
to a French *diseuse*, who had also appeared to be interviewed and had talked with wit and violence about corruption in the Chamber of Deputies. Numerous magazine
articles were written in the effort to define his charm—"the
barefoot boy in the Brooks Brothers suit," one called him;
another, "this glib, sly, funny, and occasionally infantile
Tripp, who looks like young Lochinvar and sings like a
fallen angel with laryngitis"—and there were few who,
even if unmoved, were not at least aware of it. Every night
after his weekly appearance, for instance, the telephone in
his apartment would ring, and a woman's voice, slurred
and hopeless, would plead: "Please, Tripp. Please, Trippy,
Trippy, Triptriptrip . . ." until he would finally throw
down the receiver in disgust. And all of this, whatever its
definition, Anne knew and saw, sitting in the control room
with Tripp himself visible through the glass in front of her,
his image flickering in the monitor on the wall above her
head, and there were times when neither of them seemed
more real to her than the other. Occasionally, even when
they were alone together, she discovered that for something like this very reason she would simply not hear whole
minutes of whatever he was saying to her because her
mind had been not on the Tripp actually with her at the
moment, but on the one who had once, if never again,
protested his love, and each seemed to call in question for
her the reality of the other. But as time went by, the dim-

mer of these two images became dimmer still until it disappeared almost entirely, and what she saw was little more than what the world in general saw: a young man whose heart's desire appeared to be only to charm whoever might find him most charming. It grew to be for her as if he had never been otherwise. The sunrise on the beach, the dark, autumn street, seemed only lapses in her understanding of him; the question of her response to what had happened there a less and less poignant irrelevance.

But then, at about the time when her father's appointment became generally known, there was a change and a quickening between them. As had not happened before, he began to invade other than the hours of her evening leisure, took to arriving unexpectedly at the store-front office in East Harlem where she spent her mornings doing whatever old Kuykendall might suddenly think to ask of her: going down to the courts to help a Spanish-speaking grandmother answer to a charge of littering; sorting clothes and shoes for a rummage sale; sitting at a partly charred roll-top desk and typing stencils for mimeographed announcements of "God help me, I don't know what-all, Annie!" Kuykendall would say, dropping before her a sheaf of material to be distributed throughout the parish. "Israel dies on a cross of shame and glory, and exactly three days and thirteen seconds later the tongues start wagging, the pens start scratching, the presses roll, till by now the glory's forgotten with the shame, and the cry from the cross is drowned out by the infernal clatter of typewriters. A scandal! And I add to it. I've lost my mind, of course.

Pronto viene! Stencil these!" Into all of this Tripp began to come from time to time, the neat, dark suits he wore on his program so integral a part of the public's vision of him that without them, in stained khakis and leather windbreaker, he walked with Anne the cluttered streets, unrecognized by those who were otherwise familiar with his likeness in advertisements, holding up the boxes, bottles, tubes, of the various products that had at different periods sponsored him. Once he led with her an expedition of children to see the Statue of Liberty; another time he spent the whole afternoon helping her paint the office woodwork including the charred desk; and Kuykendall liked him. He had a strength to him that his father, Rudy, had never had, Kuykendall told Anne. He had a way of making people love him, but, unlike his father, it was not a love that he crucially needed; take it away, and the chances were that you would find him still standing. To Tripp himself, Kuykendall said only: "I don't know what your reasons are, but keep coming up here." And that was the question, Anne knew; that was the cause of the change and the quickening between them: his reason, whatever it was, for coming up there to see her where she was least prepared to see him, dilettante as she was in a world of need as unfamiliar to her as her own, appalled by it, moved by it, to an extent rejected by it, for only Kuykendall welcomed her there while her co-workers, whose lives revolved entirely, as hers did only in part, around the poverty to which in one way or another they ministered, treated her with kindness, but without warmth.

"My poor, dear child," Louise von Louwe had said one evening at the opera, "the boy goes up to see you in that sad, grim shambles for the pure and simple reason that the boy's in love with you. Strike out 'pure and simple' because he's certainly not that. Just for the reason, then, that he loves you. I embarrass you? Good. Being loved is deeply embarrassing." And not being sure that you were was more so still, and not being sure that it vitally mattered to you was perhaps the greatest embarrassment of all, but the second act had begun before Anne was able to answer with this, and by the time the opportunity came again, she had thought better of it. In the affluence and tedium of her spinsterhood, Louise von Louwe sought diversion as a warrior seeks battle, threw teas and dinners like hand grenades, killed time like an enemy, and approached the subject of Anne and Tripp with a ferocity of interest. So better, Anne thought, simply not to bring it up again and, when it arose, to pretend indifference, a practice which came to affect not only what she said to Louise von Louwe, but also her conduct toward Tripp himself.

Still not speaking the word which she had at one time wished, now almost dreaded, disbelieved, he continued to confront her in divisions of her life where she had thought herself safe from him; and as his persistence grew, she made things more difficult for him. "My God, you give me claustrophobia!" she exclaimed once, partly in amusement, partly in real desperation, finding him reading *Variety* cross-legged on Louise von Louwe's front steps when she returned from shopping one late afternoon. "Go away! Kennel up!" But she could not depress the lilt of him, and even after making a transparent surfeit of excuses for not seeing him for as much as a week at a time, she would find him at the end of the week undismayed. Whatever that meant, she thought: either that he was confident that, whatever the temporary barriers, she would in the end inevitably return his love; or that he did not love her at all and had some other motive for his pursuit, a motive which she did not even try to guess until the day of her father's return when, as Louise von Louwe told her, Tripp had again and again tried to reach her by telephone.

In the middle of dinner that evening, he called once more, and despite a momentary pang at learning that it was Tripp, she left the table gladly, what with Gibbs sitting almost entirely silent, Aunt Louise and Porter Hoye chattering together like magpies, as she said to Tripp, and paying no particular attention to her at all. It was a long conversation, and the effort with which, on Anne's return to the table, Louise von Louwe did not question her about it was apparent in Louise's losing complete track of what Porter Hoye was at the moment roaring to her, so that Gibbs, who, it would have appeared, was listening to nothing at all, gave his stuttering laugh and repeated whatever it had been. Then there were several moments of silence in the flickering, candlelit air faintly scented with coffee until Anne broke it by saying that it was only the angel of death passing over. Louise von Louwe was obliged to wait for a number of hours before finally discovering what Tripp had been so eager to say.

A little snow had begun to fall, and Anne, waking up a few hours after midnight, stood at her window watching it. The flakes swarmed about the single street light like moths, and she remained there watching with the house all dark and everyone asleep as if of the entire city only she was left awake to keep vigil over it, as if in some fashion it was her responsibility to all who slept to mark for them this winter night of their dreaming. And it was almost as if she also dreamed, became part of the winter, of the swarming, soundless night until, without thinking why, with one finger she wrote the word "tomorrow" on the frosted pane and suddenly then felt that more than anything else she was hungry, a hunger that reminded her who and where she was, breaking the cold dream. Putting on a wrapper, she left her room and in the dark went downstairs, where she saw a light shining out from beneath the kitchen door. Opening it, she found Louise von Louwe sitting at a white enamel table with a bottle of milk and half of a cold chicken before her.

"Two women hungry in the night," Aunt Louise said. "As basic and timeless as mud. Sit down, my dear." Her fifty-odd years had left her round face almost entirely unlined, and her eyes were quick and appraising. She was dressed in a camel's hair bathrobe and fleece-lined slippers with her gray hair not in its usual untidy bun, but hanging loose down her back. She handed Anne a drumstick.

"Gnaw on this," she said. "It's snowing. For Heaven's sake, tell me what the boy wanted."

And who was this, Anne wondered, her eyes not yet accustomed to the light nor her mind to waking, still misted with sleep, night, snow, looking across the littered table at her elderly cousin chewing on a dead bird, grease on her chin: Aunt Louise, distant relation of her distantly dead mother asking about the young man who, as Anne remembered him for the first time since waking, jolted her fully conscious, the image of him almost blinding her for an instant. Level by level she had risen out of the depths of sleep, first to her dark room, then to the snow, her hunger, light, and now suddenly, quite as if never before, to Tripp, red-haired, gay-eyed, lean and tall as a sword, and perhaps, perhaps, loving, it came to her with a lurch of her heart, and "Oh Lord!" she said, "I'm not even *awake* yet."

"Here then," Aunt Louise said, pushing a glass toward her, "drink this," which Anne did in dazed obedience, yet not needing the flash of cold milk in her throat to come fully awake to what she had been asked.

"Oh, all he wanted," she said, "was to see Father."

"Why?"

"I don't know why. He was so eager about it, I think maybe it's all he wanted ever. I didn't ask him why."

Louise von Louwe accepted this in silence for a few moments, looking down at her glass as at a crystal ball, her hands cupped to either side of it. "Your father's a very tall man," she said. "Tall men stand out in a crowd. It's hard to resist making trouble for them."

"I hate to talk about people when they're asleep." Anne put her hand to her ankle, cold to the touch, and heard the ticking kitchen clock. "Because they can't talk for themselves. They're so helpless I could weep. Even the best of them."

"Let's talk about Tripp then," Louise von Louwe said. "I don't imagine he's asleep yet."

"The funny thing is that in his case it wouldn't matter. I can't think of him as helpless and unprotected even asleep. There's nothing to pity him for, I guess."

"Pity," Louise von Louwe brushed away a crumb from her chin and with it the word, which she repeated. "Pity. He's in love with you, is all. Why talk about pity?"

"Can you love a person without pitying him?"

"We've said the word too many times now. It doesn't have a meaning any more. Pitty cake, patty cake. Nothing. Only a sound. Say any word ten times, and it loses its meaning. A word like 'toboggan' takes only five. Do you love him? There's a question that makes sense."

"I don't know," Anne said. "How can you know?"

"I think the stomach knows first. I've always said valentines should have stomachs on them instead of hearts."

"I'm not even sure that he loves me."

"Be sure then," she said. "Mayonnaise? Cold chicken is best with mayonnaise." She pushed a jar toward Anne, who took it, and in thus tacitly agreeing with the dictum entered for a moment the world of the particular through which her cousin moved with such confidence. Louise von

Louwe knew the routes of buses and remembered birthdays, carried in her head the number of inches the sleeve of a baby's sweater should be and how many eggs were left in the icebox. This was an aspect of her which since childhood Anne had found reassuring, yet at the same time terrifying, for there was always the chance, she felt, that Aunt Louise might one day turn her eye upon her and itemize her very soul like the contents of a bureau drawer. What she saw, she named; it was a question only of how penetrating her vision.

"Of course he does," Louise von Louwe said. "Do you know any other reason for his spending time on you like water?"

"At least I'm beginning to think there must be one. I honestly believe maybe just to meet Father."

"And why?" The glazed intensity of her glance suggested that she herself knew the answer and had only a detached interest in whatever Anne's might be.

"Because of his own father, maybe. To meet the man who ruined him." The sound of her own voice in the stillness of the kitchen rang out queerly to her, the language of melodrama in which, even as she voiced it, she could not altogether believe, laughing at herself, looking at Louise von Louwe's face immobile as rock. "Don't you love action?" she said. "Even when it's tragic." And suddenly, gripping the cool enamel top of the table, she felt herself swept back into a dream which she had forgotten, had awakened from less than an hour before, and which she could not remember even now except that it possessed her

entirely so that for a few moments she belonged to no
world more real than it, a geography of search and twilight, the color of roses, Tripp somewhere, a bewilderment
of gladness and peril. Yes, yes, she thought, affirming she
could not have said what, unless perhaps the wild nostalgia
for her dream, rescued from it only by the drab tick-tock of
the kitchen. "Late," she said to her cousin, raising her face
as if into the brightness of a summer wind. "I talked to
Father after supper, and he's going to see him tomorrow—
today, in fact. Lord knows what Tripp wants. I can imagine the scene except that just because I can, I know it
won't happen that way. Tripp coming up to him and saying, 'You ruined my father and thought you could get
away with it. Take that, you old sucker!' Biffing him one.
Father slumped on the floor with his the-Honorable-Ansel-
Gibbs manner absolutely gone, and yelling for help . . ."

"Nobody ruined Rudy Tripp. I knew him, you know. He
ruined himself, was bound to from the start. You could see
it in him. He was too kind," she sighed, "or too charming
or too weak. There was something in him that begged to be
ruined. But in the end, he did it for himself. Not your
father or anyone else."

"Maybe," Anne said. "But I still think Rudy Tripp's
behind this somehow."

"Then let the boy come to me. I knew Rudy. Nobody's
ever made your father laugh the way he used to, although
he really wasn't especially clever. He was a fine swimmer
and a dancer, and he was at home everywhere. But he had
no private home inside of himself, if you understand me.

He was a tourist in life, a guest, and it was all visits for him: college, marriage, friends, everything he did, and felt. So when troubles forced him home, there was nowhere to go because he didn't have any home. Or if he ever had had, he'd forgotten the way there. I think he died of astonishment as much as anything. Who would ever have thought that of all people Rudy Tripp had no place to go home to? I can tell his son all this. Your father shouldn't be troubled now."

"I'm listening to you," Anne said, "but I had the strangest dream just before I woke up." Without any apparent awareness of what she was doing, she reached across the table and touched Louise von Louwe's hand as she spoke.

"What was it?"

"I can't remember, but it was beautiful and sad, and I'm homesick for it." Something more real, she thought, than the kitchen or winter, in sound like whispering, slow as the tides, now desperately gone.

"That's a superb remark to stop conversation with," Louise von Louwe said. " 'I had a wonderful dream, but I've forgotten it.' Anyway, anyway," frowning her way back to the tangible, she withdrew her hand from Anne's to wrap the chicken in wax paper, "whatever Tripp wants to see your father for—and I don't think you're right about it—this isn't the time for it. He has enough on his mind. Porter is worried about him. Of course Porter's always worried, but hardly a word from your father through dinner. Explain that to the boy somehow and say they can meet just as well when your father's been to Washington and the appointment's confirmed. Don't trouble him now."

"Damn it, I will! And just because it may trouble him. It's time he was troubled by me." Angry, her face grew younger as she rose, standing barefoot on the linoleum, her slippers lying where she had kicked them off under her chair. "Who is he anyway?" she asked. "I don't even know who my father is. You've always said, 'Don't trouble him,' and I never have. So how can I even know who he is when I've never troubled him into telling me? Maybe Tripp will find out tomorrow and let me know."

"There are things that have been in this icebox for so long," Louise von Louwe said, replacing the chicken, "that they no longer have names. Put on your slippers and go back to bed," she continued, clicking the refrigerator door shut. "It's wonderful to sleep with the snow falling."

"I was watching it before I came down," Anne said. "Like watching somebody with a nervous tic. Suddenly you catch yourself doing it, too. I started snowing myself up there."

"Good night, sleep tight," Louise von Louwe said. "Dream about what you'd do if what Tripp wants to see your father tomorrow for is to ask for your hand."

"Is that really what you think?" Her cousin had leaned forward to kiss her good-night, but Anne held her off, asking this. Without at first answering, Louise von Louwe turned out the lights and, swinging the kitchen door open, shot the beam of her flashlight into the dining-room beyond. Then, holding the door ajar with one arm, she half turned and shone the beam on Anne, who stood in the darkness behind her—just the face of the girl, the question still alive in her eyes.

"Anne," she said, naming the brightness before her. "And me," she said, "I," turning the light on her own face as she spoke. "You and I," she repeated, switching the light once more from herself to Anne, then back again. "We meet. An encounter. And encounters are as rare as rare. We're not unobserved either. There are ghosts. Rudy," she announced, turning her flashlight on an empty dining-room chair. "Being risen from the dead becomes him. Like a swimmer surfaced for air. Filling his strong lungs. Hair all plastered down dripping and parted in the middle. Poor Rudy. And your father. Sleepers are ghosts. See him pacing the floor of his dream. But the ghosts don't matter, the ghostly fathers. Only our meeting, you and I. That's the thing. I don't know what Tripp wants, to answer your question. My familiar gives me no particular information on the subject except that the time's not right. That I'm sure of. And that there's love involved somewhere in all this, however hard to know just where. Somewhere, anyway, between you all—Ansel, Rudy, Tripp, and you. Love. So keep your eye peeled, my dear. Be careful. That's all."

"Sometimes you scare me to death," Anne said, following her cousin's stout figure through the darkness toward the hall. "Please don't talk about ghosts. I hate them. You don't have any forebodings about anything, do you?" They had stopped at the foot of the stairs.

"Of course not, my dear. I always ride a broomstick at night. Pay no attention. Sleep well," and up they went then, separating at the top of the stairs, Louise von Louwe following Anne with the slender beam of her flashlight until she reached the door of her room. Once in bed, the girl lay watching the snow hover at her window for a while until, with her mind empty of all but the sight of the slow flakes, she fell asleep.

CHAPTER

III

"A sigh. A sigh. You're making a mountain out of a mole-hill. What significance does just a sigh have, for heaven's sakes? You collapse into a chair or something. You're tired. The breath comes out, and that's all there is to it. Some-times the breath doesn't make any more than just a noise, a groan, and sometimes words—*oh dear, oh dear,* or *well, well,* or, I don't know, anything really—but one has just about as much meaning as the other. As little, I mean. Everybody knows that." Anne had not thought that Louise von Louwe had heard her, arranging roses in a silver vase late the next morning, the scraping of snow shovels audible through the living-room windows; but then had come her answer: "Words always have meaning whether you want them to or not, even sigh words." Well, and why argue with her, Anne had thought, slipping on her overcoat and sitting down to put on her galoshes.

God help us all. The words had been Gibbs's. Actually: "Oh, I don't know," a long, almost indecipherable ex-halation, and only then, "God help us all," a sigh, as, sitting alone at the breakfast table, he had pushed his newspaper aside and indicated to Walter, the butler, that he could remove his plate. So when Miss von Louwe had come down something less than an hour later to find that her guest had already gone out and had then asked Walter how Mr. Gibbs had seemed, whether he had left any message, the report she was given consisted of those words which he had let escape just before leaving.

Seemed well enough, Walter had said, rested-looking and fine with his spectacles on and a dark gray suit; but then—these somber words. "A kind of a sigh, Madam, but as if he really meant it. I didn't think it was my place to answer. Just between you and me, Madam, you understand." Louise von Louwe understood well enough, made it clear to him with a glance, a pause, that it was also very probably not his place to have reported this at all, especially as doing so involved an imitation of Mr. Gibbs; for Walter had let his shoulders droop, his arms falling loose to his sides, as in a quite convincing approximation of Gibbs's voice, rapid and flat, he had repeated his words. Perhaps it was something that Mr. Gibbs had read in the papers, Walter suggested.

Whatever their meaning, the words traveled, gaining force as they went, initiating action. Louise von Louwe called Porter Hoye at his office, where he had only just arrived. He came to the telephone with snow still damp on the velvet collar of his Chesterfield, his face flushed with the cold, and, without admitting to any particular concern over what she told him, privately weighed the words

with great seriousness, from habit even jotted them down
on a pad of yellow paper, where again and again he found
himself confronted by them.

God help us all. A proposed combination of two large
corporations had him engaged most of the morning in
checking over the merger agreement, but in the very midst
of this, Gibbs's phrase continued to repeat itself in his
mind. Carefully scanning the newspaper, he found nothing
there that struck him as likely to have provoked it, only
the report of Gibbs's return the day before and a photograph that showed him at the airport waving his hat as he
was about to get into Hoye's car. Then, of course, there
was also the fact, as Louise von Louwe had told him, that
Gibbs had an appointment that afternoon to see Robin
Tripp—"for goodness only knows what purpose," she had
said. But Louise was, after all, a woman given by nature to
expressions of doom, Hoye knew, and easy and uncomplicated as her life in reality tended to be, she was fond of
seeing it and the lives of others as rich in peril, lions lurking
in the pantry. "If I were made of wood," she herself had
once remarked, "I would be a gallows." So despite her
present misgivings, Hoye thought, what real and factual
reason was there for believing that Gibbs's words at breakfast indicated a particularly troubled state of mind at all
no matter what he had read in the papers or how he might
dread an interview just now with Rudy Tripp's son?
Surely he had faced worse than this before and survived.
Hoye remembered standing with him on the roof of the
American Embassy in London one night during the war,

watching the bombs fall, thudding and blazing like the end of the world. For all Hoye's entreaties, Gibbs had refused to take shelter, and with the very earth shaking beneath him had quoted Caliban's "Be not afear'd; the isle is full of noises, sounds and sweet airs that give delight and hurt not," had quoted it with no semblance of wishing to make the dramatic utterance, but as if to himself and so quietly that Hoye had not been sure of hearing correctly. Gibbs endured. His opponents might call him unfit to deal with the realities of a grim century, and yet, Hoye thought, had often remarked, when the chips were down, it was, after all, breeding that counted. Gibbs was above all a gentleman, Hoye felt, and when a gentleman says: "God help us all," it is really neither God that he means nor help that he is asking.

Gibbs was a gentleman, and this counted dear with Hoye, conscious always that he was himself possibly something just short of one. Not that in terms of education and acquaintance he was not Gibbs's equal, he reassuringly believed, but, having grown up in an obscure New Jersey township as the only son of respectable but socially unambitious parents, he saw himself as possessed of the substance, but not the tradition, of gentility. In seeking to rectify this as best he could by all the more firmly establishing himself in this world that he coveted, Gibbs's world, he never in any unctuous manner emulated its ways, but with a kind of roaring good humor burlesqued them instead, boomed snobbisms, feigned horror at improprieties, was elaborately conservative in his dress, and in general endeared himself to the *haut monde*, as in his admittedly quite atrocious French he was fond of calling it, by the inverted reverence of his jesting. Successful as he was at this—partner in an old law firm, member of a half-dozen of the best and oldest clubs, the friend of men whose great-grandfathers had been friends—he strove beyond it for acceptance in the yet higher world of national affairs, and his success there depended, as he saw it, almost entirely upon Gibbs's. Specifically, it was on Gibbs's appointment to the Cabinet that Porter Hoye placed all his fondest hopes, and hence any suggestion such as Louise von Louwe's that his friend was distracted from it by some deeper concern gave rise in him to the most poignant apprehensiveness. "God help us all," Gibbs had for some reason said over his coffee, and God help us all indeed, Hoye thought, if whatever was in Gibbs's mind should, by dividing his attention, lessen his resolve to succeed. Senate confirmation of the appointment was now virtually automatic, Hoye knew, and ordinarily he would have had no qualms about it at all. But if on one hand Gibbs had long demonstrated the articulate dispassion with which he could meet the most clamorous crisis, on the other, of late, Hoye had remarked another aspect of him altogether.

He stared out of his office window as he thought, looked out at New York harbor, a coal barge roofed with snow, the water gray with winter. Gibbs's sigh written down on the pad before him, he drew circles around each of the words, drew stems and leaves on them like flowers. When the war had ended, Gibbs had retired from public life on the grounds of ill health, and it was true that he was generally overtired, that his circulation was poor, but Hoye had never felt that this justified the deep seclusion he had entered, retreating to his Montana ranch, where for two years he remained, receiving scarcely any visitors except Anne and occasionally Porter himself. Averse to all forms of physical exercise, he neither fished nor hunted nor rode. His interest in the workings of the ranch was nominal, and as a consequence there were no reassuring pictures for the papers to print of Gibbs enjoying rural life. He read a great deal, in history for the most part, particularly Toynbee and Niebuhr, and worked intermittently on an autobiographical account of the war years. Hoye had been allowed to read through parts of this, and it was only with the greatest difficulty that he had concealed his distress at what he saw. He had always regarded with astonished admiration Gibbs's grasp of nearly all aspects of total war, had heard him speak on anything from the eight-gun Spitfire to the Murmansk convoy with impressively detailed knowledge, yet in his writings there was little or nothing of this. It was introspective and digressive, a collection of impressions rather than an account of events. A drunken woman crouching in a doorway in Soho cursing into the night: "You rotten, lazy, stinking pig!" as Gibbs passed by, Gibbs stunned for an instant at the thought that she had addressed him, realizing then that she had not, then weighing the words *as if* she had: "It is a war of pigs, stinking from the sty of their own unfeeling, lazy in their humanity to a point of paralysis rotten beyond piggery."

The pride of an official at an agricultural exhibit at Victoria Station, pointing to the words "God Save the King" spelled out in stalks of vegetable marrow. "The majestic banality of the Empire . . . its king ruler over all the swans of his realm and, I am told, certain portions of its whales. If he is to be saved, it should be in the way that a bundle of old love-letters tied up in pink ribbon is saved or the ticket stub of an opera your grandmother slept through." A description of the face of Harry Hopkins as having "the look of a man who has peered deep into the dark night of his own soul for some trace of the existence of God and has found only Franklin Roosevelt." For page after page, Gibbs wrote of what was then the American policy of isolationism. Inserted in the manuscript was a photograph which Kuykendall, corresponding with him on the same subject, had once sent. It showed that portion of the black obelisk of the ninth-century Assyrian war lord Shalmeneser III which pictures Jehu, King of Israel, prostrate on the ground before his conqueror. "Such is always the fate of the nation that tries to maintain its isolationism by cautiously playing both ends against the middle," Kuykendall had written, on which Gibbs had commented: "As for the isolationist of the soul, the world does not graciously destroy him, but suffers him to live out his own isolation."

They were dark days indeed that Hoye had spent visiting Gibbs at his western retreat, reading over the pages he was in the process of writing; and they seemed to Hoye darker still for the absence in Gibbs's manner of any visible trace of the somber change which he felt to be taking place within him. For Gibbs by spoken word or act to have revealed his melancholy directly would have comforted Hoye, for then he could have challenged him on the subject, could have tried to reason him out of it. But instead Gibbs conducted himself with the same bland reserve as always, and Hoye had been obliged to conclude that the malady, whatever its nature and source, was at least for the time being beyond the reach of his therapy. And now, this January, with Gibbs's expectations at their highest and Hoye's helplessly dependent upon them, the symptoms were reappearing but no less obscurely: a mild distraction in his conversation upon arriving, a sigh at the breakfast table, and consequently, Hoye wondered, staring out at the winter sky, what could he do? Nothing, he thought, unconsciously saying it aloud to himself as he sat there in his office. If he tried taking Gibbs up on words overheard and reported to Louise by her butler, by Louise to him, Gibbs would be quite justifiably derisive. Hence "Nothing" Hoye said again, at which his secretary glanced up from her typewriter questioningly so that for the third time Hoye repeated it. "Nothing," he said. "Just a sigh."

Less than an hour later, Gibbs himself arrived at Hoye's office. Hoye had not expected him, and he entered unannounced, having simply walked by the receptionist, who, of course, knew him. He was carrying under one arm several flat packages wrapped up in brown paper and twine, and a cane. He laid the packages down on a table as he came in and stood before Hoye's desk, tall and stooped, with his head thrust slightly forward, holding the cane out before him. "It was Rudy's," he said. "Do you remember it? It unscrews."

He twisted the handle several times until it came off and then tipped out from the shank the slender glass tube that fitted inside of it. "Holds about three or four good nips," he explained. "I'm seeing Rudy's boy this afternoon, and I thought he might like to have it. There were some old pictures, too," he added, indicating the packages behind him. He had gone down to the law firm which still bore his name to dictate some correspondence, he told Hoye, and in a closet along with some other miscellaneous possessions had found these.

"We live in memory and anticipation," Gibbs said, putting the cane back together again. "The present is a kind of no man's land."

"Can I have a sworn affidavit to that effect?" Hoye had risen from his desk and put his hand on Gibbs's shoulder. His way was to roar the meagerest jest into the semblance of something far richer; but in this case the sharpness with which his little eyes looked out from his full, red face, the failure of his smile, betrayed a poverty of conviction that there was anything here to jest at. If only Gibbs would swear to anything, by that alone he would in effect create a fact with which Hoye felt that he would be able to deal. Without facts, a man was lost.

"You can have anything you want badly enough if you're willing to pay for it." Gibbs smiled. "Anything. I'm convinced of that."

"You've also got to know what you want, wouldn't you say?"

"That, too."

"And you, Ansel?"

"Know what I want? I know what I have, that's for certain—a future. A man with a future is how they describe me, my promoters. A man with a past, the opposition, and my promoters, too. Only they interpret it differently. A past sanctified by loyal public service. A past so plush and easy as to isolate me from my peers. You take your pick. I can't. I have to take the whole thing, my entire past which I am the world's foremost, if not unchallenged, authority on."

"The facts are on your side. I wouldn't worry."

"You're a lawyer, Porter. Facts don't take sides. But as far as the future's concerned, I don't worry anyway because—you're a good old friend, I can speak to you with candor—because I'm not altogether sure that I care vitally one way or the other."

"Dear God, Ansel! That's a terrible admission. Others care. I care. And the country, too, if I may say so."

"As a man grows old, he begins to lose his hair, his teeth, and his concern—for others, for the country, even for himself. He doesn't get so involved. He doesn't walk step by step through living, but begins to flap along about ten feet off the ground. He sees what's going on, mind you, but it doesn't get in his way particularly. He becomes a kind of cumbersome bird."

"A dead duck if you ask me. To talk this way . . ."

"Dying."

"God help us all, Ansel. What you need is a couple of good swigs from Rudy's cane."

"To the best of my knowledge it's been empty since about nineteen-twenty-nine."

"Has the Senate contacted you yet?"

"There was word at the office. I go down the first of next week."

"You need a rest."

"I've had a rest, two years. What I need is lunch."

"Will you do me the honor?"

"No." Gibbs ran his hand across the back of his head where the hair grew thick, thinning only on top. He gave Hoye a look of general and dimly amused inquiry. Gibbs had a young face tricked into middle age with little welts beneath the eyes, the firmly settled jaw: a slightly imperious, blunt-nosed face, but still zestful and aware. "I dropped in only long enough to depress you. I have other commissions."

"Do me a favor before you go?"

"Name it."

"Recite the seven-times table through twelve or so."

"You're serious?"

"Yes."

Hoye stood at his office window, his hands in his pockets, the loop of his watch chain glinting across his vest, and waited for his friend to begin. For a moment it was as if Gibbs did not intend to do so. Crooking the cane over one arm and tucking his packages under the other, he walked to the door and only then stopped and turned. Not the least tremor of a smile unsettled the intensity of his expression. "Seven times one is seven," he said, "times two is fourteen, times three is twenty-one . . ." They continued to face each other throughout the recital, neither of them dropping his glance. From the harbor below came the whistle of a tugboat.

"Do you want to know why I asked you to do that?" Hoye inquired when Gibbs had finished.

"No need to explain. One asks what one must."

"I thought I would find it comforting to hear you say something in specific, concrete terms again. I did. Thank you."

"Poor Porter," Gibbs said, smiling at last, his hand on the door. "I'm glad."

Gibbs ate his lunch alone. From Wall Street he took a subway to Grand Central and from there walked along pavements lined on either side by gray drifts of city snow to an Italian restaurant where the sudden warmth after coming in out of the winter day, the sounds of eating, lulled him out of any desire to read the newspaper that he had brought with him. He propped it on the table before him anyway as an excuse for not being disturbed by any acquaintance who might be there and gave himself over completely to the sound of his surroundings, the chink of silver against china, of ice in glasses, a guffaw, a command to a waiter, the drone of someone counting four, five, six hundred shares or dollars or years. If any thought of past or future crossed his mind, it left no sign upon his face; and

eating his omelet and salad, drinking his milk, he sat there
a fortress walled and moated, impervious to the occasional
glances of recognition from men eating near by, to the
solicitude of the waiter who had addressed him by name
and hovered by his chair throughout the meal. Leaving
when he had finished, he forgot his packages and cane so
that the headwaiter in his tuxedo, black as a raven against
the snow with his breath coming out in little puffs of mist,
had to chase after him with them, handing them over like
treasures, then standing for a moment beneath his own
awning to watch his distinguished patron continue along
his way. Gibbs crossed to Fifth Avenue, then walked north
along it to the square in front of the Plaza, where several
hansom cabs were drawn up at the curb, the horses blan-
keted, the drivers conferring together in their rusty top
hats. Entering the park, he walked as far as the zoo and
stopped there by the seal tank for a few minutes to watch
the seals asleep on their concrete deck. He tapped the
handle of Rudy's cane sharply against the iron railing and
roused one of them, who raised his head, flicked his silver
whiskers, yawned. "Who are you?" a small boy in a leather
helmet asked at his elbow and remained there with his
dusty face tipped up in inquiry as Gibbs moved on. At the
top of the stairs leading back to the street, he stopped for a
moment to shift his packages to the other arm, then continued the few remaining blocks to Louise von Louwe's
house. Walter, the butler, met him in the hall to say that
Miss von Louwe and Miss Gibbs were both out and that
Mr. Tripp had called to confirm his appointment for that

afternoon. Gibbs asked him to bring the young man to the library upstairs when he came, and proceeded there himself.

He sat down in the dusk of that room with its silence filtered in through the book-lined walls, through the voluminous rose damask that draped the French windows, looped full above them and falling in heavy folds to the carpet. Small and thus richly hung as it was, the furniture deep and soft, dark, an India shawl on the piano, a needlepoint bellpull to cover the one strip of wall that would otherwise have been bare, it seemed less the Victorian blunder of a room that Louise von Louwe herself had called it, than a kind of darkly heroic tent, a king's pavillion of silk and wool, hung with banners, muffled and dim. He sat there, Gibbs, with the pictures that he had brought unwrapped on his knees. Though some of them were relevant to his meeting with young Tripp, not all of them were. There was one of Corinne, his wife, placid and formal in white, her shoulders bare; another of a group of men on the deck of a man-of-war, among them the President shielding his eyes from the sun and looking up into the sky, beside him Gibbs with his overcoat collar turned up; Gibbs again, twenty-five years or so younger, and Rudy, standing in their bachelors' gowns and mortarboards, all brindled by the shadows of spring leaves; Louise sitting in the sand of a Lond Island beach with her hair tied up in a bandana and a small child easily recognizable as Anne playing at her feet. Gibbs slowly studied these and more, slipping one behind the other, discovering, perhaps, that if you look at pictures of people long enough in a poor light, the faces seem almost to come alive, to smile, to open or close their mouths. Yet not all of them, for the pictures of people who have died seldom seem to move, have a way of in some fashion dying themselves. They go flat about the face, the expressions change, especially the eyes change, assuming a kind of sameness so that Rudy and Corinne said almost the same thing through their likenesses now whereas in life they had been very different. Very long ago, they said, and very, very far away, or something like that; for something seems to pass out of the faces of photographs of the dead just as occasionally it will pass out of the faces of the living: a capacity for encountering other faces, an immediacy of eye. This was no sad dream of Gibbs's, however, for his absorption in the photographs themselves precluded dreaming, but if young Tripp or someone else had broken in upon him there and confronted him with it, he would have recognized the phenomenon as one which he had observed before. Lecturing once on King Saul, Kuykendall had touched upon it in his hearing. "We're told," he had said, "that 'the spirit of the Lord departed from Saul,' and don't think that Saul didn't know when it happened. Oh, he'd had troubles enough already, a man born to trouble—he was too handsome, too strong to escape it—but he'd always before been sustained by the spirit of the Lord, which, contrary to popular modern opinion, isn't some kind of pious deodorant, but the terrible vitality of the Creator Himself which lacerates as it sustains, and when it departed from him, he knew it, and so did everybody else.

You didn't have to be a Samuel to see it in his face in five seconds flat. Something had gone out of him that never returned, and he died one of the only two suicides in the entire Old Testament." Gibbs laid the photographs on the floor by his chair and from the hallway downstairs heard the sound of voices.

Heaven only knew what he expected to see when Robin Tripp, upon hearing an answer to his knock, first entered; but for an instant he was simply stunned both by the boy's resemblance to his father and by the dissimilarity between them, which was just sufficient to jar him into remembering all the more vividly how Rudy had looked at that age. He was almost as tall as Gibbs and slight of build, with a thin face, his head tilted a little to one side and leaning slightly forward in a kind of earnest, tentative lunge. His eyes were sharp, his hair was a deep red, and there was an air of vigor and boldness about him, yet a restraint, too, as he stopped at the door for a moment to accustom his eyes to the dim light before going to Gibbs, who had unaccountably not come to him, to shake hands, saying: "Wonderful to see you again, sir," watching Gibbs come alive with: "Not since you were a little fellow. You're so much like your father that when you first came in, if I believed in ghosts. . . ."

"You'd have handled the situation," Tripp finished, "with no less than your usual aplomb."

"I hate to think of it as a *situation*." Gibbs smiled except for his eyes, which searched for any trace of mockery in the young man's face, found nothing but a kind of reckless, admiring expectation, an eagerness to push here, pry there, until he discovered a door that would open.

"You'll want me to explain why I got Anne to arrange this when, of course, I know all you're involved in these few days."

"The past explains the present. I'm sure I don't know what else it's good for." Test, prove, try the boy, Gibbs thought, and see what door he himself might open in *him*, in Rudy's son, whoever he was, Gibbs thought—gag-man and flirt, singer of songs, young Lochinvar—as he watched him there bright-eyed and crashingly rude perhaps, by his presence alone somehow pleading with him for something, willing to go to any lengths of effrontery even to get whatever the young want of the old. "Whatever you're after, there's time enough for that," he said. "I rejoice now just in the fact that you're here. Sit down."

But Tripp did not, remained standing instead with what struck Gibbs for a moment as an almost lunatic smile, wide-mouthed, his teeth wet, white, as if at any instant he might burst into laughter; but, after all then, only the help-less smile of a boy that lingered on beyond its usefulness into his: "I suppose they're all after something."

Gibbs, too, remained standing, his arms extended out along the mantlepiece again as if they suspended him there, his head sinking slightly toward his chest, his glance to the carpet, as the unlit tent of the room grew darker with the day. Never do battle with a man when you can enlist him, make use of his services, see the possibility of loyalty in him. But for what use, this Robin, of what capacity for loyalty the famous young Tripp, riding in upon him on the crest of his giddy wave?

"You've made quite a name for yourself," he said. "I confess I've never seen you in action myself, but certainly Anne's full of enthusiasm. I always wished your father might have gone into something of more or less the same sort himself."

"From what I remember, he wouldn't have been half bad at it," Tripp said, and Gibbs thought that there was a look of something like indulgence in his eyes as if, though this was not the subject which he himself would have chosen, he was willing to go along with it for as long as Gibbs might choose.

"Your father was without a question the most," Gibbs paused for a word, shrugged slightly at the one he found, "charming person I have ever known. Do you remember him well?"

"Not really," Tripp said. "Only glimpses. I was just a child when he died."

Gibbs was on the point of mentioning the photographs that he had brought but decided against it. "Yes," he said, rather distractedly, realizing that the room had grown so dark that it was only with difficulty that they were able to see one another clearly. He switched on a lamp which stood near the fireplace, and through its red shade the light shone warmly. "Look, I'll be frank with you," he said, something approaching frankness being made possible for him simply by the irrational leap of his heart at all the richness of the room restored again with the lighting of the lamp. "More than your mother, I think, or anyone else, I've questioned how much I was to blame for his dying as he did. Don't for an instant think that because I've had other matters on my mind since, I haven't thought about it again and again. And don't think either that I haven't felt qualms about seeing you today. There's a ghost here with us, and I'm fully aware of it. I'm being candid with you."

They were sitting side by side now, Gibbs gray-suited and in appearance suddenly the lawyer, the horn frames of his glasses gleaming in the light, his expression all moderation and reason as in effect he presented his case to the young man, who to his clearer view looked less young, more solid, leaning comfortably back in his dark blue suit, his color the healthy pale of redheads. And this was the moment at which anything was possible, Gibbs thought, glancing hard at Tripp to see traces of whatever it might be, but without apparent anxiety, more resolutely, resignedly. He found himself looking forward to no matter what Tripp was to say or do, gripped by the mere potentiality of reaction because what the boy's expression lacked in the kind of intensity from which some authentic response might spring, it more than made up for simply by its vitality. Even though Tripp's eyes showed nothing so much as a faintly indolent curiosity as they met Gibbs's, his face was somehow triumphantly alive, and Gibbs thrilled to the sight of it.

"That wasn't what I came to talk about," Tripp said. "I mean I don't certainly have any objection to talking about it, but it wasn't why I asked to see you. Oh, I know," the

young man continued, "there were hard feelings between
my mother and you for a while. There was a time I used to
hear plenty of it from her, and a couple of times Anne has
gone on about it. But you know Anne. She's crazy about
soap-opera situations, and this one's just too good for her
to drop. If you want to know what I think . . ."

"Yes," Gibbs said, leaning forward, "that's what I want
to know."

"Well, sir, I'll tell you." At just the point where Gibbs
would have expected Tripp's voice to become hushed, confidential, it rose in volume. He clapped his hand softly to
his knee and spoke directly, a shade belligerently, to Gibbs
but as though others, perhaps not so receptive, were listening as well. "I'm an actor type basically," he said, his
forehead wrinkling beneath a fallen red plume of hair, "and
this is a part I could really sink my teeth into. You fire my
father, and he shoots himself, and years later I arrive on
the scene, his only son, to face you with it. I could tear
around here like a bee in a jam pot, break a few windows
and stand on my head. In fact, when the thing happened,
as a kid, I did more or less that. An uncle of mine got to the
house before the body was gone even—still lying in the
back yard near a stand of croquet mallets—and I'd loved
my father, of course, anybody could have seen that, but
having him dead all of a sudden was more exciting than
anything, just plain exciting, and I hadn't cried a drop till
this uncle of mine put his fuzzy hands on my shoulders, I
remember, and looked down at me with his eyes like sad
caramels, and it was so obvious even to a small boy that he

expected me to cry that naturally I decided that was what
I was supposed to do—I'd sensed there must be something
—and I remember smothering my face against the prickly
front of his overcoat just so he couldn't see I was half fak-
ing, and then really letting myself go. But if you want to
know, sir, I can't rise to the occasion again now, so don't
you worry. I'm not a good enough actor to be able to pretend the whole business has bothered me for years because
it hasn't—or that I blame you, I don't. If that helps clear
the deck . . ."

"And Sylvia, your mother, what about her, do you
think?" Gibbs watched Tripp smile broadly at his question.

"She hates thinking, you know. If you try to get her to,
she usually won't listen. The last time I saw her, I gave her
a long lecture about keeping her checkbook in order or
something, and when I finally finished, all she said was,
'Guess what I saw on the street today? Two nuns and a
hunchback.' " Tripp laughed. "But if she ever does think
about this the way I suppose she must sometimes, I have a
feeling she blames herself now as much as anybody. She's
changed a lot since you saw her last. Married again, you
know."

Gibbs nodded. He held one of his hands in the other,
massaging the palm with his thumb. "And what about
you? Do you blame anybody?"

"He pulled the trigger himself. I was the last one to see
him. I'd woken up early that morning and was finishing a
model airplane till it was time for breakfast, which was a

little later than usual because it was a Sunday. He opened the door on his way downstairs and looked in on me for a minute, so I could have stopped him, asked him to help me or something. But I didn't. So maybe I was to blame."

"This is unique in my experience," Gibbs said, rising to his feet and walking to the window, where he stopped for a few moments looking out into the winter evening, then turning to Tripp, who had remained where he was, his legs stretched out straight before him with his feet crossed and his hands in his pockets. "A crime is committed—call it a crime—and each of the prime suspects is inclined to believe that he himself is the guilty one. The evidence in each case is, to say the very least, inadequate. A lost job. I had to let him go, you understand. I could have done no differently if he'd been my own son, and he knew that. A model airplane to be finished by breakfast. A woman who suffered to be beautiful. She had that mirror, you remember? Queer, queer," Gibbs continued, "how the facts themselves have such an innocence about them. The croquet mallets . . ."

And this room, Gibbs thought, pausing: this particular room on this particular day, himself speaking these words to this boy, his friend's son, he thought, his own son and friend; and looking at him, young-eyed, alive, he shuddered almost with an instant of warmth. The innocence of events, he thought, following one upon the other like dumb beasts to the manger of this present instant; and if in general the present was meaningless, a wilderness, a no man's land, it was for the duration at least of this instant no longer so.

"It must have been very hard for you," Gibbs said. "I mean the shock of it, the shame . . . But you survived?"

"Maybe I was lucky it happened when I was too young to have a heart to break or a psyche to warp. Whatever's supposed to get damaged. Yes. I've survived. And I've kept on being lucky," Tripp said. "Enough after taxes to keep me in convertibles. My picture in the papers. Pretty much the girls I've wanted . . ." He cut in upon himself with a quick smile of something between complicity and apology, with his "Don't get me wrong, not a lady-killer of anything," but not before Gibbs perceived the image which it was as if the boy were trying to screen from him as he blew a mist of cigarette smoke out into the still air between them: the image of Tripp surrounded by ladies who would, of course, have found irresistible, as Gibbs thought of it, the soft jeer of his eyes, the reckless smile. If for the strange warmth of an instant's recognition Gibbs had seen him almost as a son, he saw him suddenly now as in some sense a rival as well, although for what reason he could not have explained, and said only: "Anne told me you were lucky."

"That's my girl." A joke and not a joke but, smiling, Gibbs chose to take it as such.

"By all rights you should have disliked each other on sight, old friends as your fathers were," he said.

"It's true we eyed each other with a certain suspicion at

first. It's funny really that we ever met at all. Our paths weren't the likeliest ones to cross."

"I know almost nothing about your recent path," Gibbs said. "Tell me about it."

For the first time he felt that it was the boy and not himself who stood in judgment, felt that the boy, too, was aware of it as he pulled himself straight in his seat, then gestured loosely with one hand, a kind of entreaty. "Oh, if what you want is my life story," he began, pronouncing his last words with sonorously satiric emphasis, "you'll be disappointed. The publicity people play it down because it's such a blank. High school. Then a year of boarding-school because my mother wanted the ritziest she could find, of course, and one year was all she could afford to buy for me. Then college. The first three years went off well enough. I got by, had some success writing songs for the spring musicals. Then, my senior year, the war started, and I had my own private Pearl Harbor. One by one everybody was being drafted or enlisting, so it was all just a series of farewell binges which japped me in the end. I don't think I cracked a book or went to a lecture for three months, so just before the big showdown I signed up with the Army and took off. Most of my time I spent in an I.R.T.C. head-quarters outfit in the south, compiling morning reports and sending in monthly charts of the AWOL and VD rates to the Third Service Command in Baltimore. As far as I know, they never looked at one of them, and that's just as well because I never knew beans about what I was doing anyway. But off-hours I played the piano at an officer's club, and week-end passes were automatic as long as you got your work done, so it wasn't a bad deal really. I was bored stiff most of the time, but at least I wasn't being shot at. I wouldn't have minded a taste of it, but I figured you took what they gave you. And that was Tripp's military career." He had risen and walked away from Gibbs toward the piano, where, leaning with one elbow upon it, he continued: "Our shoulder patches were red, blue, and yellow; red for the blood you never shed, they used to say. Blue for the ocean you never crossed. And yellow for the streak down your back. Joke.

"I thought of going back and finishing college after I was discharged, but I got a job disc-jockeying in the wee hours for a small Chicago station instead. I started talking a little to myself in between records, as much to keep awake as anything, and singing some of my own stuff, more or less made up as I went along. And God help me, it took. I don't know why, but it really took, you know." He rapped the piano slowly with his knuckles as he spoke. "I got an offer in New York. Eventually worked into a fancier kind of show--less singing, more talking and interviewing. And there you have it. There!" he finished, giving the piano a final rap and sitting down on the stool. "Which brings me," he began again, looking up at Gibbs, "to why I came. I have a favor to ask, sir."

"Whatever you want," Gibbs smiled at him. He stood there at the window where he had remained throughout Tripp's account, with his hands in his pockets, his shadow broken against the damask behind him, and, gazing at the boy seated before him, smiled and heard himself say that he could have whatever he wanted. "The head of John the Baptist," he added. "Half of my kingdom. But while you're there, do *me* a favor first. Play something. I've never heard you."

"No, no." Tripp said with a laugh. "I didn't come to waste your whole afternoon."

Gibbs brushed away his objection with such finality that, protesting no further, Tripp swung around to the keyboard and began to play. Whatever it was, Gibbs hardly listened at first, attending Tripp himself rather than his playing. The young man sat with his head tilted back, his eyes ceilingward, and something like jubilance in his smile as if he dreamed of music too absurd for his fingers ever to convey. Yet for all his air of self-assurance, Gibbs was instead suddenly struck by something unprotected and alone about him. There was something in the tilt of his shoulders, in the slightly hesitant lilt of his playing as it incongruously filled that dim room, that aroused in Gibbs a feeling whose immediate and unthinking translation was to stand close behind him with his hands on his shoulders and quietly, more than half to himself, to say, as in another instant he wished unsaid: "Son, son," at just the point when Tripp, whether he had heard or not, began to sing some song of his own peculiar extemporizing, his voice soft and clarion, shaping words that fell like water through the air of that room as dark as the wool of tents. It was a song about birds flying through snow and wishing for spring, as nearly as Gibbs could tell; for he heard only disconnected phrases of it, distracted by standing there with his hands on the boy's shoulders when he yearned to remove them, yet felt that, in conscience, he somehow could not. He became oddly, rather dazedly, preoccupied with what individual words he did hear—wings, snow, leaves, sky—and weighed them lawyer-like, stiff and a little embarrassed, until all at once something within him seemed to fall under their weight, and he came aware of a sharpening of his senses, especially of his sight, so that everything appeared with a splendor of detail that he had not known before: the crimson and blue design of the India shawl, the coffined harp of the piano, the glint of lamplight on the books that lined the walls, even, or so it seemed, the separate hairs that grew in whorls at the crown of the boy's head. For the first time, the room seemed endowed with a life and significance of its own, the moment with content, and once the song came to an end, Gibbs expressed his delight in it with what must have appeared to Tripp an excessive warmth, told the young man that it had carried him back, carried him back, yet not so much back to the past, had he stopped to reflect, as to the present which he had of late neglected.

"I unearthed some relics I thought you might be interested in," he said, handing over at last the photographs and cane, but instead of commenting upon them he said only: "They were your father's or of your father," and let it go at that. And only then had Tripp asked his favor.

Would Mr. Gibbs consider appearing on his program at the end of the week? Tripp knew, he said, that it was ex-

tremely short notice and that this was an extremely busy
time for him, but Senator Farwell was scheduled for an
interview then, and it would be an excellent opportunity
for them to air their differences on neutral ground, freed
of any necessity to discuss political matters exclusively.
What was more, he added, smiling, it would be an unques-
tionable *coup* for him personally to be able to secure
Gibbs's services at all when Gibbs had already made it
clear to the press that his intention was not to make any
public appearance whatever until such time as the Senate
might confirm his appointment. If he felt simply that he
must maintain that position, Tripp insisted that he must
for no reason feel in any sense obligated for his sake to
abandon it.

And yet it was, of course, no less than this that the boy
asked, Gibbs knew, and for what reason indeed should he
act against his own disinclination, he wondered, not to
mention against Hoye's admonitions to spare himself
while yet he could, not to complicate matters any further
by declaring himself on issues that might provide those
who opposed him with more material for doing so. And
what sort of interview did the boy have in mind? Would
Tripp play the piano, his hair aflame and his strong teeth
bared in laughter, while Gibbs and the Senator lumbered
about like bears at a baiting? He had never met Farwell—
by his pictures a short, stout man with a face like a wedge
—nor could he guess from his knowledge of him what
issues other than political they might find to discuss; but
in terms of the instant's wild imagining the possibilities

were limitless, and Who Killed Rudy Tripp might just as
well be one of them except that even as he paused there
about to reply to the boy's request, he realized that if that
death had involved guilt on anyone's part, he had himself
been absolved of it and by the very one who might most
justly have accused him: Rudy's son, standing before him
now, unruined and unruining. "Well, and why not?" Gibbs
said, reaching out to shake Tripp's hand. "Favor granted.
Case closed."

C H A P T E R
IV

Anne had returned home while Tripp was still upstairs in the library with her father, but she had gone directly to her room so as not to see him when he left, or so that, if a meeting between them was to take place, it would be up to Tripp to arrange it. She had been standing in front of a mirror brushing her hair when she heard him in the hall saying good-by to Gibbs and had continued to listen then as his footsteps had passed by her closed door and down the stairs. But she did not stop brushing her hair, felt the tiny crackle of electricity in it and watched it rise in wisps to the stroke of her brush as she regarded her reflection, careful only not to meet her own glance. The mirror was a full-length one, so framed that it could be adjusted to any angle, and with one foot she reached out and tipped it back now with the result that she saw herself pitched perilously backward and about to fall over with a crash into the crazily leaning room behind her, yet all the time calmly brushing her hair, wishing herself less height, more bosom, and feature by feature appraising her face. The eyes would get by was the best she could say, and, hating her nose, too long, too pointed, she puckered her mouth into the shape of whistling so that she would look less like herself and could think of other things as she finished her brushing. This she abruptly did, tapping the mirror once more, forward this time, so that all it showed were her legs and feet, the low heels of her shoes together and her toes awkwardly far apart, she thought, on the flowered carpet. She threw her hairbrush into an armchair then and lay down on her bed, where she stared at the ceiling for a few moments.

To close her eyes as then she did was not simply to shut out the world, but slowly, tired as she was, to enter another not half so well ordered, where her barely waking dream little by little took on something like substance until, as if with her eyes open, she seemed actually to see Tripp come into her room and stand by her bed without for a long time saying a word but merely looking down at her, his face impassive, until finally she asked him what had happened in his meeting with her father, and he answered that he had killed him, or that he had told him that he loved her, or that they had exchanged no words at all, but had simply sat together in silence. She showed him with her face and mind, which in her dreaming were all one, that she knew that he was lying, whereupon, smiling, he lay down beside her there and whispered softly to her words that she could not hear. In her half-dream he lay at her side like a lover, but hard as she tried, she could not dream the content of his whispered words, which were perhaps not of love at all, though warm as breath at her ear, and then, as so often happened just as she was on the point itself of sleep, it was as if she suddenly stumbled or tripped over something so that, lying there, she seemed actually to feel her whole body jolted and came totally awake to find, of course, no Tripp, no words. And then the world of waking flooded in upon her—"My toes begin to twitch," she had described it once to Aunt Louise—and she opened her eyes to her empty room, both familiar yet for an instant foreign, still cluttered with her childhood: the little glass and china horses arranged on the bureau around a silver cup she had won for riding, the photograph of her mother in cloche hat and furs among pigeons in the Piazza San Marco, pinned to one curtain an advertisement which she had cut from a magazine showing Tripp in tennis shorts with a towel around his tanned neck lighting a cigarette whose brand name was emblazoned in letters as red as his hair against the impossible blue sky behind him. He was looking up over his hands cupped around the match, his brow wrinkled, his glance inquiring, and she had said: "You want to be careful of that face of yours, you know. It's not good to have it looked at so much—TV, magazines, ads, and everything. All those eyes staring at it all the time will start leaving their mark on it, especially love-starved female eyes, because eyes are hot and they'll start melting it if you don't watch out." Except that Tripp had so many faces, she had concluded, that she supposed he could afford to lose a number of them. "Your street face," she had begun to enumerate, "your cocktail face, your publicity face, your girl face . . ." to which he had responded, smiling, by asking her which one he was wearing at the moment as they had stood on a windy corner waiting for a taxi. Suddenly uncomfortable, she had said that she did not know, and it was left for him to reply with "My Annie face, of course." And with which, she wondered, rising from her bed and about to go downstairs, had he confronted her father that afternoon?

Dr. Kuykendall was expected for dinner, and she found her father and Aunt Louise waiting for him in the living-room. Newly emerged from a hot shower, Gibbs was still flushed from it as he rose to greet his daughter, kissing her, and seating her on the sofa beside him, while Louise von Louwe acknowledged her entrance by simply glancing up for a moment from her needlepoint.

"I don't know how your spiritual mentor feels about drinking," she said, pulling a crimson thread through the petal of a rose, "so perhaps you'd better have one quickly now before he comes. Your father," she continued, indicating Gibbs with her needle, "is in a state of elation. At fifty-two, he has decided to enter the entertainment field, you know, and that is a move which for me has all the fascination of an ax murder."

Gibbs answered Louise von Louwe with a single loud laugh, speaking to Anne instead. "I met your young friend this afternoon, Annie, and we had a delightful chat. Delightful," he added, patting Anne's knee, "and . . ."

". . . he refuses to make the least comment on it,"
Louise interrupted. "Such delight is obviously not to be
shared with clods."

"I stupidly neglected to have a stenographer present to
take it all down," Gibbs said.

"I wish you'd stop talking to each other through me."
Anne took her glass from the tray that Walter passed her.
"It makes me feel like a telephone. And what's this about
entering the entertainment field?"

"I consented," Gibbs said, "to allow Robin Tripp to
interview me, together with a member of the United States
Senate, on his program day after tomorrow. Your Aunt
Louise sees me disrobing publicly, garment by garment,
to the savage rhythms of a guitar."

"I see," Louise von Louwe said, for the first time ad-
dressing him directly as she thrust her embroidery frame
to one side, "what I see. That is all."

"And that's why he wanted to talk to you?" Anne asked.

"Principally, yes. I suppose it was."

"What do you think of him?" Imagining she had heard
the doorbell ring and that it was Dr. Kuykendall arriving,
Anne asked the question abruptly, almost fiercely, in
order to have it answered before the old man came in.
Deciding then that it had not been the doorbell at all, she
asked it more easily again. "Did you get along together?
How did he look to you?"

"What she wants to know," said Louise von Louwe, "is
did he talk to you about her."

"What *you* want to know. She," Anne continued to her

father, hesitating, suddenly angry, "she's the one who wants to make a romance of this thing."

"I don't want as much as that, you know." Louise von Louwe raised her glass, stopping Gibbs before he had a chance to speak. "*Prosit*, both of you," she said. "This is such a comfortable time, the hour before eating. Don't let me spoil it just because sometimes I get a macabre impulse to spoil the very nicest things. Exorcize me. All I want is a little clarification. Don't think I'm not charmed by the boy myself. It's his *métier*, after all, and I am. Just tell me —or don't if you don't want to, of course, or can't—why he's been glittering so brightly in this house for the last four months or so if all he's wanted was to get you on his program, Ansel. If he *didn't* get around to saying something this afternoon about you, Anne."

"Such as what, do you mean?" Looking at her, large and immobile in her purple dress with a string of amber beads at her bosom, Anne felt her annoyance slip out from under her and asked her question out of nothing but purest curiosity.

"Oh, words, words," Louise von Louwe answered with a little wave of her hand. "In this case it wouldn't much matter which ones. Anything on the subject would satisfy me."

"Dear ladies," Gibbs said. "Now you've succeeded in making *me* feel like a telephone. Robin Tripp came to me for a purpose, and the purpose was not to ask for my daughter's hand in marriage, if that's what you want to know." The failure of either of them to respond to this seemed to suggest to him that it was perhaps precisely what they did want to know, and he continued quickly, lowering the glass from his lips before he had so much as sipped from it. "I'm sure your name came up, Annie, but no issue was made of it. In fact I'm pleased to report the conversation really didn't involve any issues at all, you know, except this one simple request I've mentioned. There was nothing tense about it. He even sang one of his songs for me. Damn it," Gibbs said, clapping one fist softly into the palm of his other hand, "the boy really has a way with him. There's no getting around that."

"He most certainly does," said Louise von Louwe. "Have a way with him. On that we're each in our own peculiar ways agreed. The question," she went on, leaning forward to pick from a silver dish a single peanut which she then held out before her for the scrutiny of a few seconds before placing it on her tongue like a pill, "is not so much what that way is, but for what end does he plan to use it. I for one can't escape the feeling that he's after something. In the bosom of the family I speak openly. If I'm irritating either of you, tell me."

"In any relationship between two human beings, each is always after something," Gibbs said. "In a general sense, I mean, and more often than not in a specific sense, too. Specifically, young Tripp wanted me to say yes, I would go on the air with him. He was frank about it. He said it would add to his prestige, and I'm sure it will. But you're unquestionably right, Louise, that he's after something in a general sense, too. I'm certain he is. Only who in God's name is to say what? I doubt whether Tripp could say himself."

"He's right, you know," Anne added to her cousin. "You're asking these questions about Tripp because you're after an answer, but I'm sure you're after something else, too."

"Such as the heart-warming sense of having alienated you both? Or just reassurance through your reacting to me at all that I really do exist in space and time?"

"I never know what you're after," Anne said. "Or what anybody is, I sometimes think."

"Look then," Louise von Louwe said, rising from her chair and walking toward the door to greet Dr. Kuykendall, who had not yet appeared, but whose voice she had heard in the hall, "let me register just one thing with you, and that will be an end to it. Dumb animals and certain middle-aged celibates have a way of smelling danger or thinking they do, and young Tripp is so fragrant with it that it reaches me even over a television set. Beware the barefoot boy in the Brooks Brothers suit. Both of you. *Also sprach von Louwe.*" Setting her drink down on a table, she disappeared into the hall.

Gibbs raised his head and laughed, looking at his daughter. "Are you scared, Annie?" he asked. Before she had a chance to reply, only meeting Gibbs's glance, her face slightly flushed, Louise von Louwe re-entered with her guest.

At the age of seventy, Dr. Henry Kuykendall seemed at first glance to be a considerably older man than that, with his hair thin and white, his shoulder stooped. His nose and chin jutted large and bony, and the stare of his eyes was wild and wondering until, when he smiled, he lowered them with an air of absurd bashfulness. But if the first impression he gave was that of an old man, it became apparent at closer range that the flesh of his face was firm and relatively unlined and that behind the awkward abruptness of his gestures there lay great energy. He was dressed in dark gray with a clerical collar.

"I don't believe, sir," said Gibbs, advancing to shake his hand, "that there's anyone in this country I'd rather see right now than you."

"Especially," Louise von Louwe added, "at this particular moment. We've been having a nasty, pagan row."

"We meet in the fullness of time," Dr. Kuykendall said. He held Gibbs by the arm as he spoke. "Of your time, Ansel," he continued. "I have no intention of making a speech, but . . . Let me have one of those, if I may," he pointed to Anne's glass. She poured him one, and raising it toward Gibbs, he said, " 'Before I formed thee in the belly I knew thee; and before thou camest out of the womb I sanctified thee, and I ordained thee a prophet unto the nations.' I drink to you, Ansel. To your name. You remember what Israel felt about names."

In his days of teaching Old Testament at Harvard, before being ordained at the age of fifty and taking on a parish, this had been one of Kuykendall's recurring themes, one which he touched upon again and again as he flailed and postured his way through the Pentateuch, the

historical books, the Prophets. "What are you, who, what
are you?" he would ask, suddenly stopping in his erratic
progress down the aisle of the large lecture hall and grabbing hold of some seated undergraduate by the shoulders.
"Just a lump of flesh, a blob, a thing, until I find out . . .
your name. Your name!" And he would raise his arms as if
in the wonder of discovery. "Of course. Now I know who
you are. You are . . ." and he would pause, perilously
poised on the very brink of the ludicrous, "Harry!" his
face wonderfully brightening, "or Peter or John. Israel
understood that a person *is* his name. You don't know him
until you know it. And then one day Moses asked the
Lord's name, and the Lord said, 'I am . . . Jahweh.' So at
last Israel knew the name of her God."

"I don't know what Israel felt about anything," Louise
von Louwe said, "but I will join you in that toast. To you,
Ansel," she raised her glass, "and to whatever lies ahead
for you, for all of us. Always make friends with the inevi-
table while you still can."

Anne, who had risen at Dr. Kuykendall's entrance,
lifted her glass, too, and together all three of them drank
to Gibbs, who stood there before them, smiling, his arms
hanging straight at his sides as if at attention. A little
snow mixed with sleet rattled against the windowpanes,
and Anne looked for a moment to see what it was, made
only the slightest turn of her head, her glass still raised to
her lips, and yet at the very instant of discovering the
source of the noise—it was only snow, she saw, not a
human hand, bird's wing, or ghost—she decided, and the

decision took no more than the instant, that she would not see Tripp again. So, taking another sip from her glass, she drank to that, too, moving back then with the others into the center of the living-room, sitting down on the couch next to one of them, but all the while in that state of strange remoteness which follows upon decision, scarcely noticing where and with whom she was, not hearing whatever Gibbs banteringly said to deflect attention from himself. It was, of course, the only thing to do, she thought: not to see him again. The only thing. Of all the other things of her life—the people; her job with Kuykendall; the impression, whatever it was, that she gave to the world; even the objects of that world; her room, its pictures, the clothes in her closet—of all of these, her knowing that she would not now see Tripp again was the only thing which for the moment seemed of real substance to her, and it flickered in her mind like a solitary candle. She wondered, but still remotely, dispassionately, barely hearing the queer, tense gurgle of Kuykendall's laugh as he replied to something that Louise von Louwe had said, what it would be like not to see Tripp again, however exactly she was to manage it—no melodramatic scene, she thought, but simply an unanswerable indifference. It would be, of course, to lose him; to lose perhaps worst of all just her excitement, her unending amazement, at being pursued by a young man whose fame after all rivaled in its own way even her father's. For certainly, she knew, she had loved that fame, had loved more than that perhaps, but certainly that, too, possibly that above all: the famed image of Tripp whether in black and white on the studio's monitor or in the colored warmth of flesh sitting beside her in a restaurant, wearing his famous face, his public face, or dancing with her at a night club where he was sure to be recognized, and she with him. When, as had occasionally happened, news of their having been seen together at one place or another reached the gossip column of some paper, Anne had invariably clipped it out and not pinned it, like the cigarette advertisement, to her curtain or slipped it under the glass of her dresser top, but treasured it away between the pages of an old copy of *Vogue* which she kept on the table by her bed, its covers stained here and there with the shape of her mouth where she had used it to blot her lipstick. "Your lips are marked on everything in this house. There seems to be nothing you haven't kissed," Aunt Louise had said, momentarily giving the girl a wonderful sense of being the profligate, the scarlet woman of that placid house.

Dr. Kuykendall was answering a question of Gibbs's about conditions in East Harlem; and she would not see Tripp again, she continued to think, turning it this way and that, smiling vaguely at her father, and why, she wondered, not as a way of undermining her decision but rather, simply, to sanctify it with a motive. She would not see him again because not even in her dreams of him would he betray himself to her as only once, the autumn before, he had; because his motives in seeing her father that afternoon had unforgivably and in no sense involved her; more than for any other reason, perhaps, because in turning to identify the noise at the window, she had for a wild moment thought that it might be Tripp come back, Tripp standing outside in the snow trying to attract her attention, to say all that for so long he had not said. At the sound suddenly of her own name, not from the window, but from Kuykendall sitting beside her on the couch, she was drawn again into the conversation.

"There are moments when I wonder," he had been saying, "what side Anne and I are on. There they are," he continued, mainly to Gibbs, "my flock. I hate exaggerating the poverty and suffering of their lives. Sometimes I find myself almost boasting of it, whereas it is certainly true there have been improvements in the last few years. The city's at least not totally indifferent to the problem. But the horror of it is still indescribable. Indescribable," he repeated, louder than before, his hands taut. "Their situation often seems so hopeless that I can't avoid the suspicion that for some terrible reason God has marked them out for damnation and that in trying to better their lot in one inane way or another, it's God we're working against, not for. Try that on for size." Not merely his voice but his whole presence—his stare intense, his shoulders hunched like the folded wings of some ungainly bird—confronted them in such a way that the little silence following his words seemed strained with the sense in all of them that there must be some way other than merely conversational for dealing with what he had said. It was Louise von Louwe who first acknowledged defeat by speaking.

"In the circles you move in, you could be burned at the stake, couldn't you, for thoughts like that?"

"I've been burning for forty years," Kuykendall said, his sudden smile of beaming shyness releasing them from any obligation more onerous than to smile with him. "I believe by now I'm no longer flammable."

"We all burn," Anne said, with such conviction after her long silence that she drew to herself the attention she would have preferred to avoid.

"Surely not you, Anne," Kuykendall said. "I could hardly get on without her, you know, Ansel. And I have no intention either of letting her slip through my fingers as I did you a number of years back. Though thank heaven I did, of course," he added. "It would have been a grave mistake for you to have entered the clergy."

"Imagine our Ansel a priest!" Louise von Louwe laughed.

"Oh, but don't misunderstand me," Kuykendall interrupted her. "He would have been absolutely first-rate at it, the kind of a priest I think God dreams of. A man who profoundly knows the world, renouncing it. There would have been rejoicing in Heaven, you can be sure of that."

"Then why on earth did you spoil their fun by discouraging him from the idea?" Louise asked.

"Because I saw him called to be a prophet instead. It embarrasses everybody for me to speak this way, but old men can be gauche with impunity."

"I'm not in the least embarrassed," she said.

"Well, I am," Gibbs said, "enough for us both. I like to think there's a kind of endearing nobility in a man's knowing his own limitations, and I know I'm no prophet. Not that I'm any the less grateful to you, sir, for your generous thoughts."

"I haven't expressed myself properly," Kuykendall said. "Help me out, Anne. I said I believe you were called to be a prophet, and from Moses on down the tendency for everyone so called has been to try to squirm out of the assignment somehow. They've all either said they lacked eloquence or they were too young, or asked for how long their services would be required. Now you say you know your limitations. That's just what you don't know. No man does."

"Exactly what is a prophet supposed to do?" Louise von Louwe asked, continuing her needlepoint. "It's a matter I've never been clear on."

"To ask the painful question," Kuykendall said, "and make the painful point. To hit below the belt if that's where the blow will do the most good. More than anything else, a prophet's supposed to know, profoundly know, the times he lives in and to speak what seems to him the truth about them in the most compelling way he can find, no holds barred."

"Even the way of television?" Louise von Louwe asked.

Kuykendall's momentary bewilderment at this was brought to an end by Anne, who with sudden animation explained how her father had agreed to appear on Tripp's next program with one of his principal opponents.

"Farwell?" Kuykendall expressed his pleasure by half rising from his seat at the news, sinking back into it only at a confirming nod from Gibbs. "More rejoicing in Heaven! Leave it to the genius of that boy to get the two of you together."

"Like trained seals," said Louise von Louwe.

"Every man has his hobbies," Gibbs said, "and for a long time one of mine has been not meeting the Senator, but at this particular juncture it struck me that it might be an entertaining idea."

"Oh, and a great deal more than that." As if somewhat taken aback by his own overexcitement, Kuykendall continued more moderately. "This seems to be my night for making speeches, but where else, I ask you, could you find embodied in one man more of the very principles that the appointment of someone like you constitutes such an earthquake for?"

"One of those cocky little mid-westerner men who never take off their steel-rimmed glasses even to make love at night, and have faces set like traps." Louise von Louwe made tiny little jabs in the air with her needle as she spoke. "Watch out for him, Ansel."

"I'd watch out in general if I were you," Anne said. "Tripp loves him, and he might take his side. He says he's completely unspoiled."

"And he's right," Kuykendall said. "A hundred years of painful human progress have left him unspoiled."

"You're unfair to him, I think," Gibbs said. Alone among them, his voice did not quicken and slow down at the straightaways and turns of conversation, but continued at an even pace. "I admire him for remaining totally himself. He could have let them make a demagogue of him. Potentially, he has the appeal, you know. But he didn't. He just travels his own road, casting his vote on all issues with relentless consistency and invariably getting re-elected."

"I like people to be relentlessly consistent," Anne said. "You always know where you stand with them."

"They're usually not worth standing with," said Louise von Louwe. "If you know how a book turns out, after all, why bother to read it?"

"What interests me," Gibbs said, "is why exactly he should go so far out of his way to oppose this appointment. Especially when it's so highly unlikely that he can in any way thwart it or benefit himself by trying to."

"You don't have to be a prophet to answer that," Kuykendall said, getting to his feet. "He opposes you because he distrusts you. Politically, of course, but more than that—basically, humanly distrusts you. And why?" Kuykendall in effect acted out the reply to his own question, half crouching there before his former student, pointing an accusing finger at him, drawing his face up into the parody of a snarl. "Because you went to one of the great universities east of the Alleghenies and learned a lot of ten-dollar words there and how to use them. Because you were born with a silver spoon in your mouth and never had to work to get where you are now, but had it all handed to you on a platter of the same silver as the spoon. Because you've spent all-told probably ten years or more outside the continental limits of this great nation, not only losing touch with things back here, but picking up a lot of tricky foreign ideas in the bargain, especially a lot of tricky English ideas. The bellowing watchdogs of this country are always on guard against the likes of you." Kuykendall had spoken with such rapidity that, as he paused, he had to take a deep breath, standing straight again, his expression beginning to relax, but still bearing traces of the role he played.

"You're much more charitable toward him than I can find it in my heart to be," he continued. "You admire him for always being himself, and that's just what I call him cursed for. For God's sweet sake, Ansel, be the voice that cries out against the prejudice, the self-interest, the narrowness and complacency of these Farwells."

"And yet, you know," Gibbs said, and it was by contrast like the idling hum of an engine, "he may well be all you say and still not absolutely wrong to distrust me. And his reasons, if you're right about them, aren't one hundred per cent invalid either, after all. He may be a caricature, an overstatement, of what this country is, but I venture to say that he still more accurately represents the essence of it than I do. Rising politically in it step by step, he's become an integral part of it. Whereas, on the other hand, I," and he raised his chin at the pronoun, paused at it with a kind of strange, loose majesty, "I remain on the outer edge of things. I populate the coasts and borderlands of the world. I've never had occasion or necessity to know the homely, inner details. If my views are apt to be liberal and disinterested, it may be simply that compared to Farwell I'm at heart uninterested. This country is all he has, he sees its fortunes as his fortunes, and his narrowness isn't too gross an exaggeration of its narrowness. But I am a man of the world. I don't belong any one place in particular. I don't have anything in particular to lose. I suspect such men may be quite rightly not trusted."

"Well, go to, now, go to," Kuykendall smiled as he sat down on the couch once more. "I won't bore the ladies by continuing this debate. I should add that what I've said is my own and not necessarily the word of the Lord. But when you see Tripp next, Anne, do congratulate him for me, will you? For arranging this televised encounter, because, whatever your father says now, I'm sure the fur will fly when the time comes. Commend the boy for me. Rudy would be proud of him."

To which Anne murmured something, glancing sidelong at Louise von Louwe as if she might give evidence of somehow knowing that an honest response to the request would involve saying that her plan was not to see Tripp again at all and that Dr. Kuykendall would have to deliver his own congratulations. But Louise von Louwe's attention was engaged elsewhere. She loved the idea of having serious male conversation going on under her roof and encouraged Gibbs and Kuykendall to continue theirs now by indicating to Walter, who had appeared in the doorway with his confidential smile to announce dinner, that they would be somewhat late, and by asking Gibbs

some further question about Farwell, to which Anne did
not listen. Unlike her cousin, she took less pleasure in
hearing conversation than in simply watching people
converse, observing the expressions of their hands and
faces, letting her imagination play over their pasts, the
divisions of their lives unknown to her. The result was that
she was often considered a daydreamer, inattentive,
seldom satisfactorily part of any group she found herself
in, and this was a fault for which Louise von Louwe was
particularly likely to criticize her. "You can't just sit
there," she had frequently said, "with that dazed, intent
expression you get, as if you were having a vision, not
paying attention to what anybody says, no matter how
much you say you enjoy it. A girl can't get away with just
having a good time. She must *give* a good time." But
whereas Louise ascribed this lapse on her young cousin's
part to her being indifferent to, incurious about, people,
actually no one was less so. What visions Anne had at such
times concerned only the people whom she was with. At
the mention of Rudy, she tried now to picture him, her
father, and Kuykendall, as they had been thirty-odd
years ago, in the days of their first knowing each other.

In an old trunk of Louise von Louwe's there was a piece
of tarnished silver lamé, sash or bandeau, which smelled
metallic and bitter, but at the same time fragrant with a
remnant of old perfume, and this for Anne had become so
much the smell of that era, the twenties, that she envi-
sioned her father and his friends as having breathed air
then of just this composition: silvery, tarnished, bitter as

metal, and dimly sweet. You read so much about those days, she thought. As thick as falling leaves, there were photographs just beginning to go brown with age to attest to the reality of them: the Norfolk jackets, knicker-bockers, knee-length waists, and huge fur coats. And there were the mah-jongg sets in the attics; some of the dances and songs preserved or revived, and a few of the movies and novels, although, when you stopped to con-sider, surprisingly few. But how seldom, Anne thought, did the survivors themselves reminisce about that era. That was the oddest thing of all, she found, quite as if it were all only the dream of her own generation. You heard from them of the century's teens and its thirties, the war and the depression, but rarely of the years between. Even Louise von Louwe, of usually voluble memory, was curi-ously laconic on the subject; and Gibbs, when he men-tioned them at all, for the most part mentioned only those of his activities which had not been peculiar to them. Well, and perhaps life had not been very different then, Anne thought, looking at the three of them sitting there. Yet she felt that it had been. Their very reticence on the subject, after all, suggested that it had, and then once in a great while even they admitted it. Gibbs himself had once re-marked that the mental age of the century seemed always to have approximated its last two digits and that in the nineteen-twenties everybody was more less twenty. "God forbid," he had said, "and with a deplorable sense of conse-quences."

"I remember, I remember perfectly well," Louise von

Louwe's words had dealt only with herself, her gaze softly
unfocused as she spoke, "how every single morning when I
woke up, I had exactly the same thought, which was how
was I going to have fun that day. Fun. Fun. Of course, I
still wake up with exactly the same thought, but nowadays
all the un-fun in the world gets you by the throat just
about the time you start brushing your teeth." And there
seemed to be an air of confraternity among them, these
survivors. It included even Kuykendall, Anne thought, although then as now he had surely belonged to a different
world from that of Gibbs and Louise. It was as if they had
all attended the same fantastic school where no one ever
thought to formulate a curriculum, grades were given on
the basis of *savoir faire* and charm, the endowment was all
squandered on extracurricular activities, and the head-
master lost his mind and shot himself to the tune, whin-
nied through a saxophone, of "Jada, Jada—Jada, Jada
Jing, Jing, Jing."

In rooms there are times of day that have nothing to do
with the world outside, and as Gibbs and Kuykendall
talked—Louise von Louwe prodding them forward with
an occasional question, Anne sinking back into the cinnamon-colored cushions of the couch—there was a sunset:
the warm air gathering somehow to a brilliance and a lull
that flushed their faces and made the sound of their voices
seem by contrast cool and brittle. Though winter night
outside, the day was just ending here, and by its last,
queer light Anne believed that she could at last see them
as once they had been: in some fashion younger than she

felt that she herself had ever been. There was Rudy,
Tripp's father, whom she knew only through photographs,
with something about him that begged to be ruined, as
Louise von Louwe had said the night before, swimming
and dancing his way through the silvery hours. Her own
father, having given up his momentary enthusiasm for the
ministry, and already aiming himself like a rifle for law
school and beyond, was still getting up with a hangover to
teach Sunday school in Boston. This last from Aunt
Louise, for she had known Gibbs before even Corinne,
later his wife, had, and it was she who had originally
introduced them. Anne found it almost impossible to
imagine Aunt Louise herself in those days although she
had seen photographs of her as a plump young woman
with dark bangs covering her forehead, a puffy mouth,
and long, helpless-looking arms. Only her shrewd eyes
seemed not to have changed. Looking out belligerently
from these likenesses of her flapper days, they seemed to
say: "Perhaps we are low-comedy now, but just wait until
we have come into our own in thirty years or so." Kuykendall alone, Anne guessed, had already come into his
own then. She had known him for most of her life as an old
friend and occasional visitor of her father's, and what had
almost more than anything else decided her, upon grad-
uating from college, to go to work for him in East Harlem,
had been her sense that he was a man who was all of one
piece and did not change. "Of course, he's insane," Aunt
Louise had said at the time, and to the degree to which
this might be true, Anne was certain that it had been

equally so always. In 1920, he was unquestionably as racked as he was now by, on the one hand, his fierce, disheveled commitment to a God who acted in and spoke through history, and, on the other, by his horror at the ambiguities and distortions of that history.

When they finally went in to dinner, for Louise von Louwe was unable to postpone it indefinitely as she would have liked, Anne was drawn back into the conversation again by Dr. Kuykendall, who asked her if she had told her father about her first days of working in his parish, especially about her *coup* with Lillian. Gibbs denied ever having heard anything about it at all and sent across the candles to his daughter a glance which with a kind of blurred sympathy excused her in advance for any attempt that she might make not to tell the anecdote at all, so uncommunicative had her mood seemed to be all evening, and then changed to a look of interested surprise when, on the contrary, she began with obvious relish to tell it.

The story itself was simple enough. Lillian, the reigning Negro prostitute of the block where the parish office was situated, during one of her periodic seizures of remorse came in one morning to see if any of the parish staff could help her find a job as a maid. Anne, having no idea who she was, took on her case, wrote her a letter of unqualified recommendation which she said would have brought tears to anyone's eyes by its eloquent praise of Lillian's character and aptitude, with the result that Lillian got an excellent job and had it to this day. It would have been impossible to say that Anne described the event with any

particular wit or felicity of language, but she showed
throughout such a rich if never quite resolved sense of the
comedy of the situation in so far as it involved her own
naïveté; she pictured Lillian herself with such clarity—
"She'd rave on about her troubles with her eyes bugged
out and rolling from side to side with misery until without
a single bit of warning there'd be one of those uncontrol-
lable sneezes of laughter that scrunched up her whole face
and showed her pink gums so that you just *knew* that
really, in her heart, she took the whole thing as a great,
wild joke"; above all, she, Anne, looked so young sitting
there by the light of the candles with her fair hair bright
against her gray flannel dress, speaking her piece as she
had been bidden, that Gibbs, in good spirits already, gave
out his single, explosive "Hah!" of delight when she had
finished.

"Well, Louise," he said, turning toward her, his face
florid and composed. "This family is getting back on its
feet at last. My daughter runs a placement bureau for
bawds. I do a comic turn on television. All that remains is
for you to start distilling red-eye in the basement, and
we'll really be in clover."

"With myself selling sham Bibles to Sunday-school
children to help out if the going gets rough," Kuykendall
added, at which Anne burst into laughter just as Walter
came in to remove the soup plates.

In face of such a festive turn to the evening, it was left
for Louise von Louwe to become the silent one. She
managed a smile at the outset of their laughter, but for the

most part sat there solid and immovable at the head of the table in her purple and amber, the fingers of her left hand working obscurely with the edge of the lace tablecloth as she dismembered her duckling *bigarade*. She was a gray, full-bosomed witch in the dim cave of her foreboding, and let them laugh while they might, her entire presence seemed to say: Gibbs with a fight on his hands, under the spell of a boy who had reason to blame him for his father's death; Anne, Anne, although perhaps not yet fully aware of it, in love with the boy, the barefoot boy, who pursued her for what appeared to be some curious end of his own. Louise von Louwe spoke no word of this, only continuing to eat, saying each time the conversation happened to turn her way something just short of what was required. But had she spoken her mind, Gibbs might well have admitted that for all his good humor, his odd sense of release, there was some seed of apprehension in him, too. Anne might well have recognized an instant's wild ache at the recollection that her decision was never to see Tripp again.

C H A P T E R

V

TRIPP'S program took place at ten o'clock in the evening on Friday, but Ansel Gibbs arrived at the studio a full hour in advance, as Tripp had suggested. In that way, the young man had explained, there would be time to answer any questions that Mr. Gibbs might have, show him around the studio, brief him on what few technical details it would be well for him to know, and put on his make-up. Gibbs balked at this last, and even when Tripp explained that it consisted only of panchromatic powder to correct the dark effect of his beard and a light pancake make-up to tone down his slight baldness in front, Gibbs humorously but firmly declined to submit to it, with the result that he appeared on the screen far older and less vigorous than actually he was. He consented, however, to wear a blue rather than a white shirt for the sake of avoiding glare, and when Tripp added that for this same reason it would be better not to wear a hand-painted tie, Gibbs replied that although this came to him as a considerable disappointment, he would accede to that, too, on condition

100

that the Senator also would. Porter Hoye and Louise von Louwe were to arrive in time to observe the proceedings from the glassed-in control room, but Anne insisted that she would prefer to stay at home and watch from there.

Senator Farwell, who compared with Gibbs was a veteran at affairs of this kind, did not appear until shortly before the program was to go on the air, and Tripp introduced the two men to one another in a small room adjoining the studio where the Senator, entirely bald except for a fringe of gray hair, was having his head anointed with the make-up that Gibbs had earlier refused. Describing this initial meeting later, Gibbs said that he had secretly hoped that it might have something of the same quality to it as that encounter between Alexander the Great and Diogenes, when Alexander dismounted from his horse, approaching his old enemy face to face for the first time where he sat basking by the side of the road, and magnanimously asked if there was anything in the world that he could do for him, to which Diogenes replied by requesting only that he be kind enough to step away from between himself and the sun. As luck would have it, however, Gibbs went on to explain, in the case of himself and the Senator, there was no opportunity for any such rejoinder since Farwell had greeted him with only a single word which, if his memory served him correctly, Gibbs said, was "Howdy."

In the studio itself, Gibbs and the Senator were introduced to the program and technical directors and two young engineers, and then led by Tripp to the far end of

the room, where the floor was covered with a dark carpet
upon which were arranged a desk, a sofa, several deep-
seated easy chairs, and a couple of small tables. On the
wall, framed without glass, hung a number of photographs
of Tripp in the company of various celebrities, another
showing Tripp in his staff-sergeant's uniform. Leaning
against the wall stood a guitar. There was a low bookcase
at one side of the desk in which Gibbs noticed a current
edition of *Who's Who*, a collection of American folk songs,
Alice in Wonderland, all six volumes of Carl Sandburg's
Lincoln, and several novels written by men and women
whose likenesses were among the others on the rear wall.
Off to one side stood an old-fashioned coat rack on which,
even as Gibbs was looking at it, a boy hung up a fringed
leather cowboy's jacket, a racoon coat, a plaid deerstalker
cap, and a fez. Two short walls had been built out to
either side, one hung with a Navajo blanket, the other
entirely bare except for a framed cover of *Time* enlarged to
several times its usual size, picturing Tripp with his head
tilted slightly back as though he were about to burst into
laughter, his hair a vivid red against the background of
feathery green trees with the sun in the form of a klieg
light blazing through them down upon a meadow where
men and women in full evening dress strolled with classical nymphs and satyrs and small children in gingham and
overalls. The whole three-sided room, Tripp explained, was
what amounted to the stage although they were not, if
they could, to think of it as that, but rather as somebody's

untidy living-room, the main lounge of a mental home, a Senate office, or whatever they chose.

They were to sit down anywhere they liked, Tripp told them, and could move about wherever they wanted to, never worrying about the cameras, but letting the cameras worry about them. As to the substance of the program itself, he said that it was, as he had already told them, theirs to determine. They would simply follow wherever their own conversation might lead them, avoiding specific political issues as much as possible, with Tripp himself playing a very minor role, he said, but ready to jump in if they should show signs of bogging down or if in any way things started to get out of hand, as he put it. Just then the incandescent lamps were switched on, both the ceiling and floor units, and the effect was momentarily blinding. Porter Hoye and Louise von Louwe had already taken their seats in the control room, and their expressions as they looked out through the glass were as if they were seeing the three men for the first time. They gave the impression, in fact, of not only seeing them, but of seeing around them and behind them, of indeed seeing quite through them, so brilliant was the light. Pulling up the knees of his trousers, Senator Farwell sat abruptly down on one arm of the sofa, where he remained for a few moments blinking into the blaze like some wiry, gray animal transfixed by the headlights of an automobile. Gibbs stood absolutely still with one hand raised to shield his eyes, his mouth shut tight in a deep-cut line of resigned exasperation. Only

Tripp continued, unperturbed, with what he had been saying. In fifty seconds they would be on the air; at precisely half past the hour they would go off. There was a clock above the control-room window, but they would get a signal to bring their discussion to a close. In silence then he sat down on the edge of the desk and crossed his legs as they all watched the second hand circle slowly toward the hour. Tripp wore a dark blue suit and, like Gibbs and the Senator, a blue shirt, which made his lean, boy's face seem the color of milk but richly, warmly so. Though he did not speak, his wide, mobile mouth was not totally still, but trembled faintly at the corners as though he was about to smile. Behind the glass pane, Porter Hoye glanced down at his watch like the picture of a man glancing down at his watch, and Louise von Louwe raised her hands to shoulder height and, attempting to catch Gibbs's eye, shook them, clasped, in the gesture of victory.

"This is Robin Tripp," the young man began almost dreamily, still sitting on the edge of the desk, "speaking to you from New York, which is . . . believe me, a cold, dark city this January night. The air has that soft, heavy chill to it you get when there's snow up there in the sky somewhere waiting to come down, and as far as I'm concerned, it can't start coming down too soon. I don't know about you—hardly anything about you at all for that matter—but personally I love it. It takes me back to roughly a hundred and fifty years before I was born, I'll settle for a hundred, when snow was top man around here, and if it felt like coming down thick enough, everything in

all Manhattan stopped moving except maybe the eye of a
hungry sparrow or a kid or two on a sled. But I'm not here
tonight to talk about the weather. In fact, for the next
half-hour you're going to get precious little talking from
me at all. If you're steady customers, you'll have heard me
announce last week that my guest this evening was to be
Senator Edward M. Farwell. Well, the Senator's sitting
beside me now. You'll see him for yourself in a minute. He
doesn't need anybody to introduce him, as the saying goes,
but just in case somebody's tuned in from Mars, I could
say in very general terms that he is, of course, one of the
mainstays of the right wing of our government. But do me
a favor and forget about that, will you, because we're
going to keep away from politics this evening? You know
our policy around here. Get prizefighters to talk about
Grandma Moses, scientists to sound off on the movies,
musicians to chew the rag about their days on the high-
school baseball squad. Let them talk about anything, as a
matter of fact, except their own lines because what we're
interested in on this show isn't the news, but the men behind the news. We don't want to know what they do, but
who they are. Who is Senator Edward M. Farwell? And
who is . . . But I don't want to jump the gun on myself.

"There's somebody else here with us tonight. He started
hitting the front pages again earlier this week when word
came through of his nomination by the President as a
key member of the Cabinet. He's in the city for only a
few days before heading off for the capital to appear
before a committee of the Senate, which must confirm

his nomination, and when he arrived here Tuesday, he told the press that he planned to make no public appearances at all prior to that date. I don't know just how I did it, but I trapped him into agreeing to come here this evening anyway, so it's with very special pleasure that I welcome him now, the Honorable Ansel Gibbs. It's a particular treat for me personally because Mr. Gibbs was a very close friend of my father's, and this is the first time we've met for a number of years.

"But on with the show. Who is Senator Farwell? Who is Mr. Ansel Gibbs? You can't just say, 'Gentlemen, reveal yourselves. Advance and be recognized.' That's asking too much of any man. But you can say—Senator Farwell, let's begin with you if we may, sir—you and Mr. Gibbs have in different ways both been serving our government for about as long as my generation can remember, and it would be interesting to know whether your paths have ever crossed before."

"If you mean have I ever had the pleasure of making Mr. Gibbs's acquaintance personally, my answer is that unfortunately I have not. But there was one time—"

"I saw you—"

"I was just going to say that once—"

"Yes. The Senator and I came very close to meeting in 1939, I think it was."

"Early 1940, I think."

"1939 or early 1940, in London, we met—or, that is, we just didn't meet—at a large dinner given by the then Air Vice Marshal."

"I was overseas with a committee investigating British war production."

"I believe we exchanged some suspicious glances," Gibbs said, "down the length of a very long table."

"I don't seem to remember having had any particular suspicions of anybody, Mr. Gibbs."

"I didn't mean particular suspicions. It has always struck me that Americans meeting each other abroad are apt to be suspicious of each other in a rather general way. You come across your countryman surrounded by strangers, conducting himself with great circumspection, and you can't help wondering what he's like when he's among friends at home. When you meet another American abroad, it's sometimes hard to be sure just where and how he fits into things back here."

"That is very subtle. The only ones I'm suspicious of are the ones who stay on over there. I have an old-fashioned feeling that the best place for a U.S. citizen is in the U.S."

"I believe that I would agree with you in seventy-five per cent of the cases."

"And the remaining twenty-five?"

"I'm perfectly willing to believe that they can best serve their own or their country's interests, or both, abroad."

"The trouble is they lose touch."

"This business of losing touch, Senator. I keep running into that phrase these days. I'm not sure that I altogether understand its meaning."

"I think its meaning is very simple. If you and I are friends and I go away somewhere for an extended period, we lose touch with each other. It's the same thing with a man and his country. Out of sight, out of mind, you might say."

"There are some minds that aren't so accommodating. A man may see his friend most clearly and poignantly precisely when he has gone away from him somewhere."

"That sounds a little cold and calculating, doesn't it? Give me a man with a heart who stays right in the thick of things and fights it out shoulder to shoulder with his friend or his country."

"Not all battles are won in the thick of things."

"I'm afraid this is a little too intellectual for me."

"Well, but you gentlemen have differed on one basic point here," Tripp intervened, "that I think causes a lot of people trouble. Senator Farwell, you've used a very old saying when you said: 'Out of sight, out of mind.' But there's another one which is probably just as old that says: 'Absence makes the heart grow fonder.' Are you definitely going to cast your vote for the first, Senator?"

"Well, I'll give you an example of what I mean. My mother and I were always very close. When I first went up to the Senate back in the days when you were in knickers, I don't imagine a single week went by without me writing her a long, newsy letter full of my comings and goings, all those kind of things I knew she'd want to hear. But, you know, after a few months went by and there was too much piled up on my desk for me to get home to Goshen Falls to see her, it would begin to be as if I was writing those letters to myself. I had a picture of her in my mind all the time, but that picture would just fade and fade like an old yellow photograph. Then I'd get back home some day, maybe only long enough for a cup of coffee and a cruller in the kitchen, and right away it was just like it always was. Mother said to me once, 'Ed Farwell's my boy, all right. But that young fellow up in Washington's no kin of mine.' In a way she was dead right, and I knew it. Now I just don't know whether Mr. Gibbs would agree with what I'm saying or not."

"How about it, Mr. Gibbs?"

"I think we're pretty far adrift from my original remark, which was simply that the temporary expatriate, geographically or emotionally, is apt to gain a valuable perspective. It's certainly not an original insight on my part, and I'm not going to belabor it further. But, of course, I understand what Senator Farwell has been saying about his relationship with his mother. We all know and love people who fade in our minds when we leave them, becoming flesh and blood only when and if we return, but aren't they almost all of them people with whom our relationship is based primarily on sentiment, an emotional relationship whose very substance is a matter of fairly constant personal contact? On the other hand, if I not only love my friend, but am also concerned with him as a complex, thinking human mechanism with certain ideas that challenge or confirm my own, why then I think he won't fade in my mind at all when I leave him. On the contrary, I am always in spite of myself seeing things as he would see them. When I argue from my point of view, I'm apt to have his in mind as well. And that goes for a country, too—if you take your country really seriously, that is. Not just as the wave of a flag and a lump in the throat."

"I don't know," Senator Farwell said, "but it seems to me you're commencing to say that there's something not quite bright about loving your country or your mother or your friend or just about anything else. Of course, I may be wrong but—"

"I apparently haven't made myself clear. What I intended—"

"Please let me finish."

"To love isn't always—"

"Please. Maybe I'm crazy, but when you clear away all the language out of here, it's what a man loves that he lives and dies for, and he stays with what he loves, emotionally and geographically and every which way. This 'complex, thinking human mechanism' kind of relationship has just got to take second place. Don't you agree with that, Mr. Gibbs?"

"Sometimes, Senator, you have to make the best of second place. There are even times when it may be the better of the two."

"Senator Farwell, if I can interrupt here for a minute," Tripp said. "Not to change the subject, but you mentioned a few minutes ago your home in Goshen Falls, and I wondered if you'd be willing to give us a few more . . ."

"Let's leave Goshen Falls out of it for the time being, son. I've got my teeth in something here, and I don't want to let go. Mr. Gibbs, have you ever held an elective office?"

"No, I have not."

"Well, it's an experience you ought to have. Like yourself, I'm a college man, but campaigning through the backwaters of my own home state I learned more than I ever did in any ten lectures on American government I ever heard. For instance, I learned that intelligence counts with the voters the same as it does anywhere else. But the man who gets elected has got to have more than that. He's got to have a heart, and a lot of the time he's got to wear it on his sleeve right out where folks can see it. They respect intelligence, but it's the heart they vote for."

"What are you afraid of, Senator?"

"How's that?"

"You keep trying to find cover. You let it be known that you have a heart and a mother and an occasional cup of coffee in the kitchen because everyone else has these, too. But because intelligence is a rarer commodity, you make no claims there at all as if for fear that it might make you stand out in a crowd."

"I've stood out in quite a few crowds in my day, Mr. Gibbs."

"Only as someone bigger and more successful than the rest. You're determined, aren't you, to be everyone's slightly magnified image of himself, but under no circumstances qualitatively different. We're told the purpose of this interview is to ascertain who we are. My guess is that you don't want to be found out."

"You don't stand up for election as often as I have without having that made plain enough. My record is an open book. It's well known who I am. What a lot of us are interested in is who you are, Mr. Gibbs."

"I'd be equally interested to hear your view on the subject."

"I haven't made any secret of it."

"I take it you refer to your 'I am civilization' speech."

"I had it on good report that you made such a statement once. That statement has certainly been widely ascribed to you."

"I am almost tempted not to repudiate it."

"Then you did make it?"

"I did not. But I'm tempted to make it for you now, if only because you're so confident that, like you, I'd never dare to—would never dare to admit to being anything other than what people expect their public servants to be."

"Either you make the statement because you believe it, or you don't because you don't."

"Very well, I will make it because I believe it. I am civilization. There you are, Senator."

"You know, some of my other victims on this show," Tripp said, "have told me after all the shooting was over that there's something about the whole business here that's like a sort of queer dream—this room with one wall missing and the light so strong that you see more than eyes were ever meant to. The make-up you wear, these cameras like huge, black bugs, and the faces staring in at you through the control-room window. People tell me you're apt to say more than you want to, things you may not even mean in the first place, the way you do when you're dreaming. But it isn't a dream, gentlemen. There's real snow outside waiting to fall on a real city, and over a million real people watching and listening to what you do and say in here."

"Thank you," Gibbs continued, "but I've said no more and no less than I want to. I'll even say it again for you, Senator. I am civilization, and I'm prepared to explain at least part of what that means."

"Please do. I'd like to hear that explained."

"They ran a cartoon with your speech, you remember. It showed the evolutionary process in terms of a straight line stretching all the way up from—oh, the grotesque and mysterious beginnings, the one-cell blobs and the monkeys, at the bottom, and then finally, way up at the top, me. To be civilization means to stand at the top, to be the last and best as far as things have gone to date, the educated, liberated man with his back to the grotesque mystery of his origins and his face to God knows what. Mind you, I don't stand alone up there. You're civilization, too, Senator, whether you care to say so or not."

"You're putting words in my mouth."

"It was you who started the practice. But I'll speak only for myself if you prefer. The civilized have responsibilities toward the less civilized. Politically that leads to

imperialism, of course, and on the personal scale it leads
to cynicism or despair. But that's far from being the worst
of it. To be civilization, to be civilized, is to be aware of so
many possible courses of action at any given time that no
one of them ever seems to be without qualification right.
Everything is qualified. Legal and ethical principles are
good for today, but can't be rigidly fixed for tomorrow.
There has been talk tonight about love—love between
humans and love for country. No matter how hard you
may pretend to the contrary, there is ambivalence here,
too. We know too much about the component parts of
love—the self-interest, the insecurity, the Freudian
grotesqueries. Love is no longer an answer, or if so, only
one of an indeterminate number, none of them certain.

"I don't know. If there were to be a congress of planets
—something like the U.N. celestially conceived—the
chances are that one of us, one of the ultra-civilized, would
be sent to represent this earth. You can imagine his
arrival, soberly dressed, clean-shaven, a brief case under
his arm, to hold forth in his rational, moderate tones as the
final product of all the glories and barbarities of human
history. One wonders with what single mighty assevera-
tion he would enlighten that cosmic assemblage as to the
nature of this civilization. I have no idea what he would
say. But . . . ambivalence. Ambivalence. If he were
limited to only one word, that is the one I would suggest to
him."

"No standards, Mr. Gibbs? No fixed legal and ethical

principles? No love? This is your man who *is* civilization?"

"On the contrary, all of this and any number of contrary alternatives as well."

"A man can't be many things at once."

"In all candor, I find him rarely capable of being less. It's just that which makes him civilized and civilization possible."

"Look, let's get down to the facts here. You keep talking about 'him,' about the civilized man, and civilization, and I don't know what all besides. What I'd like to hear you talk about for a change is yourself."

"Senator Farwell has at least touched on his own past for us, Mr. Gibbs," Tripp said. "I know everybody would be very interested to hear something about yours."

"What I suspect the Senator wants to hear especially is what he already well knows—that politically my past is a handicap. I was born with money, for instance. Not by any means a fortune, you understand, but enough, conservatively invested, to guarantee me a certain security for my lifetime. Consequently, I never had to work my way through college or anything else, and when I received my law degree and was subsequently admitted to the bar, I became associated very naturally with the firm founded by my father and his elder brother. I confess that I wouldn't have had it otherwise. Add to that the fact that I have never borne arms for my country. I was too young to get to France in the first war, and too old for the second. And, as the Senator has already brought to light, I have never held an elective office."

"Nobody holds these things against you. It's just the infernal pride you seem to take in them."

"I've never understood why one man shouldn't be as proud of his good fortune as another man of his lack of it."

"I think it's time for one of us to tip our hand and stop just talking words. You know as well as I do that the way this country works, Cabinet appointments are more the President's business than anybody else's, and it's the Senate's job to confirm them unless they can show a case of strong ineligibility. After what you've been saying here tonight, I think we have a case of that right now."

"I wish you would present that case."

"I will present it. You're an educated man, Mr. Gibbs, and nobody's going to question your ability when it comes to executing policy. But proud as you may be of it, you've never been in the thick of things. You've never sweated life out with the rest of us, and in my opinion you have the kind of cold, impersonal way of looking at people and history that makes me question whether you have or ever could have the imagination, the heart, the guts, to create and formulate policy. How can a man who's never had to earn his own living and whose only training has been at a rich man's college and a Wall Street law firm—now, what I want to know is how is a man like that going to be capable of suddenly pitching in and making any sense out of a world threatened by the H-bomb and by Communism inside and outside? It's like stepping out of the front parlor into a lion's den."

"I don't know how to answer a charge like that unless

perhaps by telling you something about the front parlor."

"You talk just words. You keep trying to trick me into playing word games with you."

"In the front parlor words are what we chiefly trade in."

"Forget about the front parlor. It was just a figure of speech. I'm not going to be hoodwinked into shifting this business to a discussion of figures of speech."

"If I trade in words, you trade in emotions—yours against mine, or what you call my lack of them."

"I'm not ashamed of my emotions."

"There's a difference between us. I've always been rather ashamed of my words."

"Why? Which words?"

"All of them. Because they've been so necessary. When you suggest that I'm an overly verbal person, you've put your finger on something. There have been times when I've wished I had chosen the kind of life that more clearly speaks for itself. A soldier's life. Or a priest's. Even a prodigal's. The kind of life that doesn't have to depend so heavily upon words to define it."

"You're still avoiding the issue here. I questioned your eligibility for the office you've been nominated for. You persistently refuse to give me a straight answer."

"I'm speaking about myself. That's what you asked."

"Facts, Mr. Gibbs. Not words."

"What facts would you like? In 1928 I bought a four-hundred-acre ranch in Montana. My wife died soon after we were married and left me with one child, a daughter. I have never been a card-carrying Communist. For some time now I have been engaged in writing a record of my experiences in England during the war. Roughly fifteen years ago my closest friend shot himself near a stand of croquet mallets in his back yard. There are some facts."

"This is ridiculous."

"If any fact is relevant, all of them are."

"I think what the Senator means," Tripp said, "is that you can't consider all of these facts to be equally important."

"They are all part of who I am, and that is what the Senator has asked me to tell him."

"But a ranch in Montana and the suicide of a friend," Tripp said. "Certainly you don't put them on a par with each other."

"It wouldn't surprise me if he did," Senator Farwell said.

"Simply as facts, there is no essential difference between them," Gibbs said. "The difference is not a factual one."

"What is the difference then?" Tripp asked.

"It exists only in my mind. It doesn't have any substance except the words I describe it with, and it is not a fact. The ranch in Montana is nothing—to me, that is. And to me the death of this friend is—this death is for me one of the worlds I live in."

"Why?" Senator Farwell asked.

"Because for a long time I was troubled with the suspicion that I was perhaps in some negative, partial way responsible—in much the same way that some might accuse you and others, Senator, of being partially responsible for prolonging the Second World War by your zealous advocacy of isolationism in 1939."

"You're what I call an international do-gooder. Your brand of foreign policy can only weaken us, and as far as—"

"We've been asked to keep politics out of this discussion, and I apologize for being the one to introduce the subject. I am making no charge—"

"You very clearly stated—"

"I stated, and only by way of analogy, that this is a possible charge that could be made against you. I am not pressing it myself, and I have no doubt that you could absolve yourself of it if I were to. In the case of my own conscience's charge against me, I've been absolved comparatively recently. I've become convinced that my friend was bound to take his own life whether I had come at the right moment with help or not. Looking back at it now, I can see that in any number of ways his whole life had been leading up to it, and it ended by being just about the only thing left for him. I can even believe that it may not have been the worst thing. In the long run his survivors don't seem to have suffered for it. If he'd lived, they might well have suffered a great deal more, and he with them."

"Why are you telling me all this? What's this got to do with anything."

"I'm not sure why. Perhaps just because you asked for facts, and this is one that's been on my mind for a long time. And also because it's helped me understand that, despite your anxieties on the subject, the man who says he is civilization isn't apt to do injury to other people, but only to himself. I don't think you need fear for the safety of this country in such hands. Even our policies, disapprove of them as you may, needn't cause you alarm because you can rest assured that, in the last analysis, we're never likely to try forcing them down your throats because we're never entirely convinced that they are right any more than we are ever entirely convinced that yours are wrong. For the civilized man there aren't apt to be any absolute principles or holy causes. That's what makes civilized life possible. We may not be heroes, but by and large we're also not villains—either collectively or taken one by one. Tolerant. Ambivalent. Call us what you will."

"I call you the worst kind of cynic. You don't quite believe in what you stand for, and you don't quite disbelieve in what you're opposed to."

"And that infuriates you as it infuriates a litigant to see his lawyer having lunch with the lawyer of his opponent."

"You're dead right it does. And this friend of yours who killed himself. Did he have ideas like this? It was presumably something like them that drove him to it."

"He was too young for ideas. If he were alive now at the same age as when he died, he'd be almost young enough to be my son. I remember him almost as a son."

"Before you absolved yourself, as you put it, you say you were afraid that maybe you'd had something to do with his death—very indirectly, of course?"

"I meant that if I'd only known what was in his mind, I might have been able to help him in some way."

"Was there any way you could have known what was in his mind?"

"Looking back at it, I thought that there was. Isn't that always the case?"

"How could you have known?"

"He'd always been a very modest person, for instance—extraordinarily good at a great many pleasant things, as popular a man with all kinds of people as any man I've ever known, but he was always very self-deprecating—charmingly, genuinely so. However, the last few months of his life he became boastful in a strange, belligerent way. He'd blow his own horn as if he were half daring you to wrench it away from him and break it over your knee."

"Was there anything else?"

"I remember his laugh changed. Before, he'd had a way of tipping his head back and just letting it come out, but later he'd watch you when he was laughing. I suspect he was watching to see whether you knew he wasn't really laughing at all. He also became indiscreet."

"What do you mean by that?"

"He was working for me at the time, and I had good opportunity to notice it. He tried exploiting the fact that he and I were good friends, for one thing. He betrayed certain confidences just for the sake, I think, of having it known that I confided in him. He borrowed money from his own secretary. It reached the point where for everyone's good, including his own, it became essential to let him go."

"I take it that's your way of saying you fired him?"

"I had a long talk with him. He admitted that he was

badly overtired and needed a rest. All the sweetness of the man seemed to come back that day, and he agreed to take a few weeks off and go away somewhere. It was the last time I ever saw him."

"He never came back?"

"No, no. He came back. But while he was away, it came out that he'd been talking quite irresponsibly about some highly confidential matters. Everyone was up in arms. It was impossible to keep him on—even if he'd been my own son."

"I thought you said you never saw him again after your earlier talk?"

"That is correct."

"He just came back and found out he was fired."

"Everything was explained to him. It was made clear that his salary would be continued until he had found other work. I most certainly didn't bear him any ill-feeling. Nobody did. He understood all that."

"But not from you?"

"Not directly. No. I felt it would be easier for us both that way."

"How long after this did he shoot himself?"

"I don't remember exactly. Several weeks. A month."

"Mr. Gibbs, I don't think you're talking good sense. You made the point a while back that if you'd only known what was in his mind, you could have helped him, but it seems to me that you knew what was in his mind very well and went about helping him in a mighty peculiar way."

"Senator Farwell," Tripp said, "when I asked you

gentlemen to avoid politics this evening, I didn't mean
that there was no restriction at all as to the kind of thing
you—"

"You want to know who he is, don't you?" Senator
Farwell asked. "Don't start getting cold feet just when
you're about to find out."

"I'm certainly just as eager as you are to find out and
maybe more, but there are limits to what you can put a
man through," Tripp said.

"He was the closest friend I've ever had," Gibbs said.
"I'm certain now, and so are others who loved him, that he
would have done what he did quite apart from any action
of mine or anybody else's. No one was to blame—not I any
more than all his other friends or even his wife. A man
chooses the instruments of his own destruction, and I'm
willing to believe that in some fatal, half-conscious way
that's why he chose us. But to say that we all destroyed
him is the same as to say that none of us did. Justice can't
be chopped so fine."

"Then in justice you feel you've been completely absolved, Mr. Gibbs, of any responsibility whatever."

"Yes, in justice. My son—my friend, that is—this young
man they found dead—he took his own life. There was no
one else responsible. I'm convinced of that."

"And civilization goes its merry way, Mr. Gibbs."

"Civilization survives, Senator. There's nothing especially merry about it. It may well be its tragedy—just
to survive so much that was beautiful, expendable, and
misdirected, young, that died along the way."

"Yes. You've survived a great deal. Your principles, for one thing. Your belief that what's right is right and what's wrong is wrong. Your emotions. Love even. You've said so yourself."

"It may not be a merry business to be a survivor, but there can be a kind of pride in it. There's a pride just in lasting."

"Lasting for what, I'd like to know."

"Maybe just to continue making it possible for the young to be beautiful and misdirected. I don't have all the answers."

"My mistake, sir. I was under the impression that you did."

"You forget something, gentlemen," Tripp said. "We see each other and ourselves as life-size in here. Each of us sees the other two looking just as high and wide and thick as they really are. The lights in here are brighter than the sun, and they make us seem if anything bigger and solider than life and realer than we are. But remember how we look flickering in the dark of thousands of living-rooms, bedrooms, dining-rooms, where we're reduced to black-and-white midgets a few inches high—just about big enough to saddle mice and go charging at each other with pins. When anything that size starts getting noisy and out of hand, there's just one thing to do. You fumigate. I offer this warning. We have only a few minutes left."

"I don't care how I look on a television screen," Senator Farwell said. "I, for one, am grateful for the chance of appearing in the living-rooms of the American people in any form whatsoever for the purpose of going on record as being firmly opposed to the appointment of Ansel Gibbs to any position of high responsibility in this government."

"I have a strange feeling of being on trial here," Gibbs said, "though on just what charge I'm still not certain."

"I think I've made that clear enough," Senator Farwell said. "And I agree that it's a trial. I only hope the people watching us this evening will take their responsibilities as citizens seriously enough to write to their Congressmen expressing their own verdicts. Pressure must be brought to bear."

"Mr. Tripp, this was originally your dream, as you call it," Gibbs said, "and you're not entirely uninvolved in the issues here yourself. What is your verdict?"

"I'm just the man behind the man behind the news, sir. I sing songs and ask questions. It's a long, hard pull, but the pay's not bad."

"Sing out your judgment then. I've been telling no less than the truth about myself all evening—a remarkable experience for any man—and so far I've had only one reaction. The Senator's. Sheer horror. Sing us your own feelings. I see you have your guitar in the corner over there."

"I don't sing verdicts. That's not part of my act. Besides, I don't know the chords that go with dead friends and ambivalence, isolationism in 1939 and a United Nations among the stars. It would take me hours to work them out, and our time's running short."

"You're a wise young man. Find out who everyone is, but never let down your own guard."

"Not for a minute."

"If I had a son, that would be my advice to him."

"I'm the father of sons myself," Senator Farwell said. "Three of them. Fine boys. And I'm here to say that if I can help it, and I think I can, they won't be raising boys of their own in a country run by men who have minds as cold as winter and snow where their hearts ought to be. You said you liked the snow, boy. Well, give me the good old sun any day."

"Oh, take the good old sun then, Senator," Gibbs said. "Take the sun, take all the brightness and warmth of the world, the love guaranteed against failure, coffee in the kitchen with Mother, and three fine boys—take everything brave and true and uncomplicated there is in the world. Take it because your war cry is that you already have it. Only, for God's sake, don't think I question its worth."

"I apologize for interrupting again," Tripp said, "but our time's up. This is the point where I usually say how this program's completely spontaneous and unrehearsed, but tonight that doesn't seem necessary. You might say that, like some kinds of murder, it was unpremeditated. But, seriously, I know that nobody's going to hold any grudges for words spoken in the heat of the kliegs, and, as far as I'm concerned, it's been not only extremely illuminating, but a pleasure and an honor to have—"

"It's been a trial," Senator Farwell said. "That's what it's been. And as I said before, I leave it to your listeners to—"

"Yours is the verdict I want, Tripp," Gibbs said.

"I'm sorry, but time's up."

"The verdict's plain enough as it is," Senator Farwell said.

"Tripp," Gibbs said.

"Back with you again next week, strangers out there in the flickering dark. In the meanwhile—"

"What's your verdict, Tripp?" Gibbs said.

"Yes, yes. All right. I'll give a verdict, but it'll have to wait till next week—same time, same station. In the meanwhile, this is Robin Tripp in New York wishing you all good-night and dreams to gladden your hearts."

From the control room, one of the young engineers had been gesturing hectically for Tripp to bring things to an end, and when he finally did so, racing through his last words, someone switched off the incandescent lamps so that, although the room was still dimly lit, it seemed night by comparison. The control room, on the other hand, remained bright, and for a few moments everyone in it was still, including Porter Hoye and Louise von Louwe, who sat at the window unmoving as stones. Then just the ceiling lights were switched on again, and immediately an elaborate dismantling process began as cameras were moved back into place, the lighting units checked, the furniture in the three-sided room where the interview had taken place pushed to one side, and the carpet rolled up. Gibbs, Farwell, and Tripp had all stepped out into the studio proper, but it was only with difficulty that Porter Hoye and Louise were able to single them out in the midst of all the activity, and through the soundproof glass they could hear nothing. All in pantomime they saw one of the electricians come up to shake Senator Farwell's hand, but with the powder streaked on his forehead where he had tried to wipe it off with his handkerchief, the Senator was hunched over with his fist to his mouth, violently coughing. With his free hand, he gestured the young man aside. The program director and a young woman with a clipboard and pencil stood talking to Tripp, but at a beckoning signal from Gibbs, Tripp left them to go to him. They spoke briefly, Tripp all earnestness, Gibbs with his hands clasped behind his back, his chin high. Then with a kind of mock salute, smiling, Tripp seemed to say good-by and returned to the pair whom he had left, drawing them through the crowd toward the Senator, to whom he introduced them. The Senator had stopped coughing and was drinking a glass of water, which he set down for a moment to shake their hands. Shortly after this, Tripp, leaving these three together, disappeared rapidly through a small door at the rear of the studio.

It was only at this point that Hoye and Louise managed to catch Gibbs's eye, and with a nod of his head in the direction of Farwell and just the slightest raising of his eyebrows, he indicated to them that he must speak to him before leaving. The Senator wheeled around so suddenly as Gibbs came up to him from behind that the water spilled out of the glass which he had by now retrieved, soaking Gibbs's sleeve and the front of his coat. The Senator insisted on ineffectually dabbing at it with his own handkerchief, and it was with this incident that Louise von Louwe finished describing her impressions of the whole evening to Anne much later.

"Tripp had stolen off like a shrewd, red fox," she said, "and there were the two of them left together. Everybody else seemed to draw back as though there was going to be a shooting, and, believe me, my dear, I was prepared for anything myself. And then this burlesque! Your father standing there dripping wet, with his whole career, as far as I was concerned, shattered into a hundred bits and pieces all around him, and that bald little senator pecking away at him with a pocket handkerchief. I didn't know whether to burst into tears or wild laughter. From beginning to end, it was all upside down and distorted like a face reflected in a spoon."

CHAPTER

VI

IN ANSWER to Anne's question, Porter Hoye only shook his great head from side to side twice, yet she felt greater apprehension at this than at any other point during the entire evening, which she had spent alone in the living-room, watching Tripp, Farwell, and her father on the small screen. She had asked her question in a whisper, hanging Hoye's overcoat in the hall closet while he stood close behind her, and it was when she glanced back over her shoulder for his answer that she saw him with his lips pursed, silently shaking his head from left to right. Farther forward in the hall, Louise von Louwe stood in front of a mirror unpinning her hat with a look of intense indifference, and by the door, still ajar so that the snowflakes were caught in the light from it, Gibbs was bent over, peeling off his rubbers. People must always be wrapped up and then unwrapped again, the girl thought, no matter what high purposes they might serve in between; and there was a kind of comfort in this. "What do you think?" she had whispered to Hoye only a moment before, and the gravity

of his unspoken reply was abruptly belied now by his turning away from her and roaring into the still air: "Dear
Gussy, Louise, I'm half starved!" then somehow propelling
them all toward the kitchen.

It was the kind of move that you felt he brilliantly
blundered into rather than planned. Nowhere but in the
kitchen could they have been so mercifully and naturally
relieved of the necessity, at least for a time, of making conversation. Hoye himself, with hoarse good humor, took
over the scrambling of the eggs, standing at the stove in
his iron-gray suit and starched collar, while Anne and
Louise von Louwe clattered the kitchen silver onto the
white enamel table top and set about making coffee. Gibbs
sat by the counter on a high stool waiting for the toast to
pop and then buttering it, his gaze intent on what he was
doing. It was Hoye again who thought to switch on the
tiny radio, and the music that he found, turning the volume up to where it obscured the sounds of cooking, was
some frenetic piece of Dixieland jazz which he bravely gave
evidence of enjoying even to the extent of humming along
with it off-key until Louise von Louwe passed close to him,
her hands full of egg shells for the garbage, and quietly but
with awesome clarity said: "You can strip yourself naked
and stand on your head if you want, but a wake's still a
wake." He stopped his humming at this, but the radio itself was sufficient to restrict conversation to little but the
most functional exchanges until the eggs were finished and
Hoye was dividing them into meticulously equal portions,
whereupon the music came to an end and a news broadcast

followed. Hoye was on the point of turning it off when Gibbs stopped him with a gesture, and there was thus nothing to do but sit there, the four of them, waiting, with no longer any pretense of doing anything else. Not until the broadcast was nearly over did the report come of Tripp's program an hour before. It was a late bulletin simply announcing that Gibbs's unscheduled appearance had taken place and mentioning a heated debate between him and Senator Farwell.

It was, however, enough to bring Hoye to the point of making his first open pronouncement on the whole matter, which he did rather hastily as if determined to be the one to set the tone for anything further that might be said on the subject. "Well," he began with an introductory finality calculated to discourage contradiction, "I was against it from the start as you know, but it's over and done with now, and I don't think any particular harm's going to come of it." He looked at no one as he spoke, but down at his plate and the uneaten food upon it.

"Harm?" Louise von Louwe asked him sharply. "I should think the harm's been done already. Ansel," she continued, turning to Gibbs with her fork pointed toward him, "I will never believe that you didn't for some reason do it on purpose."

"Do what? What do you think he's done?" Hoye asked, at which Gibbs, laying one hand on his friend's shoulder, interrupted with: "I've no intention of gumming my porridge in the corner while you discuss what's to become of me. I'm as grateful for that incredible half-hour as for any other I've ever lived through with the possible exception of the one in which I was persuaded to go through with it in the first place."

"The boy hypnotizes you," Louise von Louwe said. "There's something about him. I feel it myself—in the stomach somewhere. When he warned you that it wasn't a dream in there, he obviously put it into your head somehow that it was. You said things you'd ordinarily say only in your sleep, if then."

"On the contrary, Louise. I have never been so awake."

"Louise exaggerates as usual," Hoye said. The coffee began to boil over at this point, and, reaching out to turn down the gas without so much as a moment's pause in what he was saying, he gave fresh evidence of being—as from the beginning he had clearly set out to appear—the man in control of a difficult situation. "But if I may say so, Ansel, I don't believe it was a wise move to bring up the business about Rudy. Don't think for a minute they're going to let the matter rest where you left it. They'll probably try to dig up Sylvia somewhere and get her version."

"I very much doubt that," Gibbs said.

"I beg your pardon, but they will. I'm not saying that I think it's necessarily going to do you any harm, but they'll be after the facts all right."

"Will at least you eat your eggs, Anne?" Louise von Louwe said. "I hate to see them smeared all over a plate like a street accident."

"Maybe there's snow where my heart ought to be," Gibbs said, laying his hands palms down on the table, the fingers apart, "to borrow the Senator's rich metaphor, but there are no three people in the world I'm fonder of than the three of you. If it's not apparent to you what's happened to me, I owe you an explanation—you three if anybody." He looked at Anne as he spoke where she sat on the kitchen stool, her toes slipped between the rungs, leaning forward with her arms on her knees. "I'm tempted to say that it happened when Tripp was here to see me for the first time the other day, but, of course, it's not a question of any single event. Things don't happen neatly, slap-bang, like that, alluring as it is to think so. It was a process, although certainly seeing Tripp that afternoon was a crucial part of it. Oh, all I mean," he went on, taking a cigarette from Hoye, who smoked continuously, whereas Gibbs himself rarely did, "is that somehow the winter's over. I know this has its comic side. Springtime for Ansel. I've never been one to deny my own grotesqueness. But I find that after being away a very great deal longer and farther than two years in Montana, I'm back again. Not just to this city, and to you. Back to nothing Farwell would call the thick of things, I suppose. But at least to the thickness of things, you might say—to the solid present, what's happening right now—snow falling, this table under my hands, having a job again, or being about to. Somehow I've returned. That's the only word for it. I haven't lost my mind. I don't think so. A lot of it was deciding—I told the truth about that—that I no longer had this tragedy on my conscience. The boy himself exonerated me. He's obviously unscarred by it himself, though I dreaded seeing him, thinking he wouldn't be. But returning from that is only part of it. It's a much more pervasive thing. When he sang me one of his songs—some silly thing, I can't even remember what it was about—I knew that I'd arrived back in an infinitely more real sense than at the airport Tuesday. I can't be any plainer than that. Returned. So this evening with Farwell I was perfectly aware of everything I was saying. They wanted to know who I was, and I told them—not who they expected me to be, but who I precisely am—for better or for worse. Personally, I don't regret a word of it. Politically, I don't think it matters. In the long run they'll interpret what I said in terms of what they expected me to say. That's usually the way. But this is beside the point. Do you understand what I'm trying to say, not about the television program, but about myself?"

"I understand one thing," Anne suddenly said, and it was apparent to all three of them as they turned to her that there were tears in her eyes. "That politically you're ruined. Everybody understands that except you. But I don't care about that. What I care about is that he set out in cold blood to ruin you."

"Who, Anne?"

"Of course, Tripp. He made a fool of you, and it's what he must have planned to do all along. I could hardly bear to watch it."

"Come, come, my dear," Louise von Louwe said, taking her by the arm and pointlessly trying to force Anne to look at her. "I am the voice of doom in this house, and even I wouldn't go so far as to say that. Besides, you're crying."

"Why should he want to ruin me, Anne?" Gibbs asked, leaning toward her across the table. "Because of Rudy, you mean? Something like that?"

"Melodrama!" Although up to this point the sight of the girl's tears had left Hoye's face helpless somewhere between expressions, as he boomed out this single word, he could not help faintly smiling at what struck him as the ineffable accuracy of it.

"Please don't interrupt." Gibbs's voice came closer to anger than Hoye had ever heard it before. "My daughter and I are talking together. This has rarely happened, and I won't be interrupted," at which Hoye was silent, only glancing at Louise von Louwe, who almost imperceptibly shrugged. "Is that what you're saying, Anne?" Gibbs asked. "That Tripp set out to ruin me because of Rudy?"

"Yes," she said. "because of that mostly, I think, and because it's the kind of thing he'll do whether he has a reason or not. It's the way he is. I can't explain why."

"If you can't explain why, we can't take what you're telling us seriously," Louise von Louwe said. "You don't get about enough. You should be seeing more people of your own age and kind. I've told you that again and again."

"Look," Anne said. "If you won't take me seriously, I tell you what. This is no tantrum, and I'm not crying now. But do you see this?" She indicated one of the pink-and-white Meissen cups which had been set out for their coffee. Her tears were gone, and she held it in her hand for a moment; then, taking it by the handle, broke it with one sharp stroke against the edge of the table. "I'm just serious enough to do that in cold blood."

In the interval of silence that followed, Louise von Louwe bent over in her chair and started to gather up the fragments. Anne took her by the shoulder and tried to stop her.

"Don't pick them up," she said. "I'll get you another."

"Your gesture was to break it," Louise von Louwe said, "and mine is to pick up the pieces."

"Anne," Gibbs said, "this is an extraordinary accusation to make against the boy, and it's essential to know what you base it on. Did he ever speak to you of any such intention? Did he at some point give you reason to believe that he felt hostility toward me? Did he at any time discuss with you what form he expected this thing with Farwell and me to take?" The curious air of fatigue that had suddenly come over him seemed particularly incongruous in contrast to the speed with which, one upon the other, he asked his questions.

"No. None of these," she said. "It's not like him ever to say what he's really thinking. The only proof I have is what I saw, and about a million other people, too. How he got you in there and let Farwell keep on baiting you until you didn't care what you were saying. He could have stopped it any time he wanted. But that's what he's famous for, you know. Getting people to make fools of themselves. Only this time he decided to go farther than that and ruin you."

"What are you talking about? How can he ruin me?"

"You don't know what a following he's got. In that Hooper-rating thing or whatever it is, he's in the top five, and that means there are literally millions of people watching him."

"That is correct." Hoye said. "He's extremely popular."

"So if he decides to go through with this trial-and-verdict business and says next week that his verdict is you're guilty somehow, there'll be letters pouring into the Senate. And don't think for a minute that isn't exactly what he's going to do." There was a kind of soft wonder in her voice as though, in addition to everything else that she felt at this plan which she ascribed to Tripp, she was also strangely awed by it or by the sound of herself describing it.

"Guilty of what?" Gibbs had risen from his chair and stood behind his daughter now, looking down at her.

"Oh, I don't know," she said. "Of being who you are. Of saying the kind of things you did. It doesn't matter what. Whatever he says, he'll make it sound exactly right."

"I'll grant you it's possible that if he should do something like this, public sentiment might be strong enough to have some appreciable effect on the Senate and might even bring into serious question the matter of their confirming the nomination. But, of course, I flatly refuse," Gibbs said, taking her face in his hands from behind and tipping it up toward him, "to believe that he would conceive of doing any such thing or that he has any motive for doing so."

"Wait and see then," she said. "I know him."

"Everything most certainly hinges on that," Louise von Louwe said. "I don't believe you know him at all. You're only in love with him, and that's far from the same thing."

"What do you know about him, Annie?" Gibbs asked.

Sitting there in a yellow sweater paler than her hair, her clasped hands unmoving on her gray skirt, and her eyes wide, but vaguely averted under the glances of Porter Hoye and Louise von Louwe, she might have said that what she knew principally was that she would never see him again, but this she did not say because, like everything else that she might have said about him, it rose in her throat and hesitated for an instant on her lips, but then, with the faintest catch in her breath, vanished. She might have said that in New York on summer week ends the city empties, and looking down the broad avenues cleared of all but a stray car or passer-by, you can see the heat rise in a haze as fair as the haze of sun on meadows. To walk in the green dusk down side streets planted with spindly trees was always to believe that the person coming around the corner might well be a person you knew because there were so few of them left during summer, and again and again it was Tripp—in a dirty felt hat with the brim turned down against the warm rain or his red hair sleek and bright in the sun, coming on purpose to meet her or, as often had happened, walking toward her when she did not expect him at all. Except that in some remote way she was always expecting him then, and to find him anywhere at all was never entirely a surprise. Then after

they had met and were walking along the river or eating
supper in a restaurant where the waiters stood bored by
the empty tables, he had sometimes said, "Good evening.
This is a delightful surprise to be sure," so that in effect
they could meet again, a play within a play, and so on,
until sometimes they came very close to meeting truly.
That narrow, boy's face was famous enough to puzzle the
stare of children, and if only once had that wide, boy's
mouth shaped the true salutation of these last, true meetings—which was: "You know I'm in love with you,
Annie," muttered in front of a shop window full of pumpkins and candy corn one autumn night—it had often come
close to shaping words very like them in meaning or at
least had suddenly, recklessly smiled as if such words
existed somewhere and it was at them that he was smiling.
But there had been only that once, and although afterward, at Tripp's insistence, the meetings of the outermost
sort grew more frequent, the inner meetings, even without
salutation, grew less and less until finally—when she had
seen that the rattling at the dark windowpane was, of
course, not Tripp, as for one inane instant she had imagined, but only the snow—she had made her decision not to
continue seeing him at all. She could not sanely hold it
against him that in his first interview with her father he
had not asked for her hand as Aunt Louise had with
oracular elegance phrased the possibility; but surely, she
felt, he could have spoken some word or given some sign,
which Gibbs in turn would have reported to her, that at
least part of his motive in having sought out Gibbs to

begin with was simply to make himself known to the
father of the girl who at sunrise on a Long Island beach
had kissed him for his birthday, thinking him asleep, and
to whom he had some weeks later, if only once, spoken in
terms of love.

"What do you think about him, Annie?" Gibbs had
asked, standing behind her as now he still was, looking
down at her head turned slightly away from Porter Hoye
and Aunt Louise, and she could have answered by saying
that she knew that she was herself not entirely convinced
that what she had charged him with was true. Yet perhaps
she was. She found it just possible to believe—let Hoye
roar "Melodrama!" if he chose—that all summer and all
fall Tripp's chief motive had been somehow through her to
work her father's ruin. And now it would appear that he
had or, with little more effort, very easily could. She had
sat by herself in the living-room watching his program as if
in a dream at first, but waking all at once to the fact that
her father was speaking a language almost too private to
bear and that Tripp was clearly determined to do no more
than make an occasional gesture of stopping him. She was
humiliated for her father and for herself, sick with pity
and self-pity, too tired to explain. "I know you can't be
sure of him," she replied. "I know what I've told you is
true. And I'm not in love with him," she said to Louise
von Louwe. "I'm not going to see him any more."

"I have a terrific headache," Gibbs said. "It must
have been those lights." As he walked around the table to
his chair, he stepped on a piece of the Meissen cup which

splintered beneath his foot. "Everything's breaking to pieces in here," he said and sat down. Anne in pale yellow, Louise in black, Porter in a gray so dark that it amounted to black and holding a smoking cigarette in front of his face with two stained fingers: they sat stiff as waxworks around the blinding white table looking at him as the kitchen clock ticked. The top of his head felt cold, and the pain gibbered tediously. He remembered reading that Franklin Roosevelt's last words were: "I have a terrific headache," the last words of thousands upon thousands, noticed the smoke from Hoye's cigarette listing horizontally toward him across the table, and knew that he was dying. He drew himself up straight in his chair, placed the fist of one hand on the back of the other, and in a voice steady as mountains said: "I'm going to clear this thing up tonight. I'll call the boy and ask him point-blank what he means to do."

"It would be much better if I called for you," Hoye said, stubbing his cigarette out in his plate, and Gibbs started to protest but stopped as Hoye pushed back from the table, rose, and left the room.

"He takes a great deal upon himself, doesn't he?" Gibbs gave a short laugh. It was appropriate for Hoye to be present, perfectly dressed for the occasion, and perfectly prepared as always to take matters in hand. Only Hoye had eaten his eggs, Gibbs noticed, and looking at the other plates including his own, he thought what a terrible waste. "Somebody say something."

"I expect to hear a deafening crash any minute," Louise von Louwe said. "He'll never find that telephone in the dark. The chances are the dignified thing would be for me to go help him."

"What do you think, Louise?" Gibbs asked. "Ordinarily, I would simply have waited to see what happened, but under the circumstances it strikes me we might as well get hold of the boy and find out right away."

"Well after all, Ansel, what do you expect him to say?" she asked. " 'Yes, Mr. Gibbs,' or whatever he calls you, 'I'm out to destroy you, and my verdict will be that you're guilty'?"

"If that's his intention, how would he benefit by denying it?"

"You should ask your daughter these questions. This is her hour."

"I don't think you'll get hold of him in the first place," Anne told her father. "He won't answer the telephone. He almost never does. I've just said what I know he's trying to do," she added to Louise von Louwe. "For God's sake, don't think I feel triumphant about it."

The pain in Gibbs's head droned on more insistently, but through it or above it, he realized again yet as if for the first time that this was, of course, the issue: what Tripp was trying to do. "Impossible, Anne," he said, looking at her quiet there in this bright headache of a room, her eyes deeply asking some question of his, aware perhaps of what was happening to him. "I can't believe what you say. I love the boy," he said, more than half to himself, with one hand pinching a deep frown into his forehead, "as much as I loved his father."

"Oh, forget it then. Forget it!" All in a sad rush her words came to him as if from some other room in some other house, and she pressed both her hands on top of his where it lay before him on the table. "Maybe I'm crazy," she said. "I'm not sure of anything."

"It's so good talking to you," Gibbs said. "We've talked so little, you and I. It's been my fault, of course. I believe you, Anne."

"Then you do believe what she's said about Tripp?" Louise von Louwe rose from her chair and stood there black as night against the white kitchen walls, a diamond crescent glittering at her breast.

"I believe that she believes it," Gibbs said, "and on that basis I won't disregard it."

"Once a woman has been in love with a man, you can disregard anything she ever says about him. Privately she always disregards it herself." Louise von Louwe took what pieces of the broken cup she had retrieved earlier and dropped them from waist height into the garbage pail. "If you want to hear my opinion on this whole business, I will tell you."

Gibbs nodded, his hand still at his forehead.

"Grown-up people," she said, "are as a rule much simpler than you think. When you are very young, you feel you must always have a reason for whatever you do, and if you don't have one beforehand, you will make one up later. If you ask a boy why he hit his brother on the head, he will tell you it was because his brother was bothering him, but actually, if the truth were known, it was probably just because he wanted to hit him anyway. When you are young, there is so much around you that you can't explain, that you want to be able, at least, to explain yourself. So you make up reasons for everything you do, and from your reasons you find out who you are or you invent someone like your reasons for you to be. You decide, for instance, that you are a person who is bothered by his brother. But when you grow up," she continued, wiping butter from her fingers with her handkerchief, "this is no longer necessary. You have found out now who for better or worse you are, and you let simply your identity be reason enough for doing whatever you like. You do what you do because you are who you are. Tripp is still a young man—what is he? twenty-seven, twenty-eight?— but in this sense he is grown up. He knows who he is even if we don't, and he doesn't particularly need reasons any more. I won't deny that he has you right now in an extremely unpleasant position, and if he decides next week to continue this fantasy of trial and verdict, he can make it a great deal more unpleasant still. Maybe he will and maybe he won't. But who knows? That is my point. Anne doesn't know, whatever she says. I don't know. Most important of all, Tripp himself doesn't know. To say that he has some reason for doing all this, some plan for ruining you to avenge that poor Rudy, is nonsense. He is a showman, and tonight he put on a show. Next week he will put on another. Beyond that he is probably not consciously *doing* anything at all. He has no reasons, black or white. He is just a dangerous young man being dangerous."

Gibbs said nothing to this, and for a few minutes the kitchen was silent. Again he drew himself up straight until he was sitting there high and stiff in his chair, and from his pocket he took a fountain pen with which, without opening it, he traced small, invisible circles on the little space of table top cupped inside of his left hand. The pain in his head whispered on, and he made every effort not to show in his bearing how helpless he felt with Hoye making the call that he should be making. Anne and Louise sat there in silence undoubtedly turning over and over in their minds the situation to which, hard as he tried, he himself could no more than disjointedly attend. He cleared his throat—a rasping, tentative sound at which Louise von Louwe glanced up at him for an instant—and with it, briefly, his mind, so that he caught a glimpse, at least, of what was happening beyond his dying: that for one thing he was, of course, not dying at all. He thought of his law office downtown with his books in the shelves; his father's safe in one corner with the name R. B. Gibbs across its front in old-fashioned, gold letters; his secretary, a Miss Humphrey, who had retired several years before from full-time work but who returned now whenever Gibbs himself returned, wearing the same green eyeshade and the same tan cardigan buttoned up to her chin, smelling musty and resinous like an old desk drawer. The very fact that Miss

Humphrey had not notified him in advance that death that night there in the kitchen was pending, as for years she had notified him in advance of every other pending appointment, seemed to him proof enough that nothing of the sort was just now scheduled. It was Miss Humphrey who had explained to Rudy on his return from the two weeks' rest that Gibbs had prescribed that under the circumstances it would be impossible to take him back at his former job. To everyone's amusement, she had always been undisguisedly enamored of Rudy, and, once, he had taken her out to lunch and filled her with cocktails, chattering along with her in his amiable, directionless way, to the point of making it an episode that she had never forgotten but filed away in her spinster's heart and sometimes had occasion to refer to still. Remembering Rudy, Gibbs once more came up against Tripp and Anne's accusation. Each time it reoccurred to him it was as if for the first time—like recognizing a face in a crowd, then losing it and forgetting it, then seeing it again. But this time, with great effort, Gibbs kept his eye on it, as it were, followed close upon it and finally seized it, spinning it around to face him so that, truly for the first time, he saw the full, preposterous horror of it. The effect upon him was instantaneous. "Damn it," he said, almost upsetting his chair by the abruptness with which he rose from it, "I'm going to talk to him myself."

It was at just this point that Hoye flung the swinging-door open and came back into the kitchen. "I let it ring twenty-five times," he said, "and there was no answer."

"I told them there wouldn't be," Anne said. "He's there, but he won't answer."

"What would you have said if he had?" Louise von Louwe asked. "I'm fascinated to know."

"To be perfectly frank," Hoye replied, still standing by the door and talking to her past Gibbs, "it wouldn't have been my idea to call him at all. But I thought it would be a great deal better for me to, rather than you, Ansel. There's no point in letting him know you're excited, and I don't think there's any reason to be anyway. I would simply have told him that I felt he had let the discussion this evening take an unfortunate turn at the end, and as an old friend and adviser of yours, I'd like to know how he planned to go about setting things straight next week or if the press gets hold of him before that. They may, you know, with this verdict business. Personally, I don't blame him for not answering his telephone."

"Where does he live?" Gibbs asked.

"At the Carlyle," Anne said. "He has a suite there."

"What's the room number?" he asked, and as she told him, he wrote it down on the back of an envelope.

"For the last ten minutes, Ansel," Louise von Louwe said, coming up behind him, "you've sat here like the ghost of Christmas Past. Then you leap to your feet in a frenzy, and I'm now steeling myself to hear you announce that you're going to go see him this instant."

"I am going to bed," Gibbs said. "If you'll all excuse me. I'm through for the day."

"I must be off myself," Hoye swung open the door for Louise von Louwe and Anne to pass through, and as Gibbs followed them, clapped him on the shoulder, holding him back. "I'll call you from the office tomorrow. If the papers try to get hold of you in the meanwhile, take my advice and be unavailable. This is all going to blow over." The women had gone ahead into the hall, and he was left standing alone with Gibbs in the darkened dining-room. Through the French windows facing the street, they could see the snow falling. "Anne will always stand high in my books," he said. "She's a delightful girl and she's got a head on her shoulders, but she's obviously gotten herself emotionally involved with our friend. There's only one word for that outburst tonight, breaking the cup and everything. Melodrama. If I were you, I wouldn't give it a second thought. There'll be time enough to worry when the time comes. If it comes."

They were standing side by side now, looking out of the windows, and as Hoye spoke, a policeman passed, his rubber cape glistening in the light of the street lamp. Gibbs raised one hand in salutation, and the policeman returned the gesture.

"I realized tonight as never before how little I know her, but there'll never be time enough to worry about that." As Gibbs spoke, his breath misted the cold pane. "There are many things you can call what she said, and a melodramatic, emotional outburst is only one of them. She's emotional about him, obviously enough, but that only presents another question. Why? She's got a head on her shoulders, as you say, and she's not a person to get entangled with someone who's indifferent to her. According to Louise, Tripp's been far from indifferent. He kept after her all summer, followed her everywhere. Even Kuykendall's come to know him. Yet neither of the times I've seen him has he made more than the most casual reference to her. Tonight, for instance, he never asked why she hadn't come to the broadcast. It surprised me that she didn't, and it certainly must have surprised him. Suddenly it seems I'm the only member of this family he's interested in, which means either that he's transferred his affections from my daughter to me or he's been pursuing her all this while for the sole purpose of eventually getting to me."

"He certainly didn't need Anne to do that," Hoye said. "It would have been the easiest, most natural thing in the world for him to have come to you on his own, as Rudy's son."

"If all he wanted was to ask me to appear on the air with him, yes. Or if he was simply curious, as I could well imagine his being, just to meet the man who was possibly his father's best friend—who, whatever construction you want to put on it, played a major part in the last weeks of his father's life."

"What else could he have wanted?"

"He's the only one who can answer that, of course. If even he can," Gibbs said, pinching the palm of one hand with the thumb and forefinger of the other. "What Anne said he wanted, perhaps. To finish me—and just when I'd really begun. Better than that, when you come to think of it. To begin me first—to let me first see him unscarred and forgiving—and then to finish me. And in a sense to do this to Anne, too. To each of us singly and to each through the other."

"We've been friends a long time, Ansel. You can't convince me that he planned all this."

"First of all, I'm not sure I do believe it. Secondly, if I did, believing it wouldn't necessarily involve believing that it was anything he'd planned. We're apt to destroy each other with our left hands, you know—without ever clearly facing the fact that we're doing it at all, or doing so many other things at the same time that the fact's obscured."

"You can put it any way you want," Hoye said. "It's still fantastic."

"It's fantastic as a possibility, and it would be more so as a fact. Perhaps the best way to discover which is to do so fantastically."

"Sleep on it," Hoye said. He stood with his hands on his hips, looking intently at Gibbs as if from a distance or from a vantage where he himself could not be seen, but searching as the look was, it revealed far more about himself than ever it discovered about Gibbs. It was as if Hoye lived entirely in his eyes for the duration of it and left all the rest of that great face unguarded in the interim. If there was compassion there, anxious affection and concern for his friend, there was also the almost imperceptible, dry curse of a smile that deepens the lines of men's mouths when they watch their own ship sink. But "Sleep on it," he repeated, quickly taking command of that face again, "and in the morning it will all seem just like a bad dream."

When finally Hoye had left and Louise and Anne had retired to their rooms for the night, Gibbs sat half undressed on the edge of his bed with a quilt wrapped around his shoulders. He had taken off his suit coat and his shoes and then slowly had stopped and sat down, pulling the quilt about him not because it was particularly cold in his room, but because he could see that outside it was still snowing. On the table by his bed was a whisky and soda which he had poured for himself before coming up, but he left it untouched. He sat there for half an hour, hardly moving at all, until at just about quarter to two he got up, dressed again, and went downstairs. Shortly afterward, with his overcoat buttoned up to his chin, he quietly unlocked the front door and stepped out into the winter night.

C H A P T E R
VII

THE SNOW had almost stopped as Gibbs walked up Madison Avenue, but the street and sidewalk were still white with it, and at one corner he tripped on the curb, grabbed hold of a letter box to catch himself, but fell, heavily, on on both knees. Only after some seconds was he able to rise to his feet again, the pain tightening his legs as he did so, but with the streets empty and no one to see him, it was a pain which he was able wonderfully to give way to, limping grotesquely as he continued along his course. It was a pain which demonstrated to him how without pain the rest of his body was, his headache gone, and with it, totally now, his sense of having been about to die.

At the idea of death he had felt, after the first lurch of fear, nothing so much as a kind of teary helplessness. He might almost have told them there in the kitchen that he was dying except for knowing that emotion would have choked his words. But now, reprieved, the very ache in his knees witnessing to the durability of flesh and blood, he felt instead a rush of anger. It was an arrogance of anger,

controlled and articulate, that fed on the very preposter-
ousness of what, angrily, he felt himself now forced to do:
to rouse Tripp in the dark of this winter night to confront
him with what he had done and to demand an explanation
of what he intended next to do. The boy had come to him
with all his glibness and charm and, capitalizing on what
he could easily guess to be Gibbs's sense of obligation to
any son of Rudy's, had persuaded him to appear on the air
with Edward Farwell. The result of this was that in the
exhilaration of the moment, and with only token attempts
on Tripp's part to restore order, Gibbs had said tragically
more, he had come to believe as he sat on the edge of his
bed wrapped in a quilt, than ever he should have said. He
had told no more and little less than the truth about himself, but it was precisely the truth that Farwell could, after
all, best turn against him, appealing as he had to all public-
spirited citizens to rise in arms against a man by admission
so cold and unprincipled. Through all this Tripp had sat
there in the blinding light, smiling, at ease, and then at the
end had announced that yes, perhaps this had indeed been
a trial, and he would be happy to oblige with a verdict of
his own the following week. Let this verdict be guilty, put
it together with Farwell's call for vengeance, and the effect
upon public opinion, Gibbs thought, and thence upon the
Senate itself might well, as Anne in her outburst and
Porter and Louise in their comparative reluctance had
asserted, be devastating. Over the years Gibbs had viewed
his rise to national prominence with a curious remoteness
and the absence of anything like pride—he had left it to

Hoye to be proud and to the others, his family, his friends, who had in one way or another risen with him— and until now it had been a matter of some indifference to him even whether his nomination was to be confirmed or not. But as soon as he saw his chances jeopardized from without, it became another matter altogether, especially if they were to be humiliatingly jeopardized by a boy young enough to be his son who, for all he knew, might well be capable, as Anne had claimed him to be, of somehow using her as well to work his ruin. Tightening his gloved fists in his pockets as he picked his way along the snowy pavement, no longer limping to spare his knees, but perversely rejoicing in the pain, he wore his achievement like a sword, both what he had already achieved and what he was determined now should still lie ahead of him to achieve, notwithstanding the worst that Tripp or Farwell or anyone else might try to do.

For no more than an instant did he hesitate at the entrance of the Carlyle, then pushed through the revolving door and gave his directions to the elevator man with a composure and determination impenetrable enough to preclude any question as to the propriety of his arrival at so late an hour. But if the elevator man raised no such question and only set about doing neatly what he had been told he nonetheless turned for an instant toward Gibbs as they rose in their mirrored cage and gave him a glance which easily trebled Gibbs's resolve to continue with what he had planned. He saw it as the glance of a man who not merely recognized him, but had either seen or heard of

Tripp's program that evening and looked at Gibbs now
with mingled curiosity and amusement as yet another
distinguished victim of the young man's unique talents.
Gibbs returned the glance without the faintest change of
expression, standing there stiff and tall with his arms
straight at his sides, and stepped out at Tripp's floor and
rang Tripp's bell aware that the man had remained there
to see if his ring was to be answered, but not once giving
any sign of that awareness although it was some minutes
before the door finally opened. With a surprise then that
he was not quick enough to conceal, starting to speak and
then stopping, sharply striking the palm of his left hand
with the gloves he held in his right, he found that the person before him was not Tripp, but Tripp's mother, Sylvia,
who stood there in a violet dressing gown with her hair
done up in a net and saying in her mild southern accent,
"Ansel Gibbs . . . the last person on the face of this
earth! . . ."

Unflattering and indelible as Gibbs's last sight of her
some fifteen years before had been, he had tended to forget
the beauty which she had once been famous for, and which
was apparent to him again as he faced her now. On that
occasion not long after Rudy's death when he had finally
forced his way in to see her, she had been sitting up in bed
in a bedjacket all made of pink ribbons, tears streaking her
cold-creamed cheeks, and refusing, with her hands pressed
to her ears, to hear what he had been trying to explain to
her about Rudy, about what he was prepared to do in her
behalf. Although she was dressed again for bed, her face

now, although older, with a web of tiny wrinkles drawn tight about her mouth and eyes and her eyes themselves a blurred blue, was not only undistorted by grief, but so undiguisedly and delightedly surprised to see him again that much of its earlier charm returned with an intensity that took Gibbs farther back than fifteen years, to the days when she and Rudy had first known each other. During the latter months of the First World War her parents had sent her up from Savannah to Boston to live with an aunt and uncle in order to complete her education by a winter's exposure to what they considered to be the intellectual and aristocratic capital of the North, and it was there that she had first met Rudy, who was then a senior at Harvard. Rudy, who looked upon her as his first real discovery of any importance, introduced her with pride to a number of his classmates, among them Gibbs, and it was not long before she had become so popular that a song to her appeared in a Hasty Pudding show and for a time in Cambridge the name Sylvia Stowe came to mean to almost every undergraduate, whether he was favored by actually knowing her or not, the kind of vague, abandoned, game beauty that could go on dancing until the sun rose and then appear at a milk-punch breakfast as bright and new as the morning itself. Even after she and Rudy were engaged, her other admirers continued their pursuit, and not entirely without encouragement, until for a while it looked as though the engagement must surely be broken; but then, just after graduation in the spring following the Armistice, they were married in Savannah, with Gibbs as one of the ushers, and went to live in New York. Friends never doubted that she was in love with her husband, but it was a love which required a setting of large apartments, servants, and summers on the south shore of Long Island; and her demands of him, if never explicitly stated as such, were consequently so excessive that as a result he was constantly shifting from one job to another that paid more. Finally, in his mid-thirties, with the reputation of a delightful but highly undependable young man, he found himself without any job at all and accepted what amounted to little more than an impressively titled clerical position with Gibbs. It was not long after this that he shot himself in the back yard of the small house in Westchester which they had been reduced to when the city at last proved simply too expensive for them, and apart from Gibbs's one meeting with Sylvia several months later, he and she had not seen each other since.

So there were several minutes of just standing there on the threshold of Tripp's apartment staring at each other with the curiously unabashed intensity possible after a separation of many years while Gibbs apologized for his untimely arrival and tried to explain, as best he could, that he had simply been passing by and, knowing that Tripp kept late hours, had stopped in hoping to find him still up. It was not until he had finished that he realized by her carefully noncommittal laugh, the little circling gesture of her right hand that could mean either amusement, surprise, or acceptance, that she had heard little if anything of all that he had been saying and was, in fact, almost totally deaf. But now that he was here, she said, taking him by one arm and gently drawing him into the apartment, he must sit down and have a chat about old times no matter what hour it was if only he would first excuse her while she disappeared for a minute or two to make herself more presentable.

For a moment, when she had gone, Gibbs seriously considered leaving before she returned. Tripp was apparently not at home, and if he should come back while Gibbs was still there with Sylvia, Gibbs could hardly question him as he had intended, would be hard put to justify his presence in any other terms, and the situation would be impossible. But then, partly by persuading himself that if Tripp was not at home now it was probable that he had gone away somewhere for the weekend, but largely on the basis of an irrepressible curiosity to see Sylvia again, he decided to stay. He sat down on a wood chest by the fireplace, rubbing his knees where he had bruised them, and glanced about Tripp's living-room. It was a large room with white walls and a deep red rug, a grand piano in one corner, but otherwise sparsely, almost shabbily, furnished with a number of pieces that Gibbs guessed must have come from some dismantled home of Sylvia's and Rudy's. He had expected something interior-decorated and theatrical, and tried to picture the boy moving about here instead, among these rather frayed relics of his parents' past, playing the piano or sitting with his long legs stretched out, as they always seemed to be, over the arm of the sofa or across the back of the dark-stained pigskin pig which appeared to

serve as either a couch or footstool. But he found that he
could not picture Tripp at all, neither here nor anywhere,
and all that he could summon up in his mind was his likeness as it had appeared on the cover of *Time*, which he had
seen framed on the studio wall earlier that evening—his
head tipped slightly back and his smile precariously wide
as though he were about to burst into laughter.

For the first time it occurred to Gibbs that laughter was
perhaps what the boy might have chosen to greet him with
had he and not Sylvia opened the apartment door, and he
tormented himself by conjecturing, while he waited for
Sylvia, what might have lain behind such laughter: that he
had already allowed himself to be made a fool of once that
evening and, in coming here now, was only making a fool
of himself again. Yet it had seemed no foolishness when he
had started out. Only now, in tranquil reflection, did Gibbs
realize what had been the extent of his anxiety as he had
left Louise's house and the degree to which he had no less
than actually hated the boy who had with the effortless-
ness of a young athlete managed to twist out of shape not
only Anne's life, but, or so it had seemed at the moment,
the life and ambitions of Gibbs himself. Now, however,
while he waited for his old friend's widow to make herself
more presentable, as she had said, these emotions slipped
out from beneath him, and he felt himself floundering
there foolishly indeed, seeing all the events of the evening
as a kind of fever-dream from which he was only at this
point awakening to discover that in the process of dreaming he had wandered far from home and might, if Tripp

should yet arrive, be obliged to continue playing an aberrational role by which he himself was no longer convinced.

He had risen from the chest to walk briskly to the other side of the room where on a table stood a photograph of Rudy, when Sylvia re-entered. She wore the same dressing gown, but with a spray of artificial lilies of the valley pinned to its sash, and her hair, a cinnamon-colored mixture of gray and light brown, no longer in a net but brushed out fluffily to conceal the mechanism of a hearing-aid which just barely showed behind her left ear. She had put on lipstick and powder, and, with a little twitch of her violet skirt as she passed around the table, came to stand by Gibbs before the photograph of Rudy.

"Ansel, let me look at you," she said, turning him toward her and presenting herself to be looked at again now that she had had time to prepare for it properly. "I'm sure you must have some serious reason for arriving here in the middle of the night, but I'm not even going to ask you what it is. I'm just going to feast my eyes on you for a few minutes. A lot of hair's gone through the comb since the last time I had a chance to."

Gibbs, breaking away from her scrutiny under the pretext of reaching for a cigarette which he did not want, repeated the substance of his earlier explanation of why he had come, adding this time that, as she undoubtedly knew, he had been on Robin's program that evening and was interested to know how he thought it had gone. Of all of this, Sylvia appeared to hear little more than her son's name and made him the subject of her next speech. She

had been having such a lovely few days with Robin, she
said. As Ansel probably knew, she explained, she was
married again, to a Southerner this time, and living in a
little mud hut in Georgia, but she had come north to do
some shopping and have her hair done and had been staying here with her boy. He had left town after his broadcast
that night, and she herself would be flying home in the
morning. She was so terrified of airplanes, she said with a
little grimace, that the thought of getting into one always
kept her awake trembling the whole night before, and that
was why she had heard the doorbell when he rang. Gibbs
noticed as their conversation continued that she spoke almost entirely in statements or, if ever she asked a question, either supplied him with an answer which he could
simply nod to or put it in such a way that just a yes or a no
from him was sufficient. If, for his part, he kept to her
subject, whatever it happened to be, she seemed able to
gauge the general tenor of what he was saying and to respond relevantly if not directly to it, but if ever he changed
the subject, she was clearly lost. On these occasions, however, she never asked him to repeat or in any other way
admitted that she had not heard, but with the same little
wave of her hand, the same soft, aimless laugh contrived to
be understood in any one of a half-dozen different ways,
continued on some lonely path of her own. What was
originally Gibbs's surprise at her seeming to be quite unaware that he had appeared that night on Tripp's broadcast vanished with his realization that Tripp had without

doubt spoken to her of it, but that she had simply not heard.

The turns that their conversation took were thus entirely Sylvia's to determine, and if Gibbs's first reaction to this was one of frustration, he came soon to appreciate his freedom simply to listen, observe, and occasionally comment without the necessity or, for that matter, the possibility of making any greater effort. She had brought with her a silver tray containing whisky, water, and ice, and, pouring them each a highball, she settled back among the cushions of the sofa with Gibbs beside her and talked on, for the most part without interruption, until for whole minutes at a time Gibbs forgot who and where he was, why he had come, and to what he must return, and was so entirely taken up in the world of Sylvia Stowe, Sylvia Tripp, that he found it more and more difficult as she went along to step back far enough out of it to realize either that hers was only one of many worlds or that any more had taken place in the last fifteen years than what she chattered on about now. It occurred to him only that, quite apart from any sentimental attachment to them, a man is so inextricably bound to the friends of his youth that no matter how light a view, if any, he may take of them during the increasingly long and unregretted periods of their absence, as soon as they reappear, all that has taken place without them seems to become insubstantial and irrelevant by comparison.

"Oh Ansel, it's so queer to be old," she said. "I can

hardly believe it. And yet I am, you know. Nobody's sure how much. I've lied about it so often I'm not really sure myself any more. I used to tell Robin I was as old as the century, but once when he was a little boy he said to a good-for-nothing brother of mine—'just think of it. Mummy's as old as the century is, and in 1900 she was zero.' And Brother said, 'Son, in 1900 your mother was punching cows.' So that didn't work any more. And now even the century's too old for me to have as a twin. It's a losing battle. So much has happened. My boy is a famous man. Just in terms of money, he makes more in a week than his father ever brought home in a year, and his picture everywhere you look—on billboards along the public road and in any magazine you'd ever care to pick up. You'd think I'd be proud of him, and I am, but his little joke is that I'm not even interested in what he does. Of course, I'm interested, but it's all so unreal that I keep losing track of it and forget to make enough fuss over him for it. And here you are, Ansel. My own age or maybe a year or two older, and I read in the paper that you're going to be in the President's Cabinet. If I have great-grand-children, they'll be reading about you in history books. I still can't help wondering what Rudy would think about it all if somehow he could know. I had the strangest dream about him once. It was during the war, years after he died, and yet he seemed to be in the Navy, stationed on some far-off island in the Northern Sea or somewhere. He was wearing a peajacket and one of those dark blue knitted sailors' caps pulled way down, and he told me how worried he was about everything—the war, our safety, Robin's and mine. He told me to be careful. You'd think the least they could have done would be to have made it so he didn't have to be worried any more. But he was, poor lamb. I've never forgotten that dream. I don't believe in them, though. Do you? You believe old women and black mammies are the only ones who put any store by them. When Rudy died, we had a funny little nigger working for us named Bessy. You should have heard her murder the king's English. She kept cartoons of milk in the icebox and was always buying cosmeterics for her daughter who spoke French influently. She also believed in spirits. She called them spurts. On her Thursdays off she used to go in to a medium in Portchester, and in one of their sessions they got word that there was a young man who was trying terribly hard to get hold of my little black Bessy. He was very good-looking and very excited to get this message through. It was Rudy, of course, and she told me all about it later. I asked her what the message was, and you'll never guess what she said. 'Eat more apples.' Can you imagine it? And Rudy was never very keen on apples anyway. I went to her myself once, the medium, and she told me to beware of people whose names began with M, B, and G—she didn't even say whether she meant first or last names—and she tied something up in my handkerchief which she told me I was to take out in twenty-one days and throw over my left shoulder. To this day I don't know what ever became of that handkerchief. I've always thought I still might eventually come across it and find out what she put inside.

"Someday you'll have to meet my husband, Ed Muller. He would have come up with me this trip except he couldn't get away from business. Business being cotton. He has mills all over the south, and he's in *Who's Who*, so you can see I got myself a real guy again. It's not the same as young love, first love . . . heaven knows. You never find that again even if you spend all the rest of your born days looking for it. But we're dear pals, Ed and I, and I love him. He's not like you or Rudy or any of the other Harvards or Princetons. He doesn't have that easy, gay way with him, and he's a man without the slightest notion how to relax. He's farm born and bred, one of six boys and three girls, and all he has he's made on his own. He's gentle and kind and honest, and I'll never forget something Robin once said about him. It made a lasting impression on me. 'He's worth all the rest of us put together,' my boy said, and I think he was probably right.

"I don't want to pat myself on the back or anything, but all in all I think he's turned out all right, this Robin of mine, don't you? Of course, it wasn't easy being both father and mother to him because that's what I had to be —Ed and I weren't married till he was almost twenty— and in some ways I know I spoiled him silly, but in other ways I always leaned on him like a husband, and from the day his father died he had to bear responsibilities way beyond his years. It only hurts me a little sometimes that we haven't stayed closer than we have. We're still great pals, and we pay each other little visits like this one, but he's a man now, and naturally he isn't going to come to me with all his troubles any more. To look at him, you'd never think he had troubles—so handsome and sure of himself and famous—but I know he does. Rudy's death for one thing. In some queer way that's with him still. When Rudy did it, I'm sure it seemed like such a simple thing to him. He just decided the time had come for him to step out, and I'm not blaming him any more. He thought he was doing the right thing. The only thing. But, oh, Ansel, an act like that casts such a long shadow. I'll never understand how he could do it. He tried to make it look like an accident so I would get the insurance. He wanted people to think he'd gone out to shoot crows the way he sometimes did early in the morning and had just tripped over a croquet wicket, but, of course, nobody was fooled for a minute. He left me a note in a place he thought no one else would ever find it. It was the year *Gone with the Wind* came out, and he wrote it on the last page of the copy he knew I was reading. I didn't find it till almost six weeks later. He just said he loved me with all his heart, but that he was weak and no good and this would be the best way out for both of us. He said he wanted Robin to have his pearl stickpin and his watch. That was all. I'd never had an idea in the world that anything like that was in his mind. Of course, I knew he'd been terribly overtired and had had certain disappointments, but nothing like this. Why, even that last night, Ansel . . . we always had a double bed—neither of us could get to sleep any other way—and he slept that night—I've never told this to another living soul—he slept with his hand on my breast. I never even felt him get up in the morning. Then that crazy little Bessy came running in to tell me what had happened. I thought she must have gone out of her head. And it's a funny thing, but I think of his two parents, it's his father Robin looks back to most now. You notice the only photograph in this whole room is that one of Rudy you were looking at when I came back. I suppose it's because Rudy never lived long enough to make any bad mistakes with him, whereas I did. I realize now I made many bad mistakes, but how could I have realized it then? You do for a child what seems the best thing at the time.

"I'm so glad he's come to know you, Ansel. It's only right that he should, after all, and it was such a joy for me to hear how much he's been seeing of your Anne. Of course, I haven't set eyes on her myself since she was a tiny little thing, but she sounds like such a dear. Do you have a picture with you? Of course not. Only mothers and sweethearts carry pictures any more. I don't know how she feels about him—she probably has loads of other beaux—but I think he's really serious about her. It would be such fun if something actually came of it some day—such a lovely end to a long story. It would make so many people happy. A kind of vindication almost, if that's the word I mean.

"Ansel, I don't suppose I'd bring this up if I had any sense. All my life I've been saying things at night I could have bitten my tongue off for the next morning. There's something about its being dark outside—all the sharp edges of things get blurred. I'm not a very religious woman any more, I'm afraid. I think a lot of the awful things that happen in this world are harder to explain if you believe in God than if you don't. And I gather the church says that suicide is a sin while in my opinion—I know this is terrible to say—I think that if sin's mixed up in it at all, it's a sin of God's to let life do such things to people. But what I mean is I believe that, God or no God, as far as Rudy and everything is concerned, it all turned out the only way it could. I don't blame anybody any more, not even myself, and if there was a time I bore a grudge against you— there's no use pretending I didn't—that time is dead and gone. So do let's be friends again. I'll never talk your ear off this way again, I promise. You may have noticed I've gotten a little hard of hearing in my old age, and some- times I think I keep on jabbering just so I won't have to try to listen. But when I come to the city, I can call you up once in a while, and maybe when you're down in Washing- ton, you can come on down a little farther and spend a few days with Ed and me. We'd love it. And do be good to my boy. He and Ed get on terribly well together, but when you come right down to it they don't speak the same language, and what I think my Robin needs more than anything else is some wise, older man he can talk to sometimes. And now let's have one tiny little nip more, and then I'll let you go home to bed."

Gibbs took the glass she handed him and leaning slightly forward said as distinctly as he could: "I've never thought of you as anything but a friend, Sylvia. I've always had and I always will have your and your son's best interests at heart."

"Heart?" She seemed really determined this time to hear all that he had said and looked at him intently as he spoke, her lips compressed in a bewildered, self-conscious smile.

"I've never thought of you," he began again, more loudly this time, almost shouting, but at the familiar wave of her hand, the faint laugh, he stopped.

"You and I," he said, pointing at them both in turn. "We will always be friends. Friends," he repeated, and then lightly kissed his hand to her to illustrate his meaning.

"Friends always," she said, leaning back into the cushions again and for a few moments, smiling, closed her eyes.

"Here's to you, Sylvia Stowe," Gibbs said in his normal tone of voice, raising his glass to her though she could not see him. "God forgive us all."

He rose to go soon after that, but not before writing a note to leave for Tripp in which he said:

Boy: I dropped by here in some anxiety to see how you thought things had gone this evening. Why didn't you shut me up when I started getting out of hand? If they hang me to a sour apple tree, I'll hold you personally responsible. But I can't believe that all is entirely black, perhaps not even the human heart. I've had a fine chat with your mother. A. G.

He kissed Sylvia good-night at the door and walked back to Louise von Louwe's house through the night, which had become much colder and clear, the sky bright with stars and a thin, high moon. He lay down on his bed without undressing and within a few minutes fell asleep.

CHAPTER

VIII

TRIPP's program had taken place on a Friday, and on Saturday morning Dr. Kuykendall tried to reach Gibbs by telephone from East Harlem only to be told by a harassed Walter that there had been countless calls already that morning, there were about half a dozen reporters waiting across the street at that very moment, and the only information which he, Walter, was authorized to give out was that Mr. Gibbs, together with Miss Gibbs and Miss von Louwe, had left by car early that morning for a day in the country and were not expected to return until either late that night or sometime the following day. Dr. Kuykendall then tried to telephone Tripp, but no one answered there at all. With his pastoral calls to make, several hundred letters appealing for money to sign, and his sermon still to prepare for the next day, he nonetheless left the poorly lit vestry at the rear of the Church of the Holy Innocents which served as his office and bought copies of all the leading newspapers. He returned to his office with these, and with the gooseneck desk lamp twisted down to within a few inches of the printed page spent the next hour reading all that there was on the subject of Gibbs's encounter with Farwell.

The Senator had issued a brief statement from his hotel room shortly after returning from the studio, and this was reprinted in full everywhere: *I have great respect for any man who can be as frank about himself as Mr. Gibbs was to-night. It was as much of a surprise to me as I am sure it was to everybody else listening in. I nevertheless believe that his ideas and beliefs as he painted them himself are not those which this country wants in the executive branch of its government. This kind of cold intellectual approach which plays with words and dodges issues, which looks down its nose at many of the ideals that have made this nation great, may fit Mr. Gibbs for a college professorship, but not for the cabinet.*

If Mr. Gibbs [said one article] *first appeared before the television cameras looking every inch the distinguished world citizen and speaking with all his usual precision and elegance, by the time the show was coming to a close he had the haggard, flustered look of a man who had put both feet in his mouth and knew it.*

The general view [reported another] *is that Gibbs like his unnamed friend has committed suicide—political suicide. There are certainly few public figures who have ever pulled more boners in public. But there are others who say it's the smartest move he has ever made. The American people are always suckers for a man who gives the impression of having owned up to the worst.*

Whether the distinguished appointee stands to win or lose by his words last night, we rejoice in the fact that apparently genuine personal honesty can still flourish in the political scene. Whether or not you can agree with all of the rather world-weary and, in some cases, painfully blunt remarks that he made about our civilization, you can't help giving at least two cheers for the courage he showed in making them.

It is difficult to predict what effect if any the Farwell-Gibbs affair will have on the Senate's action concerning the latter's appointment to the Cabinet. The issues he raised cut across party lines and even the left-right cleavage. A great deal will depend upon what reception the Senator's appeal to the public receives, and Robin Tripp's 'verdict' is also bound to be of no small significance. Informed sources in the capital say the President feels it unnecessary to issue any official statement at this time. It is not expected that he will withdraw his nomination. Debate in the Senate, however, promises to be vigorous.

Robin Tripp, the dead-end kid of TV, must be really laughing up his sleeve this morning. By high-pressuring egg-head I-am-civilization Gibbs into putting on the gloves with two-fisted Ed Farwell, he sponsored the comedy bout of the season. Ansel went down to the count of ten in round one. But definitely. Score one up for the young maestro.

Kuykendall pushed the papers aside and tipped back in his chair. There was Inez Rosas with a son up for parole if an employer could be found to guarantee him work, once he was released. Old Mrs. Tyree had applied for money for a pair of shoes, whereas it was the staff's unanimous conviction that she would use it instead on food for the eleven dogs and three cats who shared her cellar room. Riverside

Hospital was conducting a free series of lectures on employment-counseling for ex-drug addicts. Would anyone from the Parish be free to attend? What do you preach to a congregation twenty-five per cent of which has come to church for an hour of sleep in a place with a more comfortable temperature than a doorway or an abandoned automobile rusting on its wheel-rims east of Third Avenue in the low hundreds? He picked up a mimeographed sheet headed *Minutes of Christian Action Committee, Jan. 3* and with a black carpenter's pencil scrawled across it, "Christians no longer act. They form committees," then threw it into the top of his portable typewriter case, which served as a wastepaper basket.

He left the vestry-office and walked down the few stairs into the sanctuary itself. Looking across the rows of empty pews, he could see through the window a group of Puerto Rican children playing with a kitten on the church steps. In the central aisle between the pews was the customary litter of candy wrappers, bits of newspaper, discarded orders of service from vespers the evening before. From the half-domed ceiling above the communion table the painting on plaster of the Virgin, a relic of the church's more prosperous days under an Italian Catholic congregation, still visibly stared down through the thin coat of whitewash with which it had been covered before Kuykendall's incumbency. He went to the pulpit and from the lectern took the heavy Bible and sat down with it in one of the front pews to look for a text for the next day's sermon. Unthinkingly, with his right hand he held together the pages

of the New Testament and with his left opened to somewhere near the beginning of the Old. "*Messieurs*," he had
frequently said in his lecturing days, "I don't want to
cause the pious among you undue pain, but the New Testament without the Old is in constant danger of becoming
superficial and banal. In addition to everything else he was,
Jesus was a Jew *par excellence.* He was Israel, and it is
Israel's *Heilsgeschichte,* the sacred history of the elect of
Jahweh, that you must know to know him." And that was
twenty years ago, he thought, and maybe he had been
right and maybe he had not. He let the book fall closed
between his knees and sat there staring fixedly forward, his
face like that of a tragic Punch, the nose and chin, as
Louise von Louwe had remarked, looking as though at any
moment they might meet in front of the small, thin-lipped
mouth. It was only at this point that he thought again of
Gibbs and what he had read.

In a bar on Second Avenue with a glass of vermouth and
water before him, and persuading the bartender to switch
his set from a professional wrestling match to Tripp's program, he had watched Gibbs's image, hoping always that it
would somehow become Jeremiah in the valley of the son
of Hinnom—seizing a potter's vessel of invective and
smashing it into a thousand pieces with "Thus saith the
Lord of Hosts, 'Behold I will bring upon this city all the
evil that I have pronounced against it because they have
hardened their necks that they might not hear my
words.' " And yet it had in no sense been a complete disappointment to hear instead the even accents of Gibbs ob-

liquely inveighing against a mediocrity and complacency of sentiment, the general refusal of men to admit to the tragic ambivalence of a world where what looks like the holiest cause may have perdition in it and winning is often indistinguishable from losing. Only "Go to, go to," he had kept repeating in his mind, "speak in concrete terms of the worst there is, the pain, the tedium, the despair," where-upon Gibbs began to speak of Rudy, of the worst, perhaps, that he had known, Kuykendall thought, but less than enough, less than enough. "For the most part, my prayers are sheer blubbering," he had told a generation of under-graduates, but in that bar he had soundlessly and lucidly prayed, the cheap vermouth bitter on his tongue, for a prophet to appear on the trembling, blue-white screen where instead there was only Gibbs—perhaps the best that you could hope for, he thought. And he had thought as well of Rudy: how in him he might have found his prophet—in the young power of him, in his charm that you felt like a hand when he entered a room, that he, Kuykendall, need only have somehow directed, yet had not. "Who am I to tell them to give up the latitudes of joy they were created for to become stewards of the mystery and agony of Christ?" he had asked and kept on asking until at last he had left teaching to become ordained himself, to minister to the abandoned of God, as he had put it, since he could not bring himself to recruit for His army. And still—crying out against what he called the idiocy and fraudulence of his own move, calling himself a combination of Tartuffe and Uriah Heep—he looked at the staff, clergy and lay, who assisted him in East Harlem and asked himself the same question again about them: who were they to have sacrificed their chance for joy as the world richly knows it for the sake of living and working in the squalor of these streets for a cause that might or might not stem from some sick desire in themselves for self-punishment or Heaven only knew what? Men and women alike, they all developed after a time a curious remoteness of heart, gradually showing less love of the poor than cold misunderstanding of all who did not share their poverty. They became obsessed with their own roles as dispensers of mercy, were constantly meeting in each other's rooms, which were studiedly no less bleak than the rooms of their poorest charges, and evaluating each other's and their own motives, achievements, and failures. Honey Gruber, the plump, pretty young woman in charge of doling out free clothes, developed after two years the ability of laughing rather than bursting into tears over the grotesqueness of the little knot of men she found waiting when she arrived at work every morning. But learning not to weep at them, she learned as well not to weep with longing, as once she had, for the day when at last she would marry and leave the parish for good, but tended now only to laugh at any young man who ever gave evidence of trying to persuade her to leave it for him. The demands of the Lord were great and terrible, Kuykendall had thought as he sat there watching television, and it was no wonder to him that Gibbs spoke with something less than the voice of prophecy that he had nonetheless so hoped for a time to hear from him. "To be a prophet of Jahweh," he had said to the bartender, who stood polishing a glass as he listened to Gibbs, "is to rend your garments and curse the day you were born."

Henry Kuykendall sat now in his empty church with the Bible shut on his lap, his eyes closed, and thought of all that Gibbs might have said—about cities as the sins of nations; about nations moving toward ruin with the same self-obsessed valiance as the individuals composing them; about the wrath of Jahweh speaking his awful judgments in the tongue of history with his spirit descending on the chosen and in the end destroying them; about the chosen nation of the Jews which alone at the time believed in a God who acted in history only to be itself, as a nation, demolished in history. And yet in the end you could only fall to your face in the unbearable light, Christ with you and for you, you hoped, and blubber: "Thou only art God." Kuykendall opened the Bible to the first book of Samuel and found his text—"But the spirit of the Lord departed from Saul, and an evil spirit from the Lord troubled him."—then let the book fall shut with a report that echoed the length of the sanctuary. In the vestry again he signed the three hundred letters asking for money, dropped them off with Honey at the parish office to fold, stamp, send, and lunched alone on a bar of chocolate and a glass of sweet, pink milk at the candy store at the corner.

He cut his calls short, sat with Inez Rosas while she nursed her baby and talked on and on of the goodness of her son and the evil of his companions, her voice growing gradually tinier and more persistent until it began to

pierce his ear like a pin and he rose to go, promising to find
work for the boy if he could, and leaving abruptly then to
the sound of her *"Adios, Enrique,"* which she spoke
dreamily, as though he was already miles away. Mrs. Tyree
refused to sit down for the length of his visit, but stood
barefoot on the stone floor of her cellar covered with dog-
soiled newspaper and spoke to him about shoes while her
dogs nosed at his laces. There were others whom he had
intended to see as well that afternoon, but he returned to
his office instead and began work on his sermon. With a
congregation as variegated as his—the men who had come
to sleep out of the cold, the devout ladies and few men of
the parish whose command of English was for the most
part deficient, and the seminary students who did their
field work under him and herded their Sunday-school
classes in to morning service—he found that for all tastes
the best that he could do was to retell the stories of the
Bible, which were, he pointed out to them, the stories of
themselves as well. This was his forte, and he acted them
out, frequently coming down from the pulpit and using as
his stage the center aisle, where, with a gift for character-
ization by which he transfixed the seminary students as
readily as the regular parishioners, he virtually became
Noah drunk, Abraham forcing up his hand to strike down
Isaac in sacrifice, or, as on this particular Sunday which he
was preparing for now, Saul in the dark tent of his despair
and young David at the harp. He had never yet preached
such a sermon without the painful conviction, once he had
finished, of having made a fool of himself, and even his

greatest admirers were from time to time obliged to admit that this had been very nearly, yet somehow, miraculously, never quite the case. On this Sunday, furthermore, there was not only the sermon for him to anticipate, but the bazaar.

The Protestants of the area were by no means its most numerous religious group. The Catholics outnumbered them; and then there were also the adherents of the small pentecostal churches which flourished for as long as the voluble spirit lasted and the tambourines rattled, and then disappeared to be replaced by others; and, in addition, there were those people who consulted practitioners of black magic—interpreters of dreams and dispensers of charms against disappointment in love and disease. But on the occasion of parish bazaars, Protestants appeared who had never come forward to be recognized as such before, and in numbers so large that the basement gymnasium of the Church of the Holy Innocents was filled to capacity. There was a rummage sale of clothes, shoes, toys, collected from charitable institutions and individuals all over the city; there were potato races, weight-guessing, ring tosses, a fortune teller; one section of the gymnasium floor was roped off for dancing; and free refreshments were served. "Belshazzar himself would pale at the sight," Kuykendall said, and he depended heavily upon Anne Gibbs to help him with the organization. She was in general of great help and comfort to him, being the only one of of his staff who had come to him from outside of the church in one or another of its ramifications, and who, except for her several hours a week with him, had remained outside. It was likely to be to Anne that he confided his darkest suspicions concerning his whole function in East Harlem. "Has it ever occurred to you," he had asked, "that they might be much better off without our endless meddling? Thank God at least for the likes of you who can look at us through secular eyes and tell us when we're becoming really insufferable. Only for the love of heaven never forget to tell us"—and it was Anne who had time to hear out his most impassioned indictments. "Damn it all," he had once exclaimed, "the sweet, the reasonable the pious! You go to church and listen to the preacher. Notice the gentle, other-worldly look about him, and don't miss his sensitive hands either. He'll take a cocktail, too, if you offer it to him, and he plays a dandy game of golf. He talks about injustice in ethical, Platonic terms. See what a lovely picture he paints. So perfect and so true. I nod and smile. I go away feeling all nice and clean inside. But show me a Puerto Rican boy whose hand has been held over a gas burner until his fingers are black and his eyes start to pop out of his head because he wouldn't get down on his hands and knees and kiss the American flag, and then . . ." his voice had risen harsh and raucous, "then I know what you're talking about. Then I understand what injustice means!" Anne had promised to help with the bazaar as she had helped with the last one in September, and Tripp also had volunteered to come, but now, Kuykendall thought, it was unlikely that he could count on either of them, what with Anne's having fled the city with her father, and Tripp's being apparently no less determined to remain out of sight until the furor which he had caused subsided.

So early Sunday afternoon, still shuddering at the memory of his sermon on Saul and David, he set about managing as best he could without them. People had already begun to gather in front of the church door waiting for admittance while he and the crew-cut young rectors who assisted him supervised the preparation of the gymnasium. With the help of Honey Gruber and the other permanent social workers, they strung red and yellow crepe-paper streamers around the walls, mixed an enormous bowl of grape juice and water, instructed the parishioners who were to run the various entertainments, and out of a considerably scratched and outmoded collection of phonograph records picked several dozen for the dancing. At half past two they opened the doors, and within minutes the large floor was at least half filled. Kuykendall stood at the foot of the stairs to greet them as they entered, and to his surprise one of the last to come down was Tripp.

In an O.D. rubber raincoat and his Army boots still wet with snow, he shook hands with Kuykendall as a group of Negro children came pushing through past him, and apologized for being late. He had gone out Friday night to his agent's on Long Island, he explained, but, of course, he had intended to come in to the bazaar today as he had promised, and needed now only to be told what to do. "Unless of course," he said, grinning up at Kuykendall as he bent over to brush the snow out of his trouser cuffs, "you happen to share everybody else's opinion that I'm a scheming S.O.B. who ought to be excommunicated, gelded, and burned at the stake."

In that case, Kuykendall told him, they were likely to go up in flames together. Was Anne there by any chance? the young man asked then, but before Kuykendall had a chance to reply, a group of high-school girls, recognizing Tripp, crowded around him so that Kuykendall was left alone to call Honey Gruber over to see what task they could assign to him. Everything had been pretty much parceled out by now, she said, standing there in her sneakers with her hair done up in a tight blonde bun, and eying Tripp, still surrounded by admirers, with a look of uncertain speculation. But there was one thing that she had seen done with great success on similar occasions elsewhere, she said, which he might be willing to undertake. But probably he would not, she added as he broke away from the girls to come up to them, and she had to be coaxed by Tripp even to say what it was. The three of them stepped into a small storage room where the gymnasium equipment was kept, and with a kind of flushed overexcitement she explained that first you took a poncho and hung it from the ceiling, securing the bottom to the floor with a string or wire so that you had in effect a fixed rubber screen with a hole in the middle. Then you got somebody to sit behind it on a high stool with his head thrust through the hole, and for five cents people could buy three balls of rolled-up newspaper dipped in water to throw at the head from a reasonable distance. "It's fair for you to duck if you can, and their aim is usually lousy anyway, and it doesn't hurt even if it does hit you," she said, at which Tripp, grabbing up a basketball, bounced it against the wall twice and then threw it at Honey, who caught it hard against her breast. "You've got yourself a sucker," he told her, and with a look of amused horror from Kuykendall, they stepped out onto the main floor again and, going off in search of a clear area at its far end, were lost to sight in the crowd.

The arrival of such a celebrity, as was Robin Tripp to them, only momentarily distracted those who had noticed him enter, and as soon as he was gone, they mingled again with the others while Kuykendall stayed by the door to greet anyone else who might still come, and viewed the proceedings from there. Only a few faces among them all were not familiar to him, and for the most part he had not only seen them before, but had in one way or another had dealings with them. There were the boys in their late teens who, so long as they stood, as now, somewhat aloof from the others, constituted a danger of which no one in the entire room was totally unaware. Everything depended upon the nature of whatever it was that first caught their attention as a group, and if it should turn out to be the least sign in anyone of authority that they were being especially watched, in some way discriminated against, or, worst of all, made fun of, the trouble they could cause might be grave. Consequently there was an almost visible relaxing of every face in the room as soon as Spook, a tall Negro boy who had left school at sixteen after some success as an amateur boxer and was their acknowledged leader, asked one of the girls to dance, whereupon, one by one, the others followed him. At the rummage table, women held clothes out at arms' length to look for holes. Inez Rosas's oldest son, brother of the one eligible for parole if first a job could be found for him, held a thin, fierce-eyed Czech named John Brno under the arms and lifted him experimentally, in an effort to guess his weight. Brno lived on the same block on which was Honey's office, and was always either muttering somber threats against the parish or brushing away tears of gratitude to it. He was a very angry, very sentimental man, and in his daily progress up and down the block, sometimes drunk, sometimes sober, he always took along with him his son Johnny, a pale, undersized boy of thirteen, whom he called upon to express whatever the emotion was which his father currently felt but was characteristically too overcome to describe. Kuykendall noticed that Mrs. Tyree was also there in bedroom slippers augmented by rags wrapped under her insteps and tied around her ankles, drinking one paper cup of grape juice after another as she watched a group of men tossing rubber rings from Mason jars at a table littered with packages of cigarettes, toothpaste, chewing gum. And it was all of these, Kuykendall thought, who had sat in his church that morning and heard him tell the story of Saul and David. Unconsciously he grimaced at the memory.

Standing between the two front pews, he had let his arms hang limp at his sides, his shoulders stooped and his head bowed, and in a voice so low and desolate that even the Sunday-school classes stopped fidgeting to listen, had said: "Saul was the first king of the Jews and a proud and mighty man, but he sat in the gloom of his black tent and knew that the spirit of the Lord had left him and an evil spirit of the Lord had come to trouble him. God had commanded him to do certain terrible and frightening things, and Saul had not been able to do them. God had told him to kill Agag, the king of the Amalekites, but Saul did not hate Agag enough to kill him, and the prophet Samuel had to instead. Agag fell to his knees," Kuykendall had continued, half crouching there, throwing his arms up as if in supplication, his voice almost breaking as with sudden force he cried out, " 'Surely the bitterness of death is past!' but the prophet Samuel hewed him in pieces with Saul standing by. I believe myself that if Saul, who had not hated Agag enough to kill him, had loved him enough to save him, God would not have punished him for his disobedience. But Saul had neither loved nor hated enough, and the evil spirit of the Lord came upon him, and he sat sick and alone in his black tent knowing that he was not the man that God and the prophet Samuel had wanted him to be. But then—what was that strange, sweet sound he heard?" By this time Kuykendall had walked halfway down the aisle, and at these words he spun around, his hand cupped to his ear, his stare wild and questioning. "What was the sound the king heard? It was the sound of a harp. Can you hear it? Listen. Listen. It's the sound of soft, summer rain when for days the sidewalks have been scorching hot and the air is filled with dust. It's a sound like the smell of food when your stomach aches with hunger. Once you heard that harp, nothing was ever so sweet again because it was the boy David who played it, and suddenly Saul forgot all troubles, and for a while it seemed as if the evil spirit of the Lord had departed from him." And what sense had they made of that? Kuykendall wondered now, standing by the door as he watched the progress of the bazaar.

"Is this a Christian church," a voice asked from behind him, "or the Darktown Strutters' Ball?" and turning quickly around, he saw Louise von Louwe standing in the doorway. "It's still snowing in the country," she continued, "and we were afraid if we didn't leave soon, we wouldn't be able to get out at all and Ansel would never make it to Washington tomorrow. Anne said she was expected here anyway, so we've all come to you for sanctuary." She stood there in a Persian-lamb coat with a black felt hat pinned to her hair by a garnet, her face pale with cold. Even as she spoke, Gibbs and Anne appeared in the doorway behind her.

The realization that Louise would now be confronted by John Brno, that Gibbs was within a few minutes of coming face to face for the first time with Mrs. Tyree, that, in general, worlds so remote from one another could so fantastically collide, left Kuykendall momentarily with nothing to say at all; but Anne with her own explanation, her own apology, gave him time to collect himself, and with a comic shrug of helplessness at the kermis before them, he made them welcome. Having as his last memory of Gibbs the tired, aging face which he had seen on the television screen two nights before, Kuykendall felt now that not for years had he found him looking so well. About his eyes there was a certain puffiness that suggested lack of sleep, but the whole cast of his face looked firmer, less almost pathetically dependent for its expressions upon the expressions and words of others, and he seemed in excellent spirits. For years, he said, he had been meaning to make it his business to find out exactly what it was that Kuykendall was up to here in the city, and he was grateful for the circumstances, however tempestuous and Wagnerian, that had made it at last possible for him to do so. Dr. Kuykendall must go on with whatever his function was, and he and Louise would simply wander at will if they might while Anne, as he understood it, had duties of her own to perform. For an instant Kuykendall was filled with fear for Gibbs, almost came to the point of actually warning him not to wander out onto the crowded gymnasium floor at all. It was as if the very appearance of him—his thin hair brushed immaculately back on his forehead, his suit dark and soft against the starched white of his collar, his whole bearing so tall and kingly, so graciously and precisely just—would arouse in these people from another geography, another astronomy altogether, such emotions of astonishment, admiration, fury, that they could adequately express them only by falling upon him and tearing him to pieces. With at least half of his purpose, then, being simply to hold Gibbs back, Kuykendall chose this time to

congratulate him on his performance with Farwell. In the
stress of the moment he made no attempt, as under more
normal circumstances he might have, to add to his praise
some mention of the rather less restrained and more
specifically directed criticism which he had hoped to hear
from Gibbs but had not, and the result of this was that he
knew even as he spoke that he was evincing more enthusiasm than actually he felt. But Gibbs gave no sign of
detecting this, merely listened intently, thanked him, and,
by making no further comment, left it to Kuykendall
either to think of some other subject with which to detain
him or to let him go. Anne had by this time already gone
off to help out at the rummage table, and it was Louise von
Louwe who relieved Kuykendall of the necessity for
making any such decision by announcing that she herself
was going to "plunge in," as she put it, and Ansel might
accompany her or not as he chose. With a nod to Kuykendall, Gibbs set off after her.

Almost immediately, with Louise von Louwe having
gone off in some direction of her own, Gibbs found himself
alone in the crowd and, by edging his way slightly to one
side, was able to get near to the square of floor that had
been roped off for dancing. A number of people stood in
front of him, but he was a good head taller than the tallest
of them, and his view was unbroken. He remained there
watching for a time until a short and almost totally black
colored girl in a dress of so deep a purple that it seemed to
be of one piece with her rich skin, pushed around in front
of him and rolling her eyes in mock horror at his height

gave out the hoarse screech of a tropical bird. The couples went on dancing—the boys' faces painstakingly indifferent as though it was by some tedious accident that they happened to be holding girls in their long arms—and none of the spectators turned to see who had screamed or why, but Gibbs nonetheless softly shouldered his way farther back into the room, leaving the dancers behind him. Mrs. Tyree held out a paper cup of grape juice to him as he approached, but he failed to notice her gesture and unknowingly, as he passed by, knocked her arm with his elbow so that she spilled part of the cup down the front of her moth-eaten sweater. Over a number of heads he caught sight for a moment of Louise von Louwe apparently dickering with one of the women in charge of the rummage sale over the price or condition of something that seemed to be heavy and black with a handle to it. Kuykendall's young associate minister, recognizing him, shook his hand and said something, but Gibbs could not hear what it was. He sat down for a few moments on one of a number of wooden folding chairs lined up along the wall.

It was Porter Hoye who had suggested that he leave the city the day before, and with Louise and Anne he had driven out to an inn in Connecticut where he had spent most of the time in his room, watching the snow fall and reading the newspapers. Louise had called Walter twice to discover what was happening there, and Hoye—the only person entrusted with the details of their whereabouts—had telephoned Gibbs periodically to keep him informed in the matter of reactions, as they gradually became known, to what had been said on Friday night. He had himself been approached from several different quarters, Hoye said, to identify Rudy, but interest in that question was less than he had expected it to be and seemed already to have died for lack of nourishment. In a few days, he reassuringly told Gibbs, the whole business would have blown over. Louise had brought her needlepoint, and Anne had claimed to have letters to write, so for the most part they had met only for meals, served not downstairs with the other guests, but on a bridge table in the small living-room which separated Gibbs's room from his daughter's. Their conversation was limited largely to conjectures as to the probable duration of the snow, and it was as if in the meanwhile it had fallen cold and deep in their very midst, each snowbound from the others, snowblind to all but their own unspoken preoccupations.

So it was out of deep winter that Gibbs had come into the August of this crowded room, and as he sat there in his chair on the edge of things, he was suddenly filled with the desire to identify himself with the breathing warmth of it —the air fragrant with garlic, cigarette smoke, wet rubber, the musty sweetness of hair and clothes. He craved to thrust himself into the hot heart of the crowd, somehow to press himself against all their bodies at once, soiling himself with the perspiring flesh of them, jostled by their buttocks and shoulders, knees and arms, lost in all this humid, clamoring, unclean kennel of summer. He rose from his chair and made his way toward the most crowded part of the room that he could see—faces craning, nodding,

mouthing about him as in a dream—and came to a length
of floor that lay under a somewhat lower ceiling behind the
far basketball net. The main floor was fluorescently lit and
almost as bright as day, but here there were only a few
caged bulbs on the walls so that all that he could clearly
see at first was a little mob of people, most of them children, watching what appeared to be a kind of billboard at
the far end of this oblong, cavelike extension. At intervals
a cry of applause would go up, then a shifting toward the
front of the group, a silence, and another cry. More like
dwarfs than children, Gibbs thought, with the faces of men
and women on small, wiry bodies, they pushed about him
from all sides, intent on working their way forward, while
a young woman with her hair done up in a blonde bun kept
trying to maintain some kind of order above the shrill
excitement of their voices. With some difficulty Gibbs
managed to squeeze forward himself until he could see that
in front, roped off at some distance from the billboard,
there was a table with a bucket of water upon it and a
mound of old newspaper rolled up into balls. A small
colored boy stood there with his right arm raised way back
above his head preparing to throw one of these, which,
even as Gibbs watched, he did, and as Gibbs's eyes became
more accustomed to the light, he saw that in the center of
the billboard or screen, protruding from a hole, was a
human head which bobbed to one side to avoid the missile.
Twice more the boy threw, and twice more the head
bobbed. Then another boy stepped forward, the process
was repeated, and this time there was again a shout of

applause signifying, Gibbs concluded, that the target must have been hit. Curious to see whose head it was, he pressed his way to the front despite the angry protests of the children about him, and only then was able for the first time to behold it clearly.

For an uncanny moment it seemed to him that it was Rudy's head, and he had the giddy, weak sensation of looking over the edge of a high cliff, half fearing, half wanting, to fall. But then he recognized it as Tripp's—his neck bare, his hair tangled and wet on his forehead, his teeth white and his eyes narrow and bright as he grinned. Briefly, everything else seemed to disappear until all that was left for Gibbs was the boy's face, the boy's widemouthed smile disembodied there in the dim light. Gibbs tried to catch his eye. Perhaps, though he could not be sure of it himself, he even called his name, made some wild gesture with his hand. Then suddenly, as if having known all the time that he was there, Tripp looked his way, and their eyes met. It was then that the boy laughed.

His laughter was sharp as a sword, high-pitched and loud, with all of joy in it, wanton and young, yet taunting as well, an insolence of mirth that cut the room into a hundred pairs of eyes, Gibbs's among them, bulging with shock at the triumph and challenge of it. It was the cry of a bird circling high above the heads of its pursuers, a shout of scorn from the battlements, a peal of high bells ringing the new year in and the old away. Gibbs heard it as the laugh of a boy who had managed somehow to emerge unruined from the wreckage of the past to deride that wreckage and all involved in it, who, gay-eyed and careless, was destined brilliantly to succeed where all else failed, and roughly thrusting aside whoever blocked his way, he pushed forward to the table in front. A thin Puerto Rican girl stood there now, and taking her by one arm he virtually lifted her aside, grabbed up one of the wet paper balls and hurled it at Tripp. Still laughing, the boy ducked to the right, missing it, and Gibbs hurled another, this time catching him on the side of his neck. Another missed, then another, and then he hit him squarely on the forehead, on the cheek, the mouth, until the children set up a wild shouting and people from the main gymnasium floor pressed in to see what was happening. In his passion, Gibbs upset the bucket, the water flooding the length of the table and off its sides, but sopping the paper wads in what was left, he continued his hurling until from behind him Kuykendall, who had come in with the others, took him by one shoulder to stop him. Without looking to see who it was, Gibbs tried to wrench himself free and in doing so partly ripped the arm of his coat from its seam. Then, as suddenly as he had started, he stopped.

In the effort to withdraw his head from the hole, Tripp had pulled the poncho loose from its moorings and kneeled there now with it hanging loose about him. His face was dripping wet as if from tears, and all in one rush Anne, who had accompanied Kuykendall, ducked under the rope and ran up to him. She crouched beside him and pressed his head down against her throat so that as the children, their excitement still at high pitch, began hurling the wet paper, it was she who shielded him, hit here and there about her head and shoulders. She turned from him, crying out for them to stop, then back to him again, and she stayed there by him until Kuykendall, facing the crowd with his arms raised ceilingward, began to restore order. Still on his knees with his face tipped up to hers, Tripp heard her whispering, felt her hands warm in his wet hair, then rose from the floor and with one arm about her waist led her out into the gymnasium proper, where they passed unnoticed through the main part of the crowd which had remained there. With everyone else now watching Kuykendall, who stood with his back to the rope, angrily trying to subdue their clamoring and belligerent overexcitement, which threatened to spread out to the adults, Gibbs alone was aware of their departure. Flushed and perspiring from his exertion, he remained absolutely motionless on the edge of the jostling mob.

When Kuykendall finally succeeded in quieting them and the poncho was hung up once more with one of the high-school boys to replace Tripp as target, everything returned more or less to normal, and after some searching Kuykendall found Gibbs with Louise von Louwe at the foot of the stairs that led up to the street. Louise remained largely silent, the collar of her Persian-lamb coat turned up against the cold to come, while Gibbs spoke only briefly, his face expressionless. He was appalled, he said, at the trouble he had caused, at the spectacle he had made of himself. To plead that he must have been more overwrought than he had realized by the events of the last days might constitute a kind of excuse, he told Kuykendall, but inadequate in view of what had happened. "If the boy really wanted to know who I am," he said, "I'm sure he feels he knows all there is to know now."

"Who you are, who you are," Kuykendall repeated, more to himself than to Gibbs. "I've asked myself that question often enough. There was a time I thought it might be you who were going to speak the word of judgment to this generation. I even looked for another Jeremiah, another Isaiah, but what I found was only Ansel Gibbs. I shouldn't say 'only.' It's not as bad as that sounds. It's also not good. It's the way things are, that's all, and that's what we're usually left with, hope and blubber and pray as we will. I'm sorry" he said, "sorry for you and for all of us," and suddenly then his expression which, until a moment before, had been funereal almost to the point of caricature, fell apart into his absurd, self-conscious child's smile. "But after all, there was a time I thought I might have amounted to something myself," he said, "and all I've ever been is Kuykendall."

CHAPTER

IX

"ALWAYS," Tripp said. "Always and always. Every time I came into a room full of people, it would happen again. The eye would start to revolve—slowly like the light of a lighthouse. Sweeping the horizon. Was she the one? How would she be? . . . not just to go to bed with—though that, too, God knows—but to get out of bed with, to wait for trains with, to be bored stiff with and fight. Maybe I'd only see her for three minutes at some sweaty cocktail party, but that was plenty of time to ask myself all those questions and more. Everybody does it. You'd be surprised."

For thirty blocks they had walked, down the snowy pavements through East Harlem, and then suddenly, at exactly 96th Street, into the world of Park Avenue. "There should be some border to cross—passports, customs inspection, money declaration, something. It shouldn't be so easy," Anne had said, and then on down Park Avenue, where the doormen stood behind their glass doors, keeping warm, and a little boy in a blue snowsuit

197

with red tassels on the tips of his mittens and his wool cap
waded out waist deep into a high, white drift until, without warning, his knees buckled under him, and he sat
there in the snow, trilling like a bird. The sky was a soft
pearl-gray, and the winter dusk began to gather early. The
lights were lit on the Christmas trees down the center of
Park Avenue. The tires of cars hushed or clinked with
chains along the white streets. When the bells of St.
Ignatius Loyola started to ring, they seemed to have the
cold, gray city all to themselves. No other sound competed, only faint human sounds—children dragging their
sleds back from the park, people hurrying home and talking to themselves as all women and most men in New York
do: oh God, God . . . and I said to her . . . tomorrow,
tomorrow . . . good-by . . . all cut to pieces by the
gaudy peal of the high bells. And then just at dark, as they
neared the Carlyle, the two shafts of windows on the
Grand Central Building, one vertical, one horizontal, lit
up in the form of an enormous cross, and a shelf of snow
blew off the roof of an apartment building, floating down
on them like mist.

"The first thing I can remember about myself is my
feet," Tripp said. "I'd noticed them before, I suppose,
but then one day I realized they must be mine. Annie,
Annie. . . ."

They lay side by side on his red carpet, the room smelling dimly of steam heat, the shabby furniture religiously
still, and Rudy's wing chair turned with its back half to

them. "People kiss so they won't have to look in each other's eyes," one of them said.

"Will you just tell me one thing?" Anne asked, her voice rhyming with the whisper of the mantle clock. "Why has it taken so long? . . ." and he watched the tiny pulse in her throat, felt the little space of warmth between his hand and her hair, and he knew that to tell her the answer to that would be to tell her everything.

He had shown her his apartment. Rooms in a hotel, no matter how elegant, have so much history that it amounts to their having no history at all, and these were his and as if they had been his always. His dirty laundry lay in a heap on the floor of his bedroom closet, somewhere at the bottom of them his shoes, a tennis racket, a large manila envelope full of letters from Sylvia Stowe to his father, love-letters, which she did not know that he had. They had written to each other as "Blessed": "Blessed, I thought of you this morning while I was . . ." and in Tripp's kitchenette, itself the size of a closet, there were a case of scotch, a case of gin, a tape recorder on the cover of the stove. In his bedroom on a shelf above his desk were a dozen orange-backed cardboard containers full of clippings about himself. "In the beginning," he told her, "I always played the same game with people. You'd meet somebody somewhere. You'd talk, and the game was to see how long they'd take to find out who you were, damn it, without your ever telling them. If you had to tell them, it didn't count. It meant you weren't anybody yet anyway." And he showed her around the rest of his apartment. She had seen the living-room before, but that was all. "All my life I wanted a drawerful of money. Just money," he said, and he pulled open a dresser drawer and showed her a pile of coins. "That's so you won't think I have to marry for money," he said, and taking a fistful of them, opened the bedroom window and threw them out into the winter night. "That's to show you how rich I am," he said.

"That's an awful thing. They might hurt somebody."

"Money never hurt anybody."

"I'd rather have you sane than rich."

"I'm sane and rich both," he said.

And now they lay there on the carpet the color of young kings; he had shown her where he lived, the secrets of his rooms, and now she had asked to see himself. "Why has it taken so long?" she repeated, and he looked up at her, his thin face flat against his bare arm, as if to make sure who it was that had asked such a question. "Blessed," he said, "do you want to hear the whole business?"

With his shirtsleeves rolled up and wearing a pair of khaki pants, Tripp sat up then, holding his knees to his chest. Anne lay beside him, leaning on one elbow, her head in her hand, and they were both barefooted, their shoes drying near the radiator. "There's nothing I don't want to hear," she said.

"Well, first there was my feet," he told her, pushing at her knee with his toes. "They're the first things I can remember being aware of. Then you. If you want to hear the details, I'll tell you, but you don't know what you're asking."

"I'm not asking who you are, though till this afternoon I would have. I'm asking who you've been up to now, all these weeks, and before."

"That's just it," Tripp said. "I was never sure myself. We were always on the move—like Okies heading west, but, oh God, what fancy Okies. My father would go ahead first and find a house he thought my mother would consider suitable—something with trees around it and a driveway and rooms for servants. Then she would follow along with me and a nurse, the silver all strapped up in a wicker hamper, and their clothes, trunks of them, and the furniture, the piano nobody knew how to play. Oh, the works," Tripp went on. "Nobody would have ever known to look at us that the reason we were pulling up stakes was because we'd gone broke where we were and my father had to switch to a new job that paid a few more bucks a week. So I never had a hometown or anything—how the public relations people hate that!—and I went to a different school almost every year of my life. So I was always the New Boy. Have you ever been a new boy?" he asked.

"Something like that sometimes."

"Then maybe you know what I'm talking about. A new boy's supposed to prove himself, but I never bothered much with that. I found out it was a whole lot easier to prove how much I was like whatever I thought the old boys wanted me most to be. If you get me. I got to be a regular chameleon—a kind of nine-, ten-, eleven-year-old lizard with a hide that could change colors in ten seconds flat. I had red hair so they'd usually get the idea I must be a hell-raiser, and then I'd raise hell till my tongue was hanging out—pick fights, razz the teachers, everything. But I was skinny and unco-ordinated, too, so sometimes they'd figure out because I wasn't much fit for anything else, I must have a brain. I went along with that, too, and in one place I got to be head boy of my class. They gave me a gold star or a roll in the hay with the principal's wife or something. Anyway, that's the way it went for so long that the day finally came when I didn't know which of all the people I'd been I really was. I could change my personality quicker than a hat, and it's still true. When I'm with men like your father or old Kuykendall, I'm the bright, prom-ising young man. When I'm on the air, I'm Mr. Medioc-rity himself—no better and no worse than the best or worst who's watching me."

"And when you're with me?" Anne asked. "Now?"

"Maybe now I'm myself," Tripp answered. "But don't bet on it. Even I'm not sure."

"But what about what I asked?" she said. "About why it's been so queer all these months—you keeping after me till I was ready to scream, never saying anything, only once . . ."

"I'll get to that," Tripp said. "But first my secret, inner history. You asked for it, and I'm all wound up. I'll spare you no details. You know this business about how before it's born the human fetus in the womb is supposed to run through all the evolutionary stages—a blob, a fish, a monkey, all in nine months? Well, it's the same thing when love happens. You go back to the beginning and come up through all the people you've ever been so you know who you are who's loving now and down on his knees asking to be loved back. I've done it before, and I'm doing it again now with you."

"Oh, don't make this too sad and complicated, Tripp," she said. "I can take only so much in a week. Only so many problems," and as she spoke, she rolled over so that she was lying face down beside him, her head in her hands and her shoulders hunched.

"O.K.," he said. "I'll give it to you uncomplicated and no sadder than the facts. Facts can't be sad anyway. I'll give it to you in a few short, snappy scenes—like a movie preview. Coming next week. For adults only. The theater goes dark. The curtains light up like a sunrise. They part. The screen starts flickering all silver and gray. Movies are dreams. Are you with me, Annie?" He leaned over and, brushing aside the hair, touched the back of her neck with his nose. She nodded without speaking.

"The first scene is in a kitchen at night. There's a man playing the part of a young husband, a woman playing the part of his pretty wife, and a boy about eight, their son, who's playing the only part he knows at this point—which is himself. The man is always trying to make just a little more money because they're always living on just a little more money than they have. They like things nice, he and his wife, and they have rich friends, and they forget they're not rich themselves until all of a sudden someday the phone is shut off because they haven't paid the bill, or the nurse quits because they're three months behind with her salary. Right now the man is wrapped up in a sure-fire scheme to make a million. He's heard about a couple of guys who think they've invented a kind of heat-proof glass—this is in the days before there was such a thing—and he's sunk a good-sized piece of his capital in their project to manufacture a few samples. He's brought one of these back with him tonight. It's a baby's bottle which you can put in boiling water and then in ice water without its so much as cracking. His wife and son have come out here in the kitchen to watch him demonstrate it. There's a pot of water on the stove. There's a dishpan full of ice cubes in the sink. The man's standing by the stove waiting for the pot to boil. His wife is sitting at the kitchen table looking pretty and brave and trusting. The little kid, who knows a hell of a lot more than they think he does about what happens when bills aren't paid and nurses have to take care of him without a salary, is standing by his mother watching his father. At last the water boils. The young husband takes the baby-bottle and holds it up like a magician who's just pulled a rabbit out of a hat. With a string tied around its neck, he dips it into the boiling water. Then he pulls it out and lays it in the dishpan with the ice cubes. There's a pop like a rifle going off, and the bottle breaks in three pieces. It's a scene that has everything," Tripp said. "Suspense. Pathos. The wife laughs a little, then cries. And humor, too. The boy is so humiliated for his father that he runs up and tries to kick him on the shins, so his father picks him up, laughing, and holds him upside down and shakes him till twenty-five cents and a yo-yo fall out of his pocket. The camera irises out on the yo-yo, which rolls into the dust under the stove."

Tripp had risen in the course of this and stood now by the window, looking down at the street many stories below. Anne had remained on the floor, although leaning up against the wing chair now, and consequently, though with his back to it, Tripp felt represented in the room, as if he had another heart beating there, another pair of hands and eyes. "It's getting ready to snow some more," he said. "There'll probably be forty days and forty nights of it, and that'll solve everybody's problem."

"The rain didn't," Anne said.

"That was because of Noah," Tripp answered, turning to her again, " and we don't have a Noah."

"What's the next scene?" Anne asked. There was only one lamp lit, and she sat near it, the light falling on her hair, so that the room seemed to belong more to her now than to Tripp, who remained by the dark of the window.

"The next scene is left out of the preview," he said. "In some ways it's bigger and more dramatic than the one you just saw, but it doesn't really add too much to it. The time is an early spring morning five years or so later. A twenty-two goes off, and the noise it makes isn't much louder than a baby-bottle breaking in a dishpan of ice. It doesn't even wake the young wife, who's upstairs in bed. Their son is in his room gluing a model airplane together, and when he finds out what's happened, he doesn't kick his father's shins this time, but he's humiliated for him in a lot the same way, only worse. Except that because he's older than when you saw him last, he's had time to develop other feelings about his father, too—love and fear and respect plus this humiliation for him because no matter how hard he tried, it seemed he was always messing things up and getting in bad. So when the son looks out of the window of his bedroom where his mother has made him promise to stay and sees what used to be his father lying on the wet grass down below, all these feelings are frozen in mid-air, so to speak. In time the chances are they'd have melted together into one—the love and fear and respect and humiliation all finally turning into one complicated but single feeling about his father that he could have eventually dealt with somehow. But this way they're frozen stiff while they're still separate, and they stay separate that way for years and years to come, which is very confusing for the boy and causes him no end of trouble and grief. It's like having three or four fathers at once, all very different, very dead, and very apt to haunt him in his dreams and in between times, too. So you can see how at a tender age he picked up quite a few parts to play, all suggested by his different dead fathers—the one he feared, the one he loved, the one he respected, and the one he felt so humiliated for that for a long time the only tears he shed over him were tears of awful embarrassment. This is a very complicated psychological scene," Tripp said, "and that's why it's left out of the preview.

"But the next scene isn't complicated at all," he went on, still standing by the window so that when Anne looked at him, she saw herself as well, reflected in the dark pane, "and it takes place in a bedroom. You better say in a whole lot of bedrooms and some of them not bedrooms at all, sometimes not even in rooms, but on lawns, on beaches. Do you want to skip this scene?" he asked.

"I hate all the years I didn't know you," she said. "I wonder if we ever met before."

"I can't remember, but I bet we did." Tripp came over and sat down in the wing chair which she was leaning against, shifted her toward him so that she sat now with her head tipped back against the seat cushion between his knees. "I remember seeing your father a couple of times in those days. He and my father used to clown around together. I remember once we had a Swedish cook who kept threatening to quit because she was lonely and didn't have any friends, so our fathers sat down and wrote her a letter as if it came from some guy who'd seen her in town and was crazy to meet her. It kept her going for weeks."

"I can't imagine Father clowning around somehow," Anne said. "I think he must have been born civilized." She laid her hands on his bare feet.

"Rub," he said. They sat there for some minutes in silence while she did as she was told, Tripp softly, comically moaning as he gazed down at her shoulders through half-closed eyes. It was only six-thirty by the mantle clock, yet there was the sense of its being late at night.

"Whatever sex is," he said, "having your feet rubbed is

exactly the opposite. Sometimes I think even better. That's what the next scene was about."

"Having your feet rubbed?"

"No," he said. "Sex."

"Oh, let's have it then," she said.

"You asked for it," he said. "When the boy with the three or four dead fathers is around fifteen or so, his mother starts telling him he's the best-looking thing since Valentino—a regular Greek god, in fact. To coin a phrase. She's a Southern lady and doesn't mean any harm by it. Maybe she even believes it, and after a while he starts thinking himself that maybe she's got something. They're living in Georgia now in a house her family owns, and he's going to the local high school. Have you ever been to a local high school?" he asked.

She shook her head.

"Well, in a local high school the opportunities for an adolescent Greek god are sometimes unlimited. In the gym of this one, the girls' and boys' locker rooms are separated by a wall with a door in it. There are separate entrances plainly marked *Girls* and *Boys* too in case anybody might ever make a mistake, and the connecting door in between them is kept locked tight. But there are ways of getting through tightly locked doors, and it's in those locker rooms that our boy gets his early training. If he doesn't know quite what to do at first, coming from a respectable family and having no living father to brief him on the ways of the world, there are plenty of opportunities for instruction. The older boys are very generous with their knowledge, and some of the older girls don't mind providing entirely gratuitous demonstrations. There's nothing simple and old-fashioned about what they do either. They have eager young minds, and they're crazy about experimenting. Sometimes three or four couples will experiment down there together with the air full of steam from the showers, smelling of sweat and Absorbine Jr. and perfume from the Five and Dime, and by the time this skinny, redheaded Greek god is seventeen and about to be sent up North for a year of prep school to give him polish, he's seen everything there is to see, and there's damned little he hasn't done. He finds he has certain natural gifts in this direction, and he carries around what's called in his local-high-school circles a monkey on his back. The opportunities for this kind of thing in prep school are strictly limited, but when he gets to college, the field broadens out again, and in the Army he finds it's really wide open. He's learned to play all kinds of new parts by this time. His mother tells him he's her best friend and adviser and almost a husband to her, and that's one part. People have found out he's fairly handy with a guitar or a piano, so they're always after him to sing something he's made up or play something, and that gets to be another part. And then there are still all the parts he learned when he was a kid—somehow living up to, or living down, all his fathers —so after a while it gets to be where sex seems to be the only place where he doesn't have to play a part at all— where he can forget all his lines and his fathers and the chords and words of his damn songs. So this scene, as I said, is a bedroom scene, only it doesn't all take place in bedrooms, and it's a 3-D, technicolor production with a cast of hundreds. Look," he said, leaning way forward in his chair so that for a moment his mouth touched her forehead. "I'll stop any time you get bored or want to go out and be sick or anything."

"I'd like something to eat," she said, "if you have anything here. And, Tripp," she began again, looking at him, straight and somehow lost, "I don't care what you tell me. Whatever you want. I won't be sick. But don't do it in this movie way. Say 'I' and 'we' and 'they.' Will you for me?"

"I'll do anything you want," he said. "And I'll feed you. I don't carry much in the way of food here, but there must be something. You're sure you don't want to go out?"

"I ought to call home," Anne said, "and let them know where I am."

"They know where you are," Tripp said.

So when he began again, it was sitting beside her on the couch with a glass platter full of olives and cocktail onions, crackers, cheese, and two glasses of milk on the coffee table in front of them.

"I'll tell you about an old woman named Kitten Dory," he said. "This was just after I'd gotten out of the Army, and I had a job disc-jockeying for a small Chicago station. They gave me a week off at Easter, and I flew down to Savannah to spend it with my mother and Ed, the man she married about the time I was a junior in college. The second day I was there, all hell broke loose in the smelling-salts, old South way my mother specializes in. I'd sent some clothes to the cleaners, and they called up later to tell Mother I'd left some belongings in the pocket of a coat. So she drove down to pick them up, and the idiots gave her the works—some money, some cigarettes, and a package of gadgets I was in the habit of using on some of my more colorful nocturnal adventures. She had a private show-down with me and in the course of it made it clear that as far as she was concerned, I was turning into a regular satyr, and God knows there was more truth in that than she ever guessed. She cried and said I was weak like my father, that it was her fault, she hadn't brought me up right, but she'd had to do it all alone and she'd done the best she knew how. And she had, you know," Tripp said. "I keep making her sound like the villain of all this, but she wasn't. There aren't any villains. But anyway," he went on, "she was terribly upset, and she decided one thing my father and I had both lacked in our lives was religion. She's never been a particularly religious person herself—and she has her reasons—but when she was going through change of life and afraid for a while that things weren't going to work out between her and Ed as well as they finally did, she was more or less straightened out by an old woman who claimed she wasn't a Christian Science practitioner or a faith-healer, but who was really some of both. So mother persuaded me to go see her while I was down there over Easter, and that's where Kitten Dory comes in.

"Nobody knew much about her past, but Kitten didn't need one. She might as well have sprung full-blown on the

world with a voice that could open a can of sardines and a
personality like a pneumatic drill. But I don't want to
make a gag out of her. Whatever she was up to, she was
dead serious about it. I had to wait in her sitting-room for
about a half an hour before she let me see her in her office,
and I remember looking in her bookcase while I waited.
There was *Science and Health, The Prophet,* a collection of
hymns, and crammed right in among them was a ten-
volume set of the *Business Encyclopedia*—everything from
double-entry bookkeeping to investment banking. She
knew what she was doing, all right. But anyway, she finally
called me in, and then I saw Kitten for the first time.

"She was wearing white the way she always did—a
white dress like a nurse's uniform, white shoes, and white
cotton stockings—the fattest woman I've ever seen, with a
great pale moon of a face and blue hair. Almost the first
thing she said to me was that she was seventy-five years
old, but she knew she didn't look a day over fifty because
everybody told her so, and as a matter of fact she didn't.
And then she started to get down to cases. She called me
'Baby'—that's what she called all her patients, or whatever they were—and, 'Baby,' she said, 'I'm not going to
try to make you into one of my convertibles, but for your
darling Mom's sake I just want to sound you out a little.'
I remember that business about sounding me out a little
because it was a good twenty minutes before I could get a
word in edgewise. You've never heard such a line as she
had. You could tell she'd been using the whole thing complete for the last twenty years or so, and one illustration

came spilling out after another with jokes inserted to make you feel at home and know what a good Joe she was, and she kept referring to 'that guy,' pointing at a big pencil sketch of Jesus she had hanging on the wall that made Him look like a sick fairy. The gist of it all was that unhappiness and pain don't really exist because everything is part of the infinite mind of God. She said at different times how she herself had had cancer of the stomach, all the bones in one leg crushed by a truck, and one lung gone, but she was still going strong because she knew what 'that guy' meant when he said the truth would set you free. It was the same for lusts of the flesh as for disease, she said with her eye on me, and then she used her favorite example of all which cropped up a couple more times before she was through. 'Baby, look at yourself for a minute if you don't think it'll make you lose your lunch,' she'd say, 'and then one by one take away all the qualities that make you you—beauty, symmetry, strength, vitality, power,' and I don't know what all. 'And what have you got left? A blob. Nothing. Baby, all you've got left is a great big blob of nothing, and how is nothing going to be able to go around tomcatting after a bunch of girls, how is nothing ever going to get cancer and pain and die? Baby, I'm here to tell you God is all in all and we're part of that all, so how is God in us ever going to get sick and die? It's all just a bad dream whether you know it or not, and it's time you woke up, don't you think?' Then she began all over again about 'take away beauty, symmetry, strength,' and so on.

"I was inspired then. I don't know where it ever came

from. I'd just gone to see her to keep peace in the family, and it didn't make much difference to me whether what she was talking about made sense or not. But, as I told you, it was Easter time, and I suddenly realized this day I was seeing Kitten was Good Friday. My knowledge of the Bible was shaky, to say the least, but at least I knew what had happened on Good Friday so I started trying to ask her how she explained that. You could see she wasn't used to being interrupted, and it looked for a minute as if she was going to lose her place and have to start all the way back at the beginning again, but then she got hold of herself and went sailing off into whatever she'd been saying. When you tried to say something yourself, she'd just keep right on talking, so finally I really yelled at her and asked if she knew what day it was. She said of course she did and started to go back to where she'd been when I yelled again and asked her how she explained 'that guy' dying on a cross, with nails through Him. 'Baby,' she said, 'He didn't die. That's what Easter's all about.' So I said if He hadn't died, He'd at least put on a damned good imitation of it— sweating blood beforehand, nailed up by His feet and hands, at the last minute yelling out that this all-in-all God had left Him holding the bag. If He hadn't died, I asked her, what was all this hocus-pocus about being risen from the dead, 'crucified under Pontius Pilate, dead and buried.' I knew that much. And I could see she was starting to get mad, although she kept on calling me Baby, and she said she could see I was the kind of person who loved to dwell on the ugly and unpleasant. Then I started getting mad myself. I said I didn't like to dwell on them particularly, but I knew for sure they were real as hell and no dream. That was right, she said. They weren't a dream. They were a nightmare—lust, suffering, death, all of them. I told her if they weren't real, nothing was real and she damned well knew it, but then she went through the 'take away beauty, symmetry, strength' routine again, and that was when I really blew my top. God knows why. It wasn't a subject I'd ever gotten excited about before, but I told her that if you took away the beauty, power, vitality, strength, and everything else from Kitten Dory herself, what you had left was what was sitting there in front of me now—an old woman with blue hair who, no matter how many cancers and crushed bones she'd managed to live through so far on plain guts, in a few years was going to be dead. I remember pointing my finger at her and saying two or three times in a row, 'You're going to die, Kitten. You're going to be dead as the day before yesterday.'

"I thought now I'd have a real fight on my hands, but the next thing I knew she was crying. She asked me how I could say such a thing after all she'd done for my darling Mom. I couldn't believe it. I thought she must be kidding me. But they were tears all right, and I beat it out of there as fast as I could. I've never felt like such an absolute heel. Whether you agreed with her or not, she was a brave old bird, and she'd done lots of people including my mother a lot of good, and who was I anyway to tell her what religion was all about? It was just that I couldn't let her get by with saying that the lusts and sufferings and deaths in the world weren't real, and if this Jesus of hers didn't suffer and die like everybody else, then He was never really one of us, and Christianity's based on a masquerade. But don't think what I said had any permanent effect on Kitten. She was back on the job bright and early the next morning. I was the only one who came close to being permanently affected.

"I even began to think that my mother had come close to something like the truth. Maybe it was not having any religion in their lives that had had something to do with all my fathers being dead, with my running around like a stud bull. If either one of us had ever believed that there could be a God who had somehow, ahead of us and for us, been through everything we were going through, it might have made a difference, and I even started trying to pray sometimes. But my praying was really a mess. I could never figure out what sin was except that in my case I decided it must have something to do with sex. So when I prayed . . . I don't know. Just praying about sex, sex would start swelling up like a wave trying to drown out the prayer I was making. Right in the middle of it, all sorts of pictures would begin drifting through my mind—dirty pictures, I mean; pictures of what used to go on in the locker rooms and lots of other places—till I figured out the prayer God was getting must look like the kind of photographs they pass around at stag dinners and I'd better give the whole thing up. But then I decided if He was going to take a look at me at all, He might as well know the worst and probably knew it already, so I'd barge ahead with the dirty pictures flying and just hope for the best. It wasn't exactly one of the great conversions, and I don't suppose I've been to church more than a half-dozen times in the years since, but some things got easier after that, and the monkey on my back started taking longer and longer vacations. In a way Kitten was wrong and in a way she was right. There's no point dwelling on the ugly and unpleasant things of the world, as she said, but before you can beat them you've got to know how real they are. Then maybe they get less real. So there you have the complicated religious scene," Tripp said, "and now you know about Kitten Dory."

"Have you ever seen her again?" Anne asked.

"I ran into her on the street down there once not so long ago. She pulled me into a doorway and with her big, nurse's hand tight around my wrist recited a poem she'd made up—all about sunlight and God and a baby's smile."

"Kuykendall would love that. Have you ever told him any of this?"

"Only you," Tripp said.

"There's nothing I can say to it all," Anne said. "I mean I can only just listen or ask questions. There's nothing I can contribute. You don't mind, do you?"

"How about you?" he asked. "Do you mind what you've had to listen to?"

"No, except that it seems awfully far away. I can see you in all these situations, but you'd act so differently now. Kinder," she said, "more honest, and less complicated."

"Success," Tripp said. "Money and fame and a name in the world. All the things that are supposed to make you cold and unapproachable, conceited, phony. Don't believe a word of it. When a man's got money, he can afford to be kind. That's not supposed to sound cynical. It just happens to be true. When he's a success, a name, it's easy for him to be himself—as honest and uncomplicated as he wants. It's not only skin-deep with him either. It's more than just a part. He really starts to *become* honest and kind and uncomplicated. Comparatively, of course. It's all comparative. But it's true. The best thing in the world for a man is to succeed."

"My successful Tripp," Anne said. "My honest and kind and uncomplicated Tripp."

"I haven't even worked my way up to being just two-faced yet. I've still got three dozen of them at least. But I still may get there. Especially if you stick with me."

"But why didn't you ask me to stick with you before?" she asked. "Why did it finally have to be me who broke down—this afternoon, with water all over your face, being wrecked there, till I couldn't stand it any longer? I'd sworn to myself I'd never see you again, you know. I'd never have gone today if I'd known Kuykendall had asked you. Why, Tripp?" She sat there on the couch beside him, turned around to face him with her bare feet tucked beneath her, a glass of milk forgotten in one hand.

"Because I didn't know which of us was after you," he said, "or what he was after you for. I've been talking your ear off to show you who you were up against without knowing it—all three dozen of me, and my fathers."

"Was my father mixed up in it, too, somehow?" Anne asked.

"Oh yes," he said. "Of course, he was. I was dying to meet Ansel Gibbs's daughter—just to see what she was like, and then for the drama of it, too. I wasn't one to miss that . . . the next generation meeting, friends, long after the shooting was over. Like Kitten's poem—the babies gurgling happily in the sun with God smiling down. Then when the daughter turned out to be you, I saw there was going to be more drama than I'd bargained for."

"You saw it right away?" she asked. "The first time?"

"On the beach that time. My birthday. I told you that."

"Yes, but I wanted to hear it again. But Tripp," she said, all this excitedly, her smile blurred, "tell me . . . why did you suddenly stop after that, as if you'd never said anything at all?"

"I was afraid maybe I was just making the most of a dramatic situation, that both of us were—thinking we were in love because it would give such a bang-up ending to the whole thing. Thinking—oh, there's never any end to it, you know—that in the long run you'd probably be miserable with me, and being afraid that maybe in some queer way that's what I wanted—to bring a kind of dramatic justice to pass. This was all the actor, the part-playing, in me, because when you came right down to it, I never blamed Ansel Gibbs. My father lost his job, but so what? He'd lost plenty already, lost them or left them. A man doesn't shoot himself for any one reason. I don't think reason enters into it at all. He just does what he had to do, that's all. Your father had no more to do with it than a hundred other people. Less, for that matter."

"Then you weren't out to get him or anything?"

"Of course I wasn't. But—"

"What?"

"The first time I met him—that afternoon in your house —he told me more or less that he blamed himself. He asked me if I blamed him, and I told him the truth, which was that I didn't, but even as I was telling him that, the whole thing came back at me again as a terrific possibility. I mean, I thought what a great scene it would have been if I had blamed him. So though it wasn't real, it kept on existing as a possibility, a kind of dream, do you follow me? A dream he and I had both dreamed together. And I could feel it doing something queer to the air between us just the way it had already done something queer to the air between you and me."

"Was that why you asked him to be on your program then—as part of the dream?"

"No," Tripp said. "I just knew it would be a real feather in my cap if I could manage to get him, especially with Farwell. And my God, he was fine, Annie! You know that, don't you?"

"I didn't think so at the time, I know that," she said. "I thought you'd made a fool of him, and on purpose. At least I partly thought that, and by the time I got through with him, I think he thought so, too. I made a terrible scene in the kitchen afterward, that same night."

"Well, you're wrong," Tripp said. "You know he came over here to see me still later, don't you? After your scene, I guess."

"No! He never said he did. I thought he went to bed."

"I wasn't here, but, of all people, Mother was. She left a note that he'd come and they'd had a wonderful talk about the good old days. He left a note, too. I just picked it up this morning on my way in from the country—sweet as a rose, not a word of reproach in it. I think I've still got it somewhere if you want proof."

"Then why," Anne asked, "why, will you tell me, did he do that ghastly business this afternoon? If there'd been rocks instead of paper balls, he'd have still thrown them. He wanted to kill you. I thought he'd lost his mind. Or that I had. It was uncanny, awful . . ."

"If you asked him now," Tripp said, "I'll bet he couldn't tell you himself. The whole thing down there was a nightmare anyway. And God knows he's on the spot. What he said Friday night was magnificent, but Farwell's out to get him for it. The newspapers are after him. I think for a minute something just broke in two, and he had to beat hell out of somebody. I was the nearest, so he tried to beat hell out of me. That's all it was, and I only hope he feels better for it."

"I think it's much worse than that. I told him you were out to ruin him, and he thinks you are. For the first time in my life, I think, I made him listen. And then there's this verdict of yours. How does he know it's not going to be Guilty and that all your adoring fans won't go rushing off to Western Union to wire their Senators? Porter Hoye tells me some have already. Tripp, tell me something," she said, "honestly, no two faces, no dreams—what's your verdict?"

"That's simple," he said, and he took her chin in his hand as he spoke, holding her face before him. "I think in his own way he's seen what Hell looks like, and he's survived to tell the tale. Not everybody does. I admire him as much as any man I know."

"And is that what you're going to say when the time comes?" Tears had come to her eyes, and one of them touched Tripp's hand as he held her there.

"Yes," he said, and perhaps for the first time in his life then he was spared the moment of thinking that now the time was precisely right, then taking advantage of it, but all in one instant willed and moved together so that literally before he knew it, he was lying there close to her, his mouth discovering her face and hair. He had told her of all the people who he had been and was and of all the parts he had played and was playing still, and if in conscience he could not go on to claim that with her he played no part at all, he could say at least that with her he was able to play so many parts at once that perhaps they added up to himself. He could say that each of them was just sufficiently true so that, taken together, they made truth enough even to love with.

C H A P T E R

X

THE TWO days following Tripp's broadcast were for Porter
Hoye a period of such gloom that he positively welcomed
as diversion the few distasteful tasks that he became involved in on Gibbs's behalf. Having persuaded him to
leave for Connecticut early Saturday morning, Hoye called
him there several times during the course of the day to
keep him informed of events in the city and roared into the
telephone with as much conviction and cheer as he could
muster that all was going well and the worst was already
over. In turn, he himself received a number of calls from
the papers asking him if he could enlighten them as to Mr.
Gibbs's present whereabouts, or identify for them the
suicide who had come up in the discussion with Senator
Farwell, and to both of these questions he repeatedly de-
clared that he had no statement to make whatever. He also
tried at intervals all Saturday to get hold of Tripp, but
finally decided that, like Gibbs, the young man had fled
the city, undoubtedly not to return until the turmoil which
he had caused had somewhat subsided. Louise von Louwe's

butler, Walter, further complicated matters by calling him
up after each fresh sally with the reporters who continued
to hover near the house in hopes of catching Gibbs on his
return, and asking with increasing excitement whether
there wasn't something he could tell them that would send
them all home and leave him in peace. "Just stick to your
guns, man!" Hoye had again and again told him. "You're
only the butler, and you don't know a damned thing."

He conducted all these affairs from his law office, to
which he had proceeded after breakfast Saturday morning
not because he had any pressing work to attend to there,
but in the belief that those familiar surroundings, that
atmosphere of the legal and precise, would serve to make
more tolerable the hopelessly disorganized activities in
which he was engaged. None of the other partners was
there, only two of the younger associates who were clearly
delighted to be found working overtime by a senior member of the firm; and between telephone conversations he
found numerous excuses to call on them for this and that,
taking considerable comfort in the deference with which
they did his bidding. He went even so far as to take them
to lunch with him at Fraunces Tavern and over his eggs
benedict discoursed at some length on the rewards and
rigors of following the law as a profession, reminiscing
about the days of his own apprenticeship in the office of
Mr. Justice Holmes. By late afternoon the telephone had
stopped ringing, the companionship of the two young associates had begun to pall, and it was only then that he

decided to leave the office and seek release from the tensions of the day elsewhere.

Porter Hoye did not often have recourse to what he considered to be the depraved self-indulgence of a Turkish bath, and when on occasion he did so, it was a mission which he would embark upon with all the devious precautions of a thief. Instead of going to the Racquet Club or the University Club, where he would inevitably meet men of his acquaintance, he went instead to the Hotel Taft, where, although there was always the possibility of being recognized, there was no chance at all of being recognized, he felt confident, by anyone whose good opinion he valued. Furthermore, at the desk of the bath itself where you deposited your valuables and signed the register, he never gave his own name, but always an alias, to the choice of which he had originally devoted considerable thought. Refusing to pass himself off as merely Mr. Brown or Mr. Green from some undistinguished locality, he became for the length of those clandestine visits P. H. Mortimer of Tuxedo Park, a name and title which secured for him, he felt, no more and no less than the same degree of attentive respect to which his own identity would have entitled him had he been willing to disclose it. It was as Mr. Mortimer that the attendants all knew and addressed him, and his secret pleasure in this was no small part of the bath's therapy. Thus it was to the Hotel Taft that he made his way this late winter afternoon of Gibbs's absence in the country, and within a short time of arriving there sat in a deck chair in the intense dry heat of the first tiled room, stark naked except for a wet towel which he wore wrapped around his head like a turban. As the sweat began to roll down his wide cheeks and grizzled chest, his characteristically florid face turning an even deeper and more incandescent red, he gave serious thought to his fortunes as they were involved with those of Ansel Gibbs.

It was by no means a simple matter. First of all there was his genuine concern for Gibbs's individual predicament quite divorced from his own. To witness what he feared to be the ruin or near-ruin of a brilliant career, which long friendship had given him the chance to observe from its earliest beginnings, caused him a degree of pain— in part sentimental, in part almost aesthetic as at the defacement of some noble monument—which wrinkled his bulging brow as an attendant handed him a paper cone of ice water and replaced the wet towel on his head with a fresh one. He responded with only a grunt to the "Long time no see, Mr. Mortimer," and sipped the ice water in silence. Whether Gibbs knew it or not—and as usual Hoye yearned for some sign from his friend that indeed he did know it, some momentary break in the clouds of his bland impassivity—he was precariously close to political destruction. If this caused Hoye a twinge of unselfish pain, it also made him inwardly shudder at the spectacle of his own irrepressible sense of gratification at the thought that as the years went by, it would be he, Hoye, who would continue to have a place in the world, whereas all that was left for Gibbs would be to retire to his ranch in Montana

and to take up where he had left off with the somber
memoirs of the days of his ascendancy. To the degree to
which, throughout more than half a lifetime of knowing
Gibbs, Hoye had always had to suppress a feeling of being
somehow in competition with him, he could not help seeing
in this vision of what the distinguished Gibbs might soon
be reduced to, the still further vision that it was he, the
comparatively plodding Hoye, who would in the end
emerge the winner. And yet he was robbed of the guilty
but delicious sense of full triumph by knowing full well
that, win or lose, Gibbs simply would not care. In all ways,
this was what disturbed Hoye most. It was one thing for
Gibbs to be ruined by not having cared enough to hold his
tongue with Farwell, to do the proper and expected thing;
but it was still another thing for him to be ruined and still
not to care, not even to care that it was Hoye, the carer,
who remained afloat while he himself carelessly sank to the
bottom. When the air began to burn his nostrils as he in-
haled it, Hoye left the hot room with these unpleasant
thoughts and padded across the damp tiled floor to the
edge of the swimming-pool.

"The sight of all those withered old rumps," he had
once remarked to one of his few friends who knew that he
occasionally patronized Turkish baths, "soothes me the
way some people are soothed by an ocean voyage," but he
was hardly aware now of the presence of anyone else in the
whole long room as he inched his way into the cold, chlo-
rinated water until he was crouching in it up to his chin,
his arms stretched out to either side in the absent-minded

beginnings of a breast stroke. This business of not caring, he thought, was one of the most readily identifiable aspects of being all that he meant by the word 'gentleman'; but quite out of keeping with his usual success at making his own gentility seem all the more unmistakable by the roaring and boisterous way in which he burlesqued its appearance in others, try as he might he could not burlesque this most evasive of its manifestations. It was not solid enough, this not caring. It was not a thing, but the absence of a thing. It was a kingly indifference to most of whatever perplexed and troubled other men. And if Hoye was incapable of burlesquing it, he was even more helpless when it came to any attempt to emulate it, for there was no escaping the fact that socially and professionally and in every other way that counted with him, he himself cared desperately. Gibbs did not, and before him, Hoye thought as he slowly swam out into the middle of the blue pool, Rudy Tripp had not.

Hoye had watched the effortless and indifferent way in which Rudy Tripp had won extraordinary popularity at college; more particularly he had watched him drift into a far closer relationship with Ansel Gibbs than any that Hoye had been able to manage in those distant days. He had watched the enchanted ease with which he had discovered, made famous, and eventually won Sylvia Stowe, whom Hoye still thought of as the most beautiful woman he had ever seen; and through Gibbs he had followed his later career as he left one job after another, yet always managed to float to the surface. When Hoye had first learned of his suicide, although a mixture of envy and disapproval had prevented his ever particularly liking him, he had with everyone else felt momentary horror and shock at the news; but later, if only to himself, he could not resist remarking that this or something like it was inevitably and, in all probability, justly, the fate of such arrogant indifference. And yet if Hoye, who in one way or another competed with everyone, felt for years that he, the carer, had ultimately and without question triumphed over Rudy, the careless, he could not help but wonder now whether this was really so. Such was the state of his mind as he reached the far end of the swimming-pool that he saw Rudy Tripp dead, committed to that final indifference, as triumphing over him still—not only by troubling Gibbs's memory to the point of making him fatally speak of his death to an unseen audience of millions, but by having fathered a son who had grown up himself to menace Gibbs and, through Gibbs, to menace Hoye as well. Finally, this son had obviously all the easy indifference of his father before him and of his father's friend Gibbs, and by the time Hoye began to pull himself up the ladder out of the cold water, he saw himself as the eternal dupe—conscientious, industrious, factual—of all the airy and uncaring princes and kings of the world.

Once out of the pool, Hoye stood at its edge with an enormous white towel draped about him and watched the few other bathers. For the most part in their fifties or sixties, they moved about with elaborate unconcern at their own nakedness while Hoye looked at their round shoulders and sagging paunches, their welted, blue-veined legs and the pallor of their skin, and despised them for the solicitude that they lavished upon bodies long past repair, despised himself for being one of them. Unlike P. H. Mortimer of Tuxedo Park, Porter Hoye of New York in the winter and a cottage in the Long Island dunes in the summer looked upon youth and vigor as the two prime virtues. Although unskilled at any sport—he played an exuberant but erratic game of tennis and seldom broke one hundred in golf—he nonetheless thrust his way through life itself with the robust intensity of a middle-aged athlete determined to make up in vigor for what he lacked in youth, so that the Turkish baths could seem no less to him than an ignominious lapse, and he cringed now at the sight of his partners in ignominy. But once begun, the ritual of the bath was not easily broken, and he allowed an attendant— they all looked white and shriveled to him—to lead him into one of the cubicles across the swimming-pool from the heat rooms, and there he lay face down on a marble slab while the attendant with a long-handled brush began to scrub his legs and back with soap and water. Lulled by the soft rubbing, he enjoyed a few moments of something very close to sleep but richly responsive to bodily sensation, until with a sad lurch he came awake again to the thought of the events from which he had come here seeking release.

Perhaps things were not so black as they seemed, he thought. The papers, after all, had been far from unanimously unfavorable. The enmity of Senator Farwell was in itself something less than a death-blow. There was

no reason to believe that the accusations that Anne Gibbs
had cried out against young Tripp were any more than the
vituperations of a girl crossed in love. Perhaps, even as he
had just a few hours before tried to reassure Gibbs again
over the telephone, all might indeed turn out well, and yet
it was in large part upon Gibbs that this would depend—
upon his discretion of act and word, upon his directness
and forcefulness with the Senate committee, above all
upon his simply being sufficiently determined that to win
was what he profoundly wanted. There, Hoye thought,
was the dilemma. He had read, he had heard, about men
going through a kind of menopause of their own, suddenly
running away from their families, their careers, to chase
after love or ambition or oblivion after years of respectabil-
ity, and perhaps this new, dark turn of Gibbs's mind, Hoye
pondered, was related in some fashion to this—this preoccupation with the lost and intangible, this determination somehow to express what Hoye saw as the dim and
shifting worst of himself, this indifference to whether he
won or lost. Whether Gibbs's appointment to the Cabinet
was to be confirmed or not might ultimately depend for
the most part on Gibbs's whim, and there, for Hoye, was
the full horror of the situation because on that whim his
own fortunes, of course, depended as well.

Oh, if Gibbs should lose, Hoye knew, and return to his
ranch and his memoirs, he, Porter Hoye, would continue
to have a place in the world—his practice, his clubs, his
social involvements—and would in that sense emerge the
victor, but such an undistinguished, quiet little place it

was compared to the one which he would inherit if Gibbs should choose instead to win. The bath attendant indicated that it was time to turn over on his back there on the marble slab, and he did so mechanically, scarcely aware of the act. Through his known friendship with Gibbs, he thought, through the degree to which it was also known that Gibbs valued his counsel, his legal and administrative training, he would enjoy, should Gibbs consent to occupy the high place to which he had been called, a place little less high himself. In a hundred indefinable but significant ways, and certainly in as many definable ways as well, his stock would rise, and he would be recognized as a man on whose word grave decisions hung, whose province was not merely the State of New York and its laws, but the whole broad world of national affairs. In all probability, he would take leave of his firm and accompany Gibbs to Washington, as during the war he had accompanied him to England, in the role of special adviser. And from there—well, but who could say?

He followed the attendant then into yet another tiled room, where, from a distance of about twenty feet, two hoses were played up and down the length of his body, one hot and one cold, and when at one point the force of the water as it beat against his chest sent a spray up into his face that almost suffocated him, he puffed and shouted, hopping up and down there and waving his arms, so that for a time he was troubled by no thoughts at all. At the conclusion of this, he stepped back into the main room of the swimming-pool, feeling wonderfully refreshed and almost unbearably clean, his whole body tingling from the hoses, and he was just about to proceed to the last stage of all—a brisk alcohol rub in a glassed-in enclosure at the end of the room by which he had entered—when he noticed coming through the main door a man whom he immediately recognized as known to him, but for a few moments was unable to identify further. To his consternation then he saw that it was Edward M. Farwell.

As they had met several times over the course of the years and then again at Tripp's broadcast only the evening before, there was no question in his mind but that if they came face to face now, the Senator was bound to recognize him, and this was an encounter which Hoye was willing to go to any lengths to avoid. Quite apart from his strong disinclination to meet Farwell simply on the basis of the altercation over Gibbs's appointment, in which they were both so deeply involved, there was his horror at the idea of meeting him stark naked as both of them were and in this place where he was not Porter Hoye, as the Senator knew him, but P. H. Mortimer. His first thought was to speed out of the baths altogether and back to the dressing-rooms, but because this route would take him directly past where the Senator now stood, chatting with two attendants, he was obliged to think of some other way of escaping. It occurred to him that he could go and stand in one of the scrubbing cubicles until the Senator had established himself in one or another of the earlier stages, but before he had time to do this, he saw Farwell starting to walk slowly in his direction. The two attendants were still with him and, a cigar in his mouth, he was clearly too engrossed in whatever he was telling them to notice Hoye, but it might be a matter of no more than minutes before he did so. Consequently, rather than risk the trip directly across his path to the cubicles, Hoye dived clumsily off the edge of the pool. He hit the surface flat and hard with his stomach and chest, splashing water high to either side, and when a moment later he rose to the surface again, he saw that Farwell had stopped, apparently to see who it was that had caused such a commotion. With his chest still smarting from the dive, and chilled now by the cold water, he was thus forced to submerge again, and swam underwater as far as he could toward the other end of the pool before his breath gave out completely and once more he came up for air. As the Senator still stood in full view although no longer looking his way, and not wanting to attract any further attention, Hoye remained in the pool for some minutes more, and it seemed to him as he shivered there that his immediate predicament was not unlike his predicament in general: helplessly, ignominiously obliged to wait on another's whim, his fortunes entirely dependent upon a man to whom they were a matter of complete unconcern.

Sunday morning was bitter cold, but the sun shone brilliantly on the snow-covered city, and Hoye walked the ten blocks from his apartment on Park Avenue to St. Christopher's Episcopal Church, half-blinded by the shat-

tering brightness, but enjoying every breath of the sharp
winter air. He wore a morning coat and Chesterfield and
tipped his derby with a hearty flourish to the acquaint-
ances who, like him, had lingered too long over *The New
York Times* and were hurrying now to get to the eleven
o'clock service. The rector of St. Christopher's, a thin,
ascetic-looking man with prematurely white hair, had
been a classmate of Hoye's at Harvard, and it was partly
out of loyalty to him, partly because the church itself was
situated not far from where he lived, that Hoye kept
regular attendance there. Not even his loyalty prevented
him from admitting that the sermons were not consistently
of the first order—for two Sundays in a row the rector had
been unable to get away from the tragedy of the elm-tree
blight in New England, and on this particular morning he
used the text "Render unto Caesar the things that are
Caesar's" as a point from which to urge prompt and honest
payment of State and Federal income taxes—but Hoye
argued that the sermon was after all not everything and
that simply the beauty of the Episcopal liturgy itself invariably left him feeling better and happier for having
taken part in it, plus the fact that there was a number of
distinguished and successful men of his acquaintance in the
congregation whom it moved him not a little to see gratui-
tously bending their knees to the mysteries of a bountiful
Providence. So he left the soft gray twilight of St. Christopher's on this particular morning feeling much restored
after the strains and humiliations of the preceding day,

and had cocktails and late lunch with a couple, also of the congregation, who with tactful sympathy avoided any mention of the Gibbs affair altogether.

Sunday afternoons in New York were his particular joy because they were the one interval in the week when he felt entirely unconstrained to fulfill any obligation, and he sat on the Duncan Phyfe sofa in his living-room with the papers scattered about him on the floor and read intermittently in the current novel by John P. Marquand or simply watched the slow January dusk dim his view of the apartment building across the street. The light of his lamp shone warmly through its parchment shade, and eventually the genial, tense, and aging balloon of his face sank to his chest and after one little jerk upward, as though his body were rebelling at the self-indulgence involved in loss of consciousness, it sank slowly back, and he fell asleep. He remained asleep, the novel's back broken across his knee, until around eight when he was awakened by the ringing of the telephone.

It was Louise von Louwe. Accustomed as she was to making unsparing use of the telephone, she regarded it as primarily a means of one-way communication, and her method was to explain what she had called to say and then —sometimes waiting for a response and sometimes not—to hang up almost immediately thereafter with the result that many who had gone on speaking to her, as they thought, were startled at the end of their remarks to find themselves answered only by an empty buzz. "Porter," she said. "Louise. Come to dinner. Ansel's off to Washington tomorrow, and it was to have been a festive little *bon-voyage* meal for just the three of us here. But nobody's eating in this house any more except me. So you come. Right away," to which Hoye was given time only to say that he would.

He was received at the door by Walter, who shrugged his shoulders and raised his eyes heavenward as though words were inadequate to express the horrors to which he had been exposed for the last forty-eight hours or so, and then showed him into the living-room, where Louise von Louwe was waiting for him alone. She wore a long, black evening dress with three or four nearly waist-length strands of large artificial pearls around her neck, and her gray hair was pinned up in an even looser, untidier bun than usual. "I look as though I walk by night," were her first words as she poured Scotch for him. "I won't try to tell you all that's happened today because you wouldn't believe it, but I'll tell you some."

What she settled back to recount to him then was at first scarcely comforting to Hoye, but to hear it from her, to have it presented to him in the same even, faintly sardonic tones as with many more humdrum tribulations of the past, was in itself a kind of comfort to him, and the account thus failed to upset his Sunday sense of well-being. She spoke first of their return from the country and the visit that afternoon with Kuykendall. Without explaining what had actually taken place then between Gibbs and Tripp, she said merely that they had unexpectedly met each other there and that the sight of the young man had clearly upset Gibbs greatly. "No one can say, of course, what goes on in the heads of people like Ansel," she told him. "They live the most significant part of their lives inside there somewhere, and for us even to try to make guesses about it is folly. But if they'd met as knights on a plain instead of as gentlemen at a church bazaar, you can be sure that boy's handsome red head would have rolled in the dust. I will spare you details," she said above Hoye's plea for them, "but it was distinctly —you might say uniquely—unpleasant, and my little supper party tonight has withered down to just you and me as a result. Ansel is in the library upstairs having given word that he is not to be disturbed by anyone—not even by you, my dear, because I particularly told him I'd called you—and Anne has gone off altogether."

"Mentally?" Hoye asked. A man carries his new umbrella not merely in ¦the chance that it may rain, but in something not unlike the hope that it will, and Hoye asked his question with a swagger of expectancy just sufficient to indicate that in the event that Anne had so succumbed, he for one was not so unworldly as to be caught off-guard by the news.

"No, no," Louise said. "Geographically. Emotionally, if you like. She disappeared from the bazaar so we had to leave without her, her father and I. Then when it came time for dinner and she still wasn't back—this was before I knew that the plague had set in and there was to be no dinner—I decided to see if I could find her. The unpleasantness at the bazaar had involved *rapprochement* between her and Tripp, and I was fairly certain they had gone off

together. So I called Tripp's number and found out that
they had. She was there, and I've no doubt she's there still.
We talked at some length, and I learned a great deal. It
isn't for nothing that I summoned you here, you know.
Have a cheese?"

"Thank you," Hoye said. "I already have one."

"Take two of them at once and roll them around in there
like dice," she said. "First of all, they are in love. She
didn't tell me this in so many words, of course, but a child
who's got her head caught between the bars of her crib
doesn't have to explain the problem. I gather that at last
even Tripp has seen fit to declare himself, so presumably
the whole Meissen-breaking episode has been forgotten,
and all is well with her. If you call it well, and it well may
be. Sometimes being the specter at the feast bores me. I
also thought this might be a good chance to find out what
Tripp's verdict was to be—the *verdict*, you know—so I
asked her if she'd found out."

"And had she? You realize," Hoye began, somehow
appropriating the information as his own even before she
had reported it, managing to indicate that here she was
entering a specialized field and was in need of an expert,
"you realize," he repeated, "that this is a matter of the
gravest importance—to all of us." Still in his morning
coat, he leaned forward in his chair like a judge over a writ
of execution, searching her placid face for a reply.

"There are times when I think there's nothing I don't
realize," Louise von Louwe said. "Yes, she found out. And
she told me. Tripp's verdict is not only that Ansel's not
guilty of anything at all, but that he looks upon him as a

king among men and the bright hope of our democracy. His plan is apparently to release a statement to that effect to the papers tomorrow."

"Well," Hoye leaned back again in his chair and took a long sip from his glass. "That's certainly not going to be the end of the story, but it's damned good to hear anyway. Does Ansel know?"

"Oh yes," she said. "I went up to see him right away, feeling like the angel of the Annunciation. His daughter was in love, I told him, and to all appearances loved in return. What was more, his future son-in-law apparently loved him, too, and was going to say so publicly. And in answer . . . oh, he thanked me for telling him, and Anne had been much on his mind, he said, and he hoped Tripp was the right man for her—all of this coming out in that slow, thoughtful way he has when you know he's flying on automatic pilot. Then he asked if I'd mind if he didn't come down to supper because he wanted to make an early start to Washington in the morning and he had work to do. And that was that. I suppose it isn't the festive *bon-voyage* supper that matters," she said, taking one strand of pearls in her fingers and flipping it back and forth like a pendulum, "the lobster bisque, the filet of beef, the *crème brûlé*— history's made up of feasts that were never eaten, and you and I can still play with some of this one anyway. But something matters, I'm sure of that. Perhaps it's just that a man usually gets what he wants but never just when he wants it—often not until he's past wanting it at all."

"Now don't go putting that idea into his head," Hoye

warned. "You always exaggerate everything, Louise. He's had some kind of run-in with Tripp which you won't describe, but with Tripp's verdict what it is, it can't have been very serious as I see it. But maybe that is what's bothering him now anyway, or maybe it's just that tomorrow he goes down to Washington to face the real music, and he knows it. He has things on his mind, that's all. He doesn't have time right now to think about Anne's romances or *crème brûlé* for dinner. But don't go making a five-act tragedy out of it. He wants to fight this thing out and win just as much as we all want it for him."

"Well," Louise von Louwe said, "let's hope so. All I know is that if that isn't what he wants, I think we're the ones I feel sorriest for, you and I."

Hoye looked at her sharply at this, caught off-guard by her statement to the extent of accepting for a moment her condition. "How do you mean?" he asked.

"Not because we have so much to lose," she said. "But because the other way we'd have so much to win. Nobody would enjoy his success as much as you and I. You know that's true whether you'll admit it or not. It would be so charming not to die of boredom and obscurity."

"You're an ambitious old woman," Hoye said, raising his glass. "That I'll admit, and I drink this to you. *A vôtre santé!*" he roared.

"And to yours," she said, raising hers. "And to his—to the great man's."

"And to the great man's," Hoye repeated, and they drank together.

CHAPTER

XI

ANNE DID not return from Tripp's until long after both her father and Louise had gone to bed, and she consequently slept until about ten o'clock the next morning when, coming down for breakfast, she discovered that Gibbs had already left for Washington. "Oh, I can't bear it," she said to Louise, who had come to sit with her in the dining-room. "You mean there was nobody to see him off or wish him luck or anything? He just slunk off by himself?"

"It was not a triumphal departure," Louise told her. "He had breakfast in his room, and then we met down here for about ten minutes perhaps. I was going to wake you, but he said there wasn't time. There were several men he thought were reporters waiting across the street, and he wanted to get away before they started to storm the house. He left through the court in back, and I had the car pick him up around the block with his bags and brief case. Oh, and he left a note for you," she said. "I put it on the table in the hall."

It was a bright morning, and the snow had already begun to melt, so that drops of water seeded with sunlight trickled down the pane as Anne stood by one of the narrow windows on either side of the front door reading what her father had written.

Anne dear [she read], *I am writing this at night, and by the time you read it in the morning, I'll be on my way to Washington and all that's going to involve. I'm sorry in part not to have the chance to speak to you in person before I go, but there are some things that are easier to say in letters, at least easier for me, and so it's probably all for the best. Will you try to understand me, Annie, as I'm afraid I've never tried adequately to understand you?*

Louise was up here a short time ago to tell me that you and Tripp were together this evening and that after talking to you she felt that whatever has been causing trouble between you was over now and that it wouldn't be long before you were getting married. If my reaction to this struck her as lacking enthusiasm, it was only because, of course, the news came as no surprise to me. I suspected as much the other night when you said that you were never going to see him again, and I believe the first thing that came into my mind when I saw him at East Harlem this afternoon was that here was the man who was probably going to carry you off just when I was finally about to get to know you. As far as reason came into the picture then at all, I'm sure that was at least part of why I set out virtually to kill him, although another part of what I was out to kill was certainly not him at all but myself. Or perhaps

I wanted him to kill me. I don't know. But there's no sense trying to explain nightmares away. You have your hands full just learning to live with them.

In any case, that episode is over now, and the results haven't been entirely unfortunate. For one thing, I now believe there's every chance for your being very happy with each other. As I watched you walking out of that nightmare together, I was suddenly convinced of it. He's probably the one person of all of us who's acted without sickness or subterfuge this whole strange week, and you both have my blessing in whatever plans you choose to make. Please tell him that for me.

I also came to certain conclusions about myself there in East Harlem this afternoon. I have an appointment to see the President the morning after I arrive in Washington (which is also the morning before I'm scheduled to appear before the Senate committee), and my intention is to tell him that I don't feel able at this juncture to accept the job he's offered me. Because of their highly personal nature, I don't feel obligated to explain my reasons to him in detail, and I'll probably let the official explanation rest on grounds of ill health, which is in a way a shorthand version of the truth. But I owe a fuller reckoning than that, and I want that reckoning set down in paper and ink—if only here, in a letter to my daughter.

I am no prophet, as Dr. Kuykendall pointed out when I said good-by to him today, but that is a fact which I've long known. It's never an easy thing to accept, considering the dreams you have when you're young, but at some point or another years ago I became reconciled to being no more if no less than who I am, and I would have fought for this Cabinet post anyway. A man must do the best with what he is, and even one who falls short of greatness may still greatly work for good. But more recently, during the last few weeks in fact, more especially the last few hours, I've been brought to face some harsher realities about myself still.

A man misleads himself as much by exaggerating his deficiencies as he does by denying them, and I don't want to make that mistake here. But it's one thing to fall short of greatness—you'd have a hard time naming me six men in any given century who didn't—but to fall short of common humanity is something else again. Without flagellating myself unduly, how could I avoid, how could you or anyone else avoid, seeing that that's exactly what I've done? What else can it mean to have a friend and not to save him, to have a daughter and not to know her, to meet a friend's son and not to trust him, to have had a wife and hardly to remember her? In what other way do you explain a man who has lived his whole life on the blurred edge of things? Farwell's verdict is closer to the truth than Tripp's. This is no man to govern men. This is no man at all. I'm not sure I've ever even reached the point of really knowing a man. So I'll see the President day after tomorrow and turn down the appointment before it's confirmed. Until then, please don't speak of this to anyone.

"When I leave Washington, I think I'll go on to Montana. I have my book to finish there, my memories of the war. It's the one thing I'm good for. However atrocious a penalty you pay for my kind of isolationism, it has its meager compensations. If seeing as much falseness as truth in almost everything paralyzes you when it comes to the action of self-com-

mitment, it leaves you peculiarly fit to describe what it is you've been unable to commit yourself to, and I have words for such describing. I have been at a loss for everything else perhaps but never for words. I was made for words. I sometimes believe that I am made of words. So that's what my next step will be. When your own life begins to straighten itself out— and I suspect that it will do so more easily now with me out of the picture—come out to see me, and we will 'laugh at gilded butterflies, who loses and who wins, who's in, who's out.' You can bring Tripp if you like. But give me a few weeks first to make peace with myself. In the meanwhile, think as well of me as you can, Annie. Good-by, and

Love,

A. G.

The winter sun coming through the window reflected so brilliantly from the white letterpaper that, turning away from it, Anne was momentarily blinded and had to wait there for a few moments until her eyes became reaccustomed to the dim light. Returning to the dining-room, she found Louise von Louwe seated at the table with an open box of tightly packed dates before her. "Porter brought them last night," she said. "They look like cockroaches."

Anne did not answer, but simply sat down across from her with her father's letter open in her hand. Instead of asking about its contents, Louise continued on this track of her own.

"I've always had an eye for resemblances," she said. "Cockroaches look like dates and vice versa. When you're crossing the Atlantic on a steamer, the water you see looking down from the deck is the image of black marble—all dark and smooth and veined with foam. The smell of chicken broth is indistinguishable from the smell of sweat."

"Oh, don't!" Anne exclaimed. "Just this once. Don't you care what's happening around here?"

"Many things are happening around here," Louise said. "Porter gave me these dates which I've never been fond of. Do I eat them out of gratitude or do I give them away? This morning I noticed that there wasn't enough toilet paper in my bathroom to last out the day, and I must remember to have some more put in there. Last night I was woken up by a severe pain in my breast. I've naturally thought that it may be cancer. This is all part of what is happening. It is very real."

"And Father? His whole life hanging on the next few days? Doesn't that count for anything with you?"

"That is another part of what is happening, also very real. But never make the mistake," Louise von Louwe went on, tipping a butter knife this way and that in the sun so that it danced a reflection across the ceiling, "of letting one part make you underestimate the importance and reality of the other. Have you ever taken laughing gas?"

"No," Anne said, replacing her father's letter in the envelope.

"Well, I have. At the dentist's. It doesn't take away the pain," she said, "but it takes away your exclusive concern for the pain. You know that outside the breeze is shaking the leaves on a tree. You know that the dentist's hands smell of scented soap. You know that the drill is torturing a nerve. But none of them is any more important than the other, and that's why it's hard sometimes not to laugh a little. It's the best way of looking at the world, you know."

"All I know is that I've got to go," Anne said, finishing her coffee.

"Without telling me what's in your father's letter?"

"Without telling even you what's in my father's letter," she said. "He asked me not to."

"Then don't," Louise von Louwe said.

"The drill is torturing a nerve," Anne said, rising from her seat at the table. "I'll tell you that much."

"Only remember then," Louise told her, spearing one date with a fork, "about the leaves on the tree and the scented soap."

Tripp had arranged the night before to meet Anne for lunch before going down to the studio, and although it was barely seven-thirty when she left Louise von Louwe in the dining-room, she set out for the Carlyle anyway in the hope of finding him ready early. The snow was still banked high along the street and sidewalks, but the morning was so bright and comparatively mild that she decided to walk, and on her way she reread Gibbs's letter. Finishing it for a second time, she came to a halt by the huge window of a florist shop and remained there for fully five minutes still holding the letter open before her. In gloves and stadium boots, with the collar of her polo coat turned up and a yellow wool scarf wrapped around her neck, she cut an incongruous figure against the flowers and green leaves burgeoning through the glass behind her. It seemed to her suddenly that the letter faced her with a terrible choice: either to continue on her way to Tripp or to turn back even now and go to her father. The irrationality of this, of her conviction that to go to one of them now meant irrevocably to renounce the other, was lost to her in the rush not only of pity for Gibbs, who had gone off alone, but also of self-pity. She saw herself orphaned by his going, deserted by him at the very moment when by his own admission he had only just reached the point of being about to know her at last, at the very moment when she in turn might have come at last to know him, as now, by giving herself instead to Tripp, she would never have the chance to do again. It seemed to her a last, fatal choice between life as she had always known it, candied by her sense of being about to relinquish it, and life, precarious and unknown, with this boy whom after all she knew little better. She thought not only of her father, whose farewell letter seemed a farewell most final, but of Aunt Louise sitting in the morning light with a date on her fork, of her own room, her pictures and books, of everything familiar, safe, kind; and with the sun dazzling her eyes, she turned and pointlessly entered the florist shop, taking her lonely illusion of choice into that fragrant room crowded with flowers. Almost before she had come fully aware of where she was, a clerk with rimless glasses approached and asked what she wanted, to which "Roses," she found herself answering, "—yellow ones if you have them, please," wonderfully and all in a moment ceasing to be a person at the crisis of decision and becoming a girl buying flowers on a snowy winter morning. It was only when the clerk slid back the glass doors of a refrigerator and, showing her what roses he had, asked how many she wanted that she realized that, of course, she wanted none at all. But "A dozen," she said, and then, from nowhere, "I don't want to take them with me, though. I want to wire them to somebody. To the Honorable Ansel Gibbs," she said, "The Mayflower, Washington, D.C."

"Any message to go with them?" the clerk asked, and she wrote out "Love, Anne" for him, and after paying for them and stepping out onto the street again, found that in some fashion she had already made her decision: to send yellow roses to her father, to go herself to Tripp as now she hurried on to do.

As she walked, she tried to think of him as her husband, of going to him now because it was with him and nowhere else that her life was. She tried to imagine Tripp's being the point from which she would always go out and to which she would always return. "But it isn't so much a question of whether or not you can bear living with him for the rest of your life," Aunt Louise had once said. "Ask yourself instead whether you could bear living without him," so Anne tried to think of that, too, of going not to Tripp now, her husband, but to her father or Aunt Louise or Kuykendall. She pictured herself an old woman some fifty years hence saying to some bored descendant: "There was a boy named Tripp once whom I might have married but never did," and her ache of loss and regret at the prevision became as she walked through the melting snow the ache instead of simply loving him beyond the point where she could any longer take pleasure in the torture of such imagining. There was something almost of spring in the soft January air, and with it something of the exhilaration that she had known as a girl when June and the end of school had approached, the silly, green dream of summer, the conviction that now at last all her problems were to be solved and everything set right. She ran the few remaining steps to Tripp's hotel, and when, in bathrobe and slippers he drowsily opened his door to her, she threw her arms around him and pressed to herself not only him, but her whole vision of a life free at last from all the constraining securities of her girlhood which only a short time before in front of the florist shop she had nearly wept at the thought of relinquishing. Smelling of toothpaste, his unshaved cheek rough against hers, he held her there until all thought of why she had come and what she had left behind disappeared, and she knew only the precarious moment itself.

When he went off to shower and dress, she made coffee and toast for him, setting it out in the sun on a bridge table by the living-room window. They sat there together for some time after he had finished eating, and then he said that just before she had come, he had telephoned the papers and announced his verdict concerning Gibbs. It was substantially what the night before he had told her that it would be: there was no one in public life whom he admired more, no one whose appointment to the cabinet, he felt, would better serve the interests of the present administration or of the nation at large. Furthermore, Tripp told her, he planned to make the statement again on his program that Friday evening.

For only one moment did she hesitate out of loyalty to show him Gibbs's letter, and then she handed it to him. "He left it for me before he caught his train this morning," she said. "I didn't even get a chance to say good-by." As she watched him start it, she almost rejoiced in the betrayal of confidence as a further commitment to him, as a kind of dowry that she was bringing him. She wanted to lay the letter before him so that he might know just what it had cost her to turn her back on it and come to him instead. She wanted him to turn his back on it with her and yet not to be unaware of the great sadness of it.

But then, while Tripp was reading the letter, Anne read it again in her mind, and the words that she saw in her mind moved her far more deeply than those which Gibbs had actually written. They were her words now rather than her father's, or his translated almost beyond recognition into the idiom of her own love and need of him, and as such they made demands of her which she would have heeded from no source other than herself. Watching Tripp as he read, she saw in the letter a supplication of such poignance that she came close to snatching it back as something too painful to share even with him. To an incomparably greater extent than in front of the florist's, she understood it as demanding no less than that she go to her father totally now, in thought and feeling as well as deed. It was a demand which she could no longer refuse, and as soon as she saw Tripp finish reading, she told him of her new decision as if it had been in her mind from the beginning, as if she had never felt less than an hour before that to wire yellow roses was enough.

"Of course, I've got to go to him right away," she said. "That's what I came to tell you."

She waited for some protest from him, some recognition of the magnitude of the choice that she had made, but he only replaced the letter in its envelope, pushed it back to her across the table, and smiled.

"Blessed," he said, "it's up to you."

"But what do you think?" she asked. "You just sit there smiling."

"I don't see what good you could do. He said himself not to come till he had everything straightened out."

In silence she looked at him for a moment as he sat there in the sun, suddenly impassive, out of reach. "You just don't understand, do you? You don't get the point at all."

"What is the point?"

When he reached out to touch her hand, she withdrew it, not irritably but distractedly, looking for her answer. "The point is I've got to . . . make him change his mind," she said. "If he gives up now, that'll be the end. He won't have anything left—not even me now. Maybe nobody else thinks so, but to me it's so pathetic I can hardly bear it."

"That's quite a letter," Tripp said. "You're not going to have an easy job."

"Oh don't desert me," she suddenly begged him. "Don't act as if I have my troubles and you have yours. You've got to come with me."

"I'm not deserting you," he said, "but my God, there's nobody he'd want to see less than me."

"That's just because he doesn't know whether you're for him or against him."

"He'll know by the time you get there. It'll be in all the evening papers. I couldn't have given him more of a plug if he'd been by Abraham Lincoln, out of Mary Baker Eddy."

"The papers aren't enough," Anne said. "You've got to come down with me and convince him. He'll have to see you and hear it from you to be sure."

"Look," Tripp said, taking her by both hands and holding her so that she had to look at him directly. "It's stupid to say this, but it could be worse if I didn't. Seeing me face to face is going to make him sure only if I'm sure myself."

Then and there, she realized later, she would have risen and left him if he had not still held her hands, if he had not immediately continued speaking. As it was, in a sense she left him then anyway. What he had said did not serve so much to hurt her or anger her as simply to throw her back upon herself, to make her feel so entirely alone in her anxiety and love for Gibbs that Tripp's presence seemed less than real to her. She listened to him, but it was like listening to a stranger.

"Don't ask me what I *am* sure of about him," she heard

him say, "because I don't know myself. He's an honest man. He speaks the truth. But to Hell with all that. The world's crawling with honest men. What he's got is a mind —a sharp, mediocrity-hating beauty of a mind. So why can't I let it go at that? Except that I can't, because whenever I'm with him, all the admiration's there, but it's like a freshly painted white wall. You can't help wanting to mess it up a little. Annie," he said, and then in another, quieter voice that made her look up from the square of sunlight on the table between them, "where have you gone?"

"Where have you?" she asked in return, but even as she did so, she saw that he had come back, or that she had, and for the first time she smiled.

"I'm here," he said. "If I'm not here, I'm not anywhere."

"I know," she said. "It's all right now. And you don't have to come if you don't want to. You don't even have to explain."

"No, but I'm telling you," Tripp said. "I'd come if I thought it would help. But take the show with Farwell. I saw the way things were going all right, and don't think for a second I couldn't have stopped it. The right word at the right time and I could have had them talking about flying saucers or how to hook a trout with a dry fly. That's my business. But I didn't."

"It doesn't matter," she said. "I'll go alone, or I can get somebody else to go with me. Dr. Kuykendall or Hoye. Maybe Porter Hoye would be the best."

"It does matter," Tripp said. "Or it matters to me to

try to say it. I'm the one who let him get the idea he was on trial there in the first place, and once he's gotten that, the next step was obvious. He decided he was guilty as Hell, and that's what I wanted him to decide. I decided maybe he was guilty as Hell myself, and I wanted to clobber him with it. Except all the time I kept thinking what a great show he was putting on in there, too. Well, you explain it if you can," Tripp said. "Don't take me, take Hoye. Hoye's sure your father'd be wrong to give up now, and maybe Hoye could convince him. I'm not, and it would show."

"Have more coffee," Anne said. "That's what Aunt Louise would tell you. She'd draw your attention to a thing because she has such a knack with things. She thinks things are as important as people. This morning she was as worried about a box of dates as she was about my father."

"You'll make a fine wife," he said.

"I doubt it."

She poured him another cup of coffee, and, rising from the table, he walked into the center of the room with it.

"Take Hoye, and maybe together you can change his mind for him," Tripp said. He lit a cigarette and blew a single smoke ring which they both watched slip toward the floor, slowly falling apart in the still air.

"But what will we tell him?" she asked.

"Blessed," he said, "just your going down there will tell him plenty. But you can tell him, too, that if he falls short of common humanity the way he said, so do we all.

Tell him for God's sweet sake we all fall short. We're all
guilty as Hell. Tell him he's got courage and brains, and
a heart, too, if that's what's worrying him."

"You sound as if you believe it yourself."

"There are also things you don't want to tell him,"
Tripp said. "Don't tell him he's old and tired. That he's
said too many words and held too many views all his life.
Don't tell him he'll never be able to take a stand because
he doesn't think there's any worth taking. Maybe that's
itself the hardest, bravest stand there is, and maybe it
isn't. Maybe what the world needs most is somebody who
knows there's no such thing as a holy cause—somebody
who knows it not just cynically and hard-boiled but sweating blood and wishing to God it wasn't so but making the
best of it because it is. But maybe that's the last thing the
world needs. Above all, don't tell him that maybe the
Senator was right last Friday."

"Tripp, won't you come?" Anne asked, half blinded as
she turned from the bright sunlight to squint at him
standing in the shadows. "And tell him all these things or
not, but just come, for my sake? I'll be responsible for
whatever happens."

"Talk about faces," he said abruptly and laughed.
"You've got a planning face on if I've ever seen one. You
could be talking to anybody. A world face . . . "

"No," she said, "my Tripp face."

"All I have left is my Annie face. It's a terrible handicap."

"Then you will come?" she said, going to him. "Just for

moral support—because I couldn't go without you?"

They were standing by the table on which the photograph of Rudy rested. Tripp tapped the glass of it with one finger. "It always makes me think of that funeral scene in *Gatsby*," he said. " 'The poor son-of-a-bitch.' It goes for your old man, too. I don't know which is more complicated. To have a father or not to. The poor sons-of-bitches," he said.

"You'll come then?" Anne asked.

"It'll be on your head if I do."

"And tonight we'll be in our beds thinking back on it," she said. "It's always my most comforting thought. No matter what happens, you're bound to end up in bed thinking back on it."

They decided to take a plane that would get them to Washington late that afternoon, and Anne sent Gibbs a wire that they were coming. She then called Porter Hoye at his office and had already told him of her own plan—had already begun to explain why she thought that he, Hoye, would be, of all people, the best to assist her in it—when Hoye stopped her with: "My dear Anne, what in God's name are you talking about?" and she abruptly realized that, of course, he had no idea that Gibbs had decided anything but to accept the appointment that had been offered to him. So she found herself obliged once more to betray her father to the extent of reporting the gist of his letter to her, and even as she did so, she understood that it was Hoye, too, that she was betraying.

It was a betrayal and a humiliation for Hoye to have

to learn, almost incidentally, from her, of his old friend's decision when by all rights it was his old friend himself who should have told him; and she then made matters only worse by saying: "But of course I assumed you already knew." To this Hoye made no reply at all, and trying somehow to dress the wound that she had thus deepened, she began again to tell him how more than anyone else he was a man to whose word in this matter her father would give serious weight. "I'm making Tripp come, too," she said into the awful silence of that telephone, "but he's not going to be any help at all." Tripp was standing beside her, and she pinched his arm as she spoke. "He's not even sure Father isn't right to give up. He's just coming because I said I'd never speak to him again if he didn't. So you see how we need you—all of us. Especially Father. If anybody can make him change his mind, you can." Covering the mouth of the receiver with her hand, she looked at Tripp and groaned, and even as she did so she heard Hoye's answer.

"If you want to know what I think," he said, "your father's a plain damned fool. But go ahead. Do what you want. I have no idea whether I can get away or not. I have a life of my own, you know. My God! It was good of you to let me in on this mess. Thank you."

And then "good-by," she supposed, looking back at it, but his tone left her uncertain of his having concluded with even so minor a pleasantry as that.

C H A P T E R

XII

HOYE's first reaction to his conversation with Anne was to let Gibbs go hang himself if that was what he wanted. "I have a life of my own, God damn it!" he flung out at his secretary, a Miss Emmet, who had been taking dictation from him when they had been interrupted by the telephone. Then, in an attempt to give her some plausible context for his words, he brushed aside the pile of papers that lay on the desk before him and added: "Work isn't life. It's Hell. Why don't you go get your lunch?" It was barely noon, and Miss Emmet never left for her lunch before one, but he made his suggestion with such tragic vehemence, thrust his papers aside with such finality, that she made no protest and withdrew.

He had a life of his own, he repeated silently to himself, and for a few moments sat alone there trying to convince himself that this was true. "When Porter frowns," Louise had once said, "his features somehow all contract into an area about the size of a dime, so all you have left is a great empty waste of face," and as he rose from his desk, frowning, and walked toward the window, the accuracy of her description was never more richly demonstrated. There seemed to be only vacant face, the small features clenched inconspicuously somewhere toward its center, and when he raised his hands to his head, one might have imagined his being on the point of wrenching it loose and hurling it in featureless rage down at the street more than thirty stories below. Instead, he only massaged his temples as he gazed out over the gray harbor. A life of his own, he thought, and this was it: this city, this view, his clubs, his cottage on Long Island, the slightly amused respect of men whom with no amusement whatever he profoundly respected. It was a life, a collection at least of bits and pieces of life, and it was his own; but if you could compare it with some tangible collection—in Long Island he collected gadgets of the Colonial era: apple-corers, wool-carders, blood-letters—it was one which, without Gibbs, without all that he had long dreamed of achieving through Gibbs, lacked precisely that piece which could give it focus and meaning, which could prevent its remaining simply an assemblage of odds and ends. All that he had collected about him thus far, he never more profoundly realized, had value only as a setting for the personage who he had hoped someday, through Gibbs, to become. And now Gibbs had deserted him.

For a long time Hoye had, of course, feared that this might happen, but that had in no sense armed him against the eventuality. On the contrary, it was the very familiarity of the nightmare that struck the deepest notes of horror in him—this nightmare which he had known for so long in anticipation that he felt helplessly sensitive to all of its most extravagant ramifications now that it had arrived. Down to the last detail, Hoye knew what he stood to lose by Gibbs's move, and, worst of all, it was a move on which he had never been consulted, of which he had never even been informed except almost accidentally by his old friend's daughter. He saw himself as having been deprived of the right to attend his own execution; and once more, standing there by his office window, he tried to disassociate himself from the whole affair, to see it as Gibbs's execution, not his own, and again to say in effect good riddance. Let Gibbs hang himself if that was what he wanted; he, Porter Hoye, had a life of his own apart.

He returned to his desk and bravely, vaguely, leafed through his papers in an effort to simulate a man to whom nothing untoward had happened. He regretted having dismissed Miss Emmet, and rang for her only to be informed that she had gone out for lunch. "Dear Gussy!" he called into the intercom, "does everybody around here start feeding at noon?" Then for the first time he actually stopped to consider what Anne had called to propose— that he accompany her and Tripp to Washington and try to persuade Gibbs to change his mind.

It was absurdly more than Gibbs deserved, and it was absurdly unlikely to succeed. It was also a last ignominy: to trail along behind this girl and add his plea to hers. But it was also a last chance, and as such it forced him to put aside for a moment his attempt at indifference. Perhaps he should go, he thought, but the more seriously he considered this, the more determined he became to go alone if at all. "Tripp," he wrote down on the yellow pad in front of him, and then he scratched the name out before the ink of it was dry. To follow in Anne's wake would be humbling enough, but to follow in Tripp's as well was more than he was prepared to endure: Tripp who had had the idiocy to suggest that Gibbs might be right to give up, as Anne had reported it; Tripp, who more than anyone else had been responsible for the whole nightmare from the beginning. With a superb sense of relief, Hoye found the entire weight of his anger and humiliation shifted from Gibbs to this boy who had undermined Gibbs; and without further hesitation he decided not only to go to Washington and to go independently, but to go in time to get there before the others did. He would get to Gibbs before Anne could make matters worse with her emotional blundering and, most crucial of all, before Tripp.

Hoye was able to secure passage on a plane that would land him in the capital a good hour, he judged, before the others were to arrive, and one way or the other that would be time enough. An hour, he grimly thought as he adjusted his homburg squarely on his great head and pulled on his gloves, would be more than adequate either to win his case with Gibbs or to lose it. It occurred to him as he closed the door of his office behind him that when he saw it again, if in the meantime he had lost with Gibbs, its four walls would constitute the outermost limits of the only life left him, a life insurmountably remote from that rare and exalted one to which Gibbs alone might have gained him access. Hoye was not a man given to displays of self-pity, but as he stood out on the cold street hailing a taxi, he felt old and shaken.

Thus it was that the two attacks were planned, Anne's and Hoye's, and although they were unco-ordinated with one another, each was committed to the same objective, which was Gibbs's peace of mind, if you could call it that; and indeed it had been with a kind of peace that Gibbs had arrived in Washington that morning and gone directly to his hotel to pass the twenty-four hours still remaining before his appointment with the President the next day. He had taken precautions that no one should know of his arrival except the hotel management, and with them he had left word that in the unlikely event of anyone's trying to reach him by telephone or any other means, they were simply to take messages and say that he would be unavailable all day. So he had settled down there in that little suite of rented rooms secure in the anticipation of what seemed an almost infinite amount of time during which there was nothing whatever to do but to take stock, perhaps: to review and evaluate with the curious detachment of a traveler between trains all that had led up to the decision of which he had written in confidence to Anne. As if to impose a kind of order on his thinking, he had sat down at a desk with a pen in his hand, his journal open before him, and before long had found himself writing there in his small, even script: "There is of course no tracing a human decision to its source. You might as well try to trace the source of a wave," which would be a process, he had supposed, of breasting your way back through a nearly endless series of earlier waves until you reached at last an original swell of sea so vast and diffuse that it could no longer be distinguished from the very sea itself. When you came right down to it, Gibbs had concluded, the announcement that he had made in his letter to Anne was not so much the result of a decision whose history stretched far back into his past but, rather, the cause of one. Nothing that he could think his way back to struck him as half so crucial as those words that he had written—so well ordered, so gracious, so convincing an expression of a possible course of action that he could not now bring himself to undercut it by acting otherwise. He had skillfully written his daughter that for various reasons —none of which, as he reflected upon them now, seemed any longer to be irresistibly compelling—he would not accept the appointment, and precisely because he had written this way, and written well, he was resolved to act upon it. You become who you hear yourself say that you are. It amounted almost to that, Gibbs had thought, and he had written in his journal: "The man of words, as distinct from the man of action, decides to do that which he has been able best to phrase." Then he had leaned back in his chair, clasped his hands behind his head, and smiled dimly out at the strip of winter sky that had been visible through the window.

The result was that when Porter Hoye arrived several

hours later, it was like a warrior, armed to the teeth and
steeled for a battle to the death, coming upon his adver-
sary asleep in a hammock, as it were—not so much caught
off-guard as simply innocent of the knowledge that there
was anything to be on guard against. Hoye had called from
New York before he had left and, after being informed
that Mr. Gibbs would be out of reach all day, had left a
message that he was coming down immediately on a
matter of the gravest concern to them both. However,
that message was not sufficient, not even when coupled
with the arrival shortly thereafter of Anne's telegram
announcing that she and Tripp were also coming, to
arouse Gibbs to any sense of impending crisis. He guessed
that in both cases their motives in seeking him out now
now must have had to do with his decision, but so an-
esthetizing was the effect of having himself now simply
made the decision that in no very real way did it occur to
him that their intention might be to challenge him on it.
In his own mind he had passed beyond challenging, and
thus he was able to look forward to their arrival with some
curiosity, with a kind of mild irritation at being broken in
upon at a moment of such rare tranquility, but without
apprehension. In fact, as the afternoon had worn on and
he had completed a few notes on what he intended to say
to the President the next day, had finished his usual
exhaustive reading of the morning papers, he had even
found himself looking forward to their arrival with
pleasure, and it was this reaction that was dominant in

him when Hoye had made his grim entrance around half past four.

As far as Hoye was concerned, his most outrageous fears were instantly realized: there was Gibbs on the very eve of catastrophe, not even asking him why he had come but clapping him on the shoulder and ambling into the small sitting-room with him as though nothing mattered more than the mere fact of his being there, an old friend turning up unexpectedly toward the end of a tedious afternoon. Whereas Hoye himself had come dressed as if for burial—his black shoes glistening, his somber suit and necktie setting off his brick-red flush of January cold and doom—Gibbs faced him in shirtsleeves and slippers. Gibbs's smile alone was an affront, and if Hoye had only had less to lose by the gesture, he would have turned on his heel then and there and gone back. But back to where? That was precisely the question that stayed him, that forced his precarious smile in return.

"Anne spilled the beans," he said, "so I take it the party's over. *Fini*," he added, his voice cracking, and sank into an armchair, slamming his hands down on the leather arms and staring past Gibbs to the bare wall beyond him.

"I suppose that's one way of putting it." Gibbs half sat, half leaned on the edge of the desk and smiled. "Or you might say the party's just begun. I assumed Anne had told you. I would have told you myself except that I decided it would be simpler for us both if I didn't."

Hoye waved one hand impatiently as if to brush aside

the explanation. "That's water over the dam," he said. "I found out before it was too late, and that's all that matters."

"Too late for what?" Gibbs asked.

Hoye had transferred his stare from the wall to Gibbs's face, and under the unwavering yet somehow detached intensity of it, Gibbs felt ill at ease with his old friend to a greater degree than he ever had before. He felt, strangely, as though it was he rather than Hoye who was the visitor, the one to state his business and explain himself.

"What are your plans?" Hoye asked.

Gibbs laughed. "I hope you appreciate that I was under no obligation to let you up here at all."

"Knowing you," Hoye said, pressing a knuckle against his lower lip and continuing to look at Gibbs over it, "I'm sure you have reasons for what you're doing."

"I don't plan to go the the President tomorrow empty-handed, if that's what you mean," Gibbs replied.

"Let me ask you a stupid question," Hoye said. "Like the time I asked you to recite the seven-times table." He relaxed suddenly and for a moment lowered his small eyes. "Do you get any kind of kick out of the idea of seeing him tomorrow—the President? Just seeing him, I mean, regardless of what you're seeing him for?"

"Well, sir," Gibbs said. "The President's not a great conversationalist. I don't believe even his press secretary would claim that for him. In all candor, he's not a man I'd ordinarily go out of my way to spend half an hour with, any more than he would for me. We just don't have minds that particularly interest each other. But in so far as he's President, yes," Gibbs said, raising his chin and looking directly at Hoye. "I have enough sense of history to be impressed with the idea of seeing him tomorrow. If that answers your question."

"It does," Hoye said. "I wonder if you've stopped to consider that you'll probably never see him again, or any other President for that matter—that this is the last time you'll ever be able to move around this city like a king, with no doors barred to you, enjoying the kind of *carte blanche* you've been used to for the last fifteen years or so. If you give the whole thing up, that is."

"Just look at this face of mine," Gibbs said, and this time he was aware of the affront implicit in the smile with which he answered Hoye, who sat there frowning up at him, all hunched over on his deep chair with his nicotine-stained fingers restless on its arm. "It's a face that's all worn out and old from looking at Presidents. I've not only thought what it means to give them up, but it's a thought I rejoice in. You know that, you know that," he said, and his impulse was almost to go pat him consolingly on his great, worried brow as he said: "It's no use, old Porter. I'm only a shadow, and not even you can pin a shadow to the wall."

Hoye lit a cigarette and let the smoke cloud the air between them. "I knew I was a damned fool to come down here at all. I just couldn't stand to see this happening without making some kind of row."

"Egotist that I am," Gibbs said, "I don't think I would

have guessed that what became of me was anything you took so much to heart."

"That, and also what becomes of me," Hoye answered. "After all, you're the . . . " he paused for a word, and then, with an approximation of his usual self-caricaturing roar, finished with, "you're the star I've hitched my wagon to. I take that to heart, too, you know."

It was, for Gibbs, a moment of almost unparalleled poignance, for all in an instant he saw Hoye as he had never looked closely enough to see him before, saw that whereas for himself, Gibbs, his decision meant simply a shadow's slipping back easily and gratefully into shadows, for Hoye it meant nothing less than defeat. And was it, for that matter, as the result of anything even as positive as a considered decision that he was indirectly bringing his friend's defeat about, or was it simply as the result of his fundamental indifference happening to have taken the form suggested by his letter to Anne? Such at least he had managed earlier that afternoon to convince himself was the case, and now, looking back at it with Hoye sitting there in silence before him, he was appalled at his own wanton irresponsibility toward Hoye and not least of all toward himself. If to slip back into the shadows had really been a decision, he thought, he might at least in his own terms be justified in abiding by it no matter whom he injured; but if it had been less than that—a decision merely of words—he was guilty not only of killing his friend but of a kind of pointless suicide. "Porter, forgive me," he finally said. It had begun to grow dark outside, and reaching behind him, he turned on the desk lamp. "A man can get so entangled in the rhetoric of his own mind that he forgets everyone else—gets cut off, even from himself. I can't thank you enough for coming. I promise you that. It's made me try to remember who I am, and when I've remembered, then maybe I'll be able to tell you why I've got to do this, even though it means hurting as good a friend as I've ever had. You've just got to give me a little time."

"You know that Anne's on her way here, I take it," Hoye said, "and bringing Tripp with her. They ought to be arriving any time now."

Gibbs nodded. It was like some fantastic morality play, he thought, with himself, the Shadow King, meeting and holding court with the faculties of his lapsed humanity: Hoye the conscience, Anne the heart, Tripp the memory, perhaps, or whatever Tripp might be.

"Just watch out for Tripp, that's all," Hoye told him. "I called it melodrama at the time, but I think there was more truth than Anne knew in what she said about him that night of the broadcast. He can always get you stirred up, and he knows it. If I may say so, that's exactly what he's coming down for now."

"Then this time let's hope he succeeds," Gibbs said. "Really succeeds."

He excused himself then and retired to the bedroom where he remained for some time before returning, no longer in his shirtsleeves and slippers but fully dressed, the little rosette of the *Légion d'honneur* in his buttonhole.

There was some further conversation between them, but then they gradually fell into a silence imposed not by Hoye, who had begun to show signs of that combination of ebullience and querulousness characteristic of the convalescent, but by Gibbs, who stood looking out of the window so apparently absorbed by whatever he saw that when the telephone rang, he seemed at first not to have heard it, and Hoye reached forward and tapped his sleeve.

"Anne prepared me for Tripp, but not for Kuykendall," Gibbs said as he replaced the receiver. "But for Kuykendall, after all, there's no known way of preparing."

It had been Anne's idea at the last minute to bring him. Uncertain as to whether or not Hoye was planning to go, and equally uncertain as to what kind of support if any she could expect from Tripp, she had telephoned Kuykendall at the parish less than half an hour before they would have had to pick him up on their way to La Guardia Field and had explained what had happened. He had agreed then so readily to accompany them, had responded with such a young man's indifference to the startling suddenness of her project, that until they had stopped for him at The Holy Innocents, she had nearly forgotten that he was, of course, a man of seventy. But when they had met him there, he had looked scrawny-necked and brittle to her in his heavy black overcoat, and she had noticed his hands tremble as he had locked the vestry door behind them. Whatever his initial response had been, the unexpectedness of the journey that he was to take had by then clearly rattled him; and whereas in the context of his own parish he had always seemed to Anne wonderfully in command, at the airport waiting to board the plane, he had struck her as tense and bewildered. Tripp had had to fasten his seat belt for him, to reassure him that it was only a routine precaution, and when the plane had begun to take off, gathering speed as it howled down the runway, she had seen his fingers tighten on the arm of his seat, his eyes close in a kind of fierce submission. It was only as they had leveled off, circling slowly around to the west, that he had given any sign of regaining his composure. "Such is the power of the word, even the word of man," he had said, tapping Gibbs's letter against his knee, "that once it's spoken, anything can happen—even old priests hurtling off into the sunset," and Anne had followed his glance out towards the enormous conflagration of the sky.

They arrived then, the three of them, at Gibbs's suite— Anne entering first, followed by Kuykendall and Tripp— and Gibbs made no more show of welcoming them than to kiss Anne and merely smile and shake hands with the others as he ushered them all into the living-room, where Hoye, too, acknowledged their arrival cordially, but with few words. Kuykendall in his black clericals sat down stiffly between Hoye on one side and, on the other, Tripp, who, in gray flannels with a red carnation in his buttonhole, tipped himself slightly back in the desk chair, his hands in his pockets. On the couch next to Gibbs and facing the others, Anne wearing a hat looked strained and young.

"I'm as touched as I am unprepared by this meeting," Gibbs finally said at a lull in what few, disjointed exchanges there were, "but it strikes me we know each other well enough not to go on evading the fact that you're here for a purpose. Although in that connection, you know, you could really have spared yourselves the trouble of coming at all because in a thoroughly unsentimental way you would have been here with me anyway. Every man has his voices," Gibbs went on, stretching his arms out over the back of the couch and looking not quite at the three who faced him, but just above them, "and you are mine, whether I like it or not—voices that your absence can never shut out because for better or for worse I carry them around inside." And perhaps voices were all that they were, voices that could be as easily discounted as heard, but they were at least that, Gibbs thought in the little pause that he put forth as evidence that it was he who had confronted them before ever they had rallied themselves to the task of confronting him. "There are a hundred ways a man can isolate himself, but the voices remain," he said, smiling. "However, if you have anything to say to me beyond what I've already been hearing you tell me in my mind all afternoon, now's your chance."

"I don't know about everybody else, but I for one would like to hear what we've been telling you all afternoon," Dr. Kuykendall said.

"Yes," Hoye added, appropriating the remark. "Let's start with that."

Gibbs answered slowly, more as if to himself now than to them. "What each of you has been trying to tell me from the beginning, of course, is who I am . . . " and if he had not attended their voices before, he did so now, and each of them, as he listened, defined him in part—as the father of a daughter, for instance, of Anne, who sat there beside him as uncomfortable in the crooked little velvet band of her hat as in this situation which she had created but was now at a loss to control; who seemed almost totally estranged from him now by the queerness not only of the moment, but of all the years during which her animals and the friendly, bored servants had served her as father and mother both. Yet he was her father nonetheless and could tell at a glance, if ever he had doubted it, that she was in love with Tripp; he knew that his deepest concern should be for her and that he could wish nothing more profoundly than that, for her sake, Tripp be kind. But Gibbs was unable to accept any definition of himself as simple as that because Anne's was not the only voice that he heard, and there were others telling him who, in their terms, he also was. He was Tripp's father, too, now as well as Anne's, and Gibbs strained only to catch the tone of the boy's claim, substantiated, as it was, not only by Anne's love for him, but by Rudy's death, by Sylvia's "Be good to my boy." Was it mocking or pleading, the laughter at East Harlem or the song at dusk in Louise's upstairs library? But in either case the claim was made, and Tripp's father, too, Gibbs knew himself to be, thus Tripp's friend or Tripp's enemy, to be ruined or ruin, or both at once perhaps because that was what it meant to be a father, Gibbs thought; and he glanced at the boy now, his son, who sat so easily with his chair tipped back, watching him. Next to Tripp, Kuykendall, who had said: "You are only Ansel Gibbs," but by his very presence there asked now for incomparably more, asked him to be a voice and not only a word, not to be a shadow, but to cast one, sharp and straight across history itself. Hoye, on the other hand, said only: "You're the star I've hitched my wagon to," asked only—and who knew what it had cost him to ask it, Gibbs wondered—"Remember me."

"In other words," Gibbs said, "you've all been telling me the same thing. You each put it differently, but it all adds up to the same. You say, 'Be who we think you are.' " He passed again for a moment, glancing at Kuykendall, who had asked the question. "The truth of it is I'm afraid I can only be who I am."

"But who can you be apart from who you've been to the four of us?" Kuykendall asked. "Heaven knows, between us we must have had you running pretty much the whole gamut. What self can you possibly have except for the one you've shared with us and that we've come to know you by?"

"You force me to say it, sir. I've never shared myself," Gibbs said. "I don't want to sound ridiculous or tragic, and I know I sound a little of both, but the self I've had to come to terms with alone, the self that's forced me to make this decision you're all down here to challenge me with— I've already said this to you," he interjected to Hoye, "and written it to Anne—I couldn't share it even if I wanted to because it's almost without substance—like a shadow. It's not yes and not no. It doesn't love or hate, accept or reject. It sits on the sidelines. It looks on you— even *you*," he repeated, including them all in his gesture, "and remains appallingly unmoved."

"Do you think there's any one of us here who hasn't always known that about you?" Anne asked.

Gibbs turned to his daughter so suddenly that it was as if she had struck him, and for a long moment no one said anything.

"Then how can you in conscience, knowing that, try to persuade me I'm wrong to back out of this job now—that I'm mistaken to give it up before I've had the chance to cause something like the hurt I've already caused you, only on an immeasurably greater scale?"

"Just for your own sake, I think." Anne searched her father's face as she spoke, the little welts beneath his eyes, the straight line of his mouth drawn tight. "I don't think a person like you hurts people any more than you've ever really hurt me, but even if you do—even if you hurt the whole country or whatever you think—I'd rather that than have you hurt yourself. Because if you give up now, you'd more than hurt yourself. You'd be killing yourself. That awful letter you wrote . . . "

"I'm sure the time comes," Gibbs said, "when the best thing you can do is kill yourself. The best thing for everybody including yourself."

When Tripp spoke, just the very quality of his voice was enough to set him instantly apart from the others. It was a tenor where theirs were baritones, Anne's almost a whisper. He spoke with a kind of reedy fluency and directly, exclusively to Gibbs, his smile, too, aimed at Gibbs alone. "You know when it comes to suicide," he said, "I think I have a sort of priority on the subject—it's in my blood, you might say. And what I want to say, sir, is that I think you're absolutely right. I think the time *does* come when the best thing a man can do is kill himself, and as far as I'm concerned that time came for you whenever it was you first thought of writing Anne this famous letter we all seem to have read. But all you did then was write the letter, and now the time for suicide is past. Take it from an expert. In other words, when the chips were down, you decided to stick it out with the rest of us. You decided not to turn on the gas, but to live instead, only now you want to somehow have your cake and eat it, too. You want to reap all the benefits of being alive and dead both."

"And are you still so young you think that's impossible?" Gibbs asked.

"Of course it's possible. You just have to look around you. The streets are crawling with zombies, with the living dead. Except that in your case it seems like such a rotten waste—the waste of a life that could really have made some kind of sense, or the waste of what would have been a real beauty of a death."

Porter Hoye, who had been lighting a cigarette, threw the burning match to the floor and ground it under his toe. "My God, what are you telling him to do!" he asked. "To go home and blow his brains out like your father?"

"I'm telling him he could do worse," Tripp said.

"Don't worry, Porter," Gibbs said, smiling. "Old zombies never die—the boy's right. And I'm the kind of person who always lives to tell the tale anyway. It's probably just what I deserve."

"Then why not for once not tell it?" Kuykendall suddenly asked, interrupting Hoye, who had started to speak. "Don't, for once, let your life be just a tale you tell, just words following words and never really involving you. Why, you are—" and Kuykendall stopped there for a moment, staring at him in real perplexity, "you are— Ansel Gibbs," he finished finally with all the wonder of discovery. "There's no mistaking it. That's exactly who you are. I would have known you anywhere. And we meet," he went on. "Precisely at this moment, which is the only moment that counts, of course—now, in this particular room, and I say to you . . . go," he pronounced the word quickly and lightly, "go and *be* Ansel Gibbs. Make acts your words, and speak out to the nations because that way salvation lies—not salvation for the nations, perhaps, because after all, you're only Ansel Gibbs, but certainly salvation for you."

"You're all making it too complicated," Hoye broke

in again. "You're getting the whole thing muddled, and that's where the trouble started in the first place. There's nothing complicated here at all, Ansel. Either you take this job your whole life's been building up to and make a go of it, or you throw it over and start going to seed somewhere. It's as simple as that. Face the facts, that's all I ask. Just face the damned facts."

"Either that," Anne said, "or just throw us all out of here and do whatever you want. It's his life," she said, touching Gibb's hand but turning to the others. "It's my father's life, and maybe the best thing he can do is throw us all out."

"That would be the easiest thing," Tripp said, "and it would keep on being easy from then on out. You know that," he went on, nodding to Gibbs. "Think how easy it'll be to go to the White House tomorrow, for instance. Word will have gotten around you're coming, of course, and there'll be reporters lying in wait for you, and photographers . . . the works. But you're used to all that kind of thing, God knows, and nobody can handle it better. Then there'll be just you and the great man alone in his office—everything quiet and easy the way you like it. Just a clock ticking somewhere, and maybe a little snow blowing around outside. You'll sit there facing him and talk about your health, which a man of your age has to start thinking about, and your personal obligations. You'll tell him you're deeply honored by the trust he's put in you, but circumstances being what they are . . . And then for a couple of minutes when you've stopped talking, it may

seem to that famous, busy man that something unspeak-
ably too bad has happened. But he's got a whole country
to run after all. Meetings, memoranda, speeches. He'll
thank you regretfully with an extra warm shake of your
hand, and that will be that. As easy as tripping over a
croquet wicket with a loaded gun over your arm," Tripp
said, "only it doesn't make the same kind of sense. It
lacks fire. It lacks the touch of a master."

Gibbs had been looking at Tripp intently throughout
his speech, yet when it was finished he made no immediate
answer, but continued to look at him for a few moments
more, his chin high, his face slightly flushed. "You're a
young man of staggering presumption," he said. "My
daughter and these two old friends I've known for years,
I'm beholden to them in countless ways, and they have
every right to be here now and to state their case however
they choose. But you and I are strangers. If I ever owed
you anything for your father's sake, I've certainly paid in
full before this. You have no rights here whatever. You've
laughed at me before, and there's laughter in what you've
just been saying now. I needn't tolerate it. You understand that. Who are you to be my judge? And I challenge
you as a member of my jury. So there's only one thing left
for me to say."

He paused for a moment, and his head trembled slightly
with his effort to hold it perfectly steady. There was none
of them who had failed to see what was coming, and Hoye
sat there inanely nodding his head more and more deeply
as if to hasten the words from him, yet when at last they

came, even Hoye was stunned, and all of them except Tripp avoided looking either at Gibbs or at one another.

"I have no words," Gibbs said, "to express how profoundly distasteful I find your presence here. You have no place with us here or with me, and no right. I ask you please to get out."

Before Gibbs had finished, Tripp had risen to his feet and stood facing him. There was an unprecedented self-consciousness in his stance, and for the first time he seemed to lose control over his face. His attempt to smile failed entirely, and before speaking he gave a quick, unguarded glance about the room as if in search of something more sure than words with which to answer Gibbs. "When my father before me incurred your distaste, I believe you had your secretary tell him so," he said. "I appreciate your dealing with me directly."

"I'm going," he added and took a step toward Anne, who was still sitting on the couch beside her father. In front of the couch there was a low coffee table, which Tripp leaned over then, bending down to kiss her good-by. As he had approached, Gibbs had also risen to his feet, and suddenly at this point he reached out with both hands, grabbed Tripp by the shoulders, and with all his strength tried to push him away. Caught completely off-guard by the force of Gibbs's thrust and pitched awkwardly forward as he already was, Tripp lost his balance, and instead of simply stumbling off to the side, he tried to recover by a quick lunge of his whole body in Gibbs's direction. The result of this was that he lost his footing altogether and went crashing down on top of the table with his full weight, hitting his head on the table's edge as he fell. He tried to pull himself to his feet and then slumped into a sitting position there on the floor, his red hair darkening with blood above the right temple where the skin had been broken, his eyes narrowed and his mouth slightly ajar as he rubbed his hand up and down his long chin.

Anne and Hoye had both leaped up to help him, but they were prevented by Gibbs, who had instantly gone down on one knee beside Tripp where he remained now with his hands on the boy's shoulders. "That's all right now," Gibbs repeated several times, "That's all right," and then, as Anne came back with a damp towel from the bathroom and began to wipe Tripp's head, Gibbs spoke to Kuykendall, who had not moved from his chair. "What do you think it means now to *be* Ansel Gibbs?"

"That's for you to answer," the old man replied.

"You look awful," Hoye said, putting one hand under Gibbs's arm and helping him to his feet. "You'd better go lie down." Once Gibbs was standing, he staggered slightly and sat down heavily on the couch. "Put your head down between your knees," Hoye told him.

Tripp shook himself, pushed Anne gently aside, and got up. "This is no time for elaborate farewells," he said. "Having provided the floor show, I'll be on my way." As he spoke, he glanced down at Gibbs's bowed head and then started for the door, when Gibbs looked up, his face flushed, his eyes glistening.

"No, stay," he said.

"I think we'd better all go," Anne said, walking to Tripp with the towel in her hand.

"My God, what a nightmare!" Hoye stood there with one hand on his cheek, holding a cigarette in the other, and shook his head slowly from side to side.

"It would be a worse one for him to be left alone," Kuykendall said.

"He said himself he had his voices," Anne said. "Our voices telling him who he is. Don't you?" she asked her father. "He wants us to leave him alone."

"You know, Tripp," Gibbs said, "you can go it alone just so far." There was a curiously unguarded, almost dreaming air about him as he spoke, as if he could not hear what he himself was saying and was listening only for whatever Tripp might make of it. "Then you either join up somewhere or pay the penalty for desertion."

Tripp came back slowly and sat down beside him. "There's a penalty for joining up, too, of course," he said.

"The penalty," Kuykendall broke in, "is that you rend your garments and curse the day you were born."

"Look here," Hoye interrupted, stepping between Gibbs and Kuykendall. "I don't know what they're talking about. There's no penalty with this job. Only honor. Honor, responsibility, and power—and power you'll use a damned sight better than most. So face the facts and take it. I'm telling you this for your own sake, Ansel, not for mine. I have a life of my own, after all."

"Perhaps nobody has a life of his own," Gibbs said.

Anne dabbed at Tripp's head with a corner of the

towel. "You look like Banquo's ghost," she said. Gibbs reached out and took his hand, shaking it.

"I wish that along with apologizing, I could believe that nothing like this would happen again," Gibbs said. "I think if I could ever manage to define fully the relationship between us, I'd know all there is to know about myself. All I do know is that there's something about you that makes me always have to meet you head on. I can't detour around you by any of the ordinary routes of indifference or rejection. I don't know why. So we're bound to keep meeting head on, you and I—and more and more now as the years go by—and every time I collide with you, I collide with a part of myself, too. Lord knows where it's all going to end, but I for one wouldn't have things any different. How about you, Tripp? Will you accept things this way?"

"It's the way things are for me, too," Tripp said, smiling, "so I really don't have any choice. You'll be a hell of a father-in-law, but I'm no pushover myself—except maybe literally every once in a while. I accept."

"Bloody but unbowed," Anne said.

"And what about tomorrow?" Hoye asked Gibbs. It was no less a plea than a question, and for once he let it escape him as such, his voice so unusually low-pitched and quiet, so without his customary roar which tended to make all his questions rhetorical, that the four of them turned to him as though a stranger had spoken.

"As to that," Gibbs said slowly, "grant me at least the illusion of changing my own mind—more than the illusion," he added, inhaling deeply, "of changing more than my mind."

Kuykendall sat with his fingertips together and his chin just touching them. He stared at Gibbs as though he had been doing so for centuries and only now at last, in this hotel room on this January evening, had found the word for which he had been searching.

"Go," he said. "I speak with authority."

C H A P T E R
XIII

Louise von Louwe's original plan had been to have a celebration at the new house in Washington and to invite a number of people from all of their worlds—her own and Gibbs's, Anne's and Tripp's—but circumstances forced her to change her mind, and what she was finally reduced to was cocktails and dinner for eight in New York. "The four of us, including Mr. Tripp," she had said to Walter that morning, counting them off on her fingers, "which leaves the thumb." She crooked it slowly up and down as she stood there in the sunlit dining-room, thinking. "Mr. Hoye. Five. And Dr. Kuykendall is six, and Mr. Tripp's mother and stepfather, the Ed Mullers, makes eight. It's just the hard, bitter core, but it will have to do. My first thought had been for something a little more baroque."

The party was to have a double function—to celebrate not only Gibbs's appointment but also Anne's engagement to Tripp—and in both respects it seemed best to her to keep it small. She had reached this decision by reminding herself that as Gibbs's official hostess it was no longer possible for her to entertain more than a few people at a time, because the alternatives were either to expand her list to include a great many more than she actually wanted or to expand it to include only those whom she did want and thus to risk giving offense to others at a moment when she felt that it was particularly expedient not to do so, determined as she was at this early point in Gibbs's new career to do as well by him as she possibly could. So on the basis of this she reduced the number of guests to eight, and then she decided to move the whole affair to New York, "because when you come right down to it," she told Porter Hoye, "it's the only place I can take seriously. I wouldn't feel that an engagement announced anywhere else really counted—like a Mexican divorce or confession under torture." Neither Anne nor Tripp had wanted a large party anyway, she went on to say, and as for celebrating Gibbs's appointment, this had already been done in the form of a reception in his honor at the White House several weeks earlier, so that he might be said to have already fared as well as he could quite apart from anything that she was or was not able to do for him in addition now.

Two days after his meeting at the hotel in Washington with Anne, Tripp, and his friends, Gibbs had appeared before the Senate committee and there answered all objections raised against him. The committee's members unanimously recommended to the Senate that his appointment be confirmed, and for three hours the Senate debated the issue. All the objections which had arisen since his nomination by the President almost two weeks before were reviewed again, and in this Senator Farwell played a leading part. He read selections from a transcript of Tripp's broadcast and pointed out once more that since Gibbs by his own admission did not believe that either legal or ethical principles could ever be permanently valid, his policies were bound to be weak and vacillating as a result. He also questioned whether Gibbs had anything more than a kind of cold competence for the job, a Wall Streeter's impersonal view of men and history which might enable him to execute policy adequately, but showed him painfully lacking in the imagination and the heart to formulate it. The Senator finally drew attention to what he called Gibbs's "fancy talking . . . the gobbledygook that keeps coming out so thick and fast that when you try to pin him down to something you know he's said, he can always claim he said just the opposite, and ten to one that's in there somewhere, too." But, as one newspaper expressed it: "If Gibbs is ever devious, it is a deviousness too subtle for the average human eye," and on these, perhaps, or other grounds, the Senate eventually made its own decision and confirmed the appointment by a vote of eighty to nine.

Apart from one short trip to the ranch in Montana and a brief return to New York, Gibbs had remained in Washington ever since, moving out of the Mayflower into the large, yellow house on Kalorama Road which Louise had quickly succeeded in finding for them. Resigning from her job with Kuykendall, Anne had come down to join them there, and Porter Hoye also occupied one of its

high-ceilinged bedrooms for the few days that it took him
to find a suitable apartment for himself near by. He continued to spend one or two days each week at his New York
office, but devoted the rest of his time to working with
Gibbs as Assistant Secretary on the various problems of
reorganization that faced them during those first days of
their incumbency. Hoye also applied himself to helping
Louise von Louwe with her job of staffing and decorating
the new house, and in this, as in his assignment with
Gibbs, there was no detail too insignificant to escape his
dictum. He interviewed cooks and economic analysts, and
was as authoritative in his opinions concerning curtains
for the library windows as in his most labored memoranda
to Gibbs on the subject of departmental policy.

All in all, he threw himself into the new life provided
him by Gibbs's victory with such voracity and hoarse
enthusiasm that seldom, even in his increasingly rare opportunities for solitary introspection, did he admit to himself, let alone to anyone else, that there was something
that thieved him of full triumph. That is to say, whenever
he considered how close Gibbs had come to not accepting
the appointment at all, the triumph that *was* intermittently staggered under his knowledge of the failure that
so nearly might have been. It was true that in the end
Gibbs's rational self, as Hoye saw it, had been victorious,
but what nevertheless continued to haunt him was his
view of it as a victory in which he himself had played almost no part. Heaven only knew by what obscure process
Gibbs had finally decided to change his mind; Hoye knew

only that his own words seemed to have been without effect. This was not only sad and humiliating but also caused him the darkest apprehensions. If Gibbs had not listened to him once, there was no reason for believing that he would listen to him again. In the hotel room that Sunday afternoon, Hoye had confronted him with a simple choice between success and failure—with the facts, in other words—but Gibbs had come to his decision in some unholy realm beyond the facts, some realm where Tripp and Kuykendall, where even Anne, had seemed better able to follow than he, Hoye. Thus if ever Gibbs should show signs of being about to relapse—of being about to retreat again into that world of shadow and half-light which Hoye had so come to fear—the only people who could so much as attempt to save him would be those who were themselves able to deal with more or less than facts. That meant, of course, people like Kuykendall, Anne, and Tripp, who had bungled into rescuing him this once; but Kuykendall was an eccentric if not a downright fanatic, Anne was an emotional child, Tripp was the Barefoot Boy in the Brooks Brothers suit, and God forbid, Hoye thought, that they should be left with the job again. But if not they, who else? Certainly not himself, Hoye knew, and there was the frightening worst of it. If Gibbs was the star that he had at last successfully hitched his wagon to, it was a star whose course he was unable either to foresee or to control.

Hoye found no way of resolving this problem, but for the most part he managed quite well to thrust it out of his mind altogether. At least for the present he had, as Assistant Secretary, all that he had long dreamed of having, and then there was also so mercifully much to do that he had time for little else but to storm around Washington with his small eyes fever-bright, his great face flushed, as he breathed deep and hard of the anesthetic of doing it. "He attacks everything with such thunderous energy," Louise told Anne, "that most of the time I find myself caught up in it with him. When he's around, I can't go upstairs to the water closet without the sense of charging San Juan Hill. But every once in a while, I get a glimpse of him out of the corner of my mind, so to speak —that enormous bald head and that scrawny little neck. It's as if he unscrewed at the collar and had jelly beans inside. Dear Porter."

But Louise was the first to agree that they were jelly beans of the highest quality. He was invaluable to her in any number of ways, and never more so than on the occasion of her party in New York, flying up with her and Anne the Saturday before, going with them to meet Sylvia and her husband shortly after their arrival from Savannah later that day, and taking them all, with Tripp, to dinner at the University Club, where Sylvia, all in dove gray with white frills at her throat and wrists, had sat between Tripp and Anne, a hand of each in hers, and had spoken with increasing sentiment of this magical flowering of an old friendship until Hoye, to Louise's profound gratitude, had boomed out loudly enough to penetrate even Sylvia's deafness that they must all save their tears for the wedding and in the meanwhile bottoms up and the Devil take the hind-most. Slowly and unconsciously releasing her son's hand then and Anne's, she had floundered there for a few moments as the conversation passed her by, and only after a sudden warmth of relief at knowing that she had been spared the necessity of somehow bringing her little address to a conclusion was able to turn her thoughts to the subject that more than any other had caused her anxiety since she had first heard that there was to be such a party. She so wanted, that was, for Ed Muller to make a good impression on these friends of her youth, particularly on Ansel Gibbs.

As soon as she had decided several weeks before that she would make the trip at all, she had driven him all the way up the coast to Charleston because there was a tailor there who had worked for the New York firm which had made Rudy's suits twenty years earlier, and "Something single-breasted for a change, and dark, and a hat that's not all brim, and a Chesterfield," she had said as Ed had stood there stout and powder blue among the long mirrors. He was a gentle man, used to letting her have her own way even when it was not his inclination to do so, but on this occasion he was positively grateful for her intervention, the more so as it would have been a matter of pride with him not to have sought her advice on the subject himself. He was as eager as she was for him to meet such a man as Gibbs on his own ground, as an equal, and if driving a hundred miles and spending two hundred dollars for a blue serge suit with sloping, unpadded shoulders and a vest that cramped his breathing was the price which at her recommendation he was to pay, he still felt that he had swung a bargain. "Only don't throw a fit, Mammy," he had told her in his slow, Georgian bass, "if you catch me slipping out of these shoes all of a sudden. Hell, they know we don't go in for them much down home anyway," and to Sylvia's satisfaction he and Gibbs seemed to take to each other as soon as Tripp first introduced them in Louise's upstairs library at cocktails on Sunday evening. Although Ed Muller was actually two years Gibbs's junior, with his white hair and creased, tan face he looked ten years older as they stood there talking about the textile industry. "It's the different kind of lives they've led," Sylvia said to Tripp. "Ansel's always had easy going, but Ed's had to slave every inch of the way. But I don't know why I'm standing here talking to you," she added. "I'm going to go over and start babying that darling over there."

Everyone was standing except Anne, who sat in one corner of the couch with her feet tucked under her and a gray chiffon scarf thrown loosely over her shoulders. She was grateful that it was Sylvia who had come to join her because her deafness made it unnecessary to do much more than occasionally nod or smile in the way of response. She watched all the others talking and moving about her there, yet instead of being drawn into their midst, she found herself drifting farther and farther away from them. She had taken a nap that afternoon and while she slept she had dreamed about Tripp. He had not been Tripp as she knew him, but some small object like an orange or a ball of twine which she had kept in her pocket, treasuring it and defending it, crying over it in her dream until she had finally awakened to a sensation of loss so poignant that not even the arrival of Tripp himself soon afterward had been able at first to dispel it completely. The orange was gone, her pockets empty, and she told him about the dream as though nothing else mattered so much. "I loved you so, even as an orange," she had said. "I could keep you so safe that way. Just never go and die without me or anything, that's all, or let me without you. It didn't even matter that you were just an orange, I loved you so," to which Tripp had responded with a puff-cheeked grimace which he said was his "orange face," grabbing his knees to his chest and rolling over on his back on the foot of her bed where he had been sitting.

"Honey, nobody ever wears a thing like that unless there's a story connected with it," she heard Sylvia say to her now, sitting beside her on the couch and pointing to the pin on her dress. "Tell me about it."

"A woman named Mrs. Tyree gave it to me," Anne said. "A woman from the parish where I used to work," she repeated more loudly to Sylvia's vague laugh, the little circular wave of her hand. It was a rhinestone horse-shoe surrounding a green glass four-leaf clover across which in tiny letters ran the words "Good Luck." Anne unpinned it and handed it to Sylvia.

"A colored woman who keeps about a dozen dogs," she said. "She came to say good-by when she heard I was leaving to get married, and gave me this."

Sylvia smiled. "He's just like his father," she said, handing it back. "Rudy was always producing little horrors like that, too."

It was her last morning at the Holy Innocents that Mrs. Tyree had come. She had at last been granted the loan to buy a pair of shoes and shuffled into the office wearing them. They were a yellowish tan with a design stamped into the toes and had low heels and fringed tongues that flapped out over the instep. She had stayed too long and talked too much, had borrowed the office telephone to call the Legal Aid Society which she was trying to enlist to help her establish her claim to a small piece of property in Tennessee which she said a nephew had stolen, and then went on into all her life's troubles in general, reciting them in an almost roguish way as though they constituted a private joke which she and Anne shared together. And then with no change of tone she had shifted the subject to marriage, specifically at last to Anne's, and to Anne's departure, whereupon she had reached down into a deep paper bag full of scraps for her dogs and had pulled out the pin wrapped up in a pink Kleenex. "Reverend," she had said, giving it to her, "in this world you need as much luck as you can get, especially if it's good," and soon afterward she had left, but not before borrowing the telephone again to call an employment agency to which Anne had heard her describe herself as thirty-nine years

old and an experienced baby nurse. The whole interview
had lasted for somewhat more than an hour, but eager as
Anne had been at the time to bring it to an end and to get
back to her mimeographing, once it was over, she remembered it vividly for days. She marveled at the ease with
which she had been able to leave not only Mrs. Tyree but
the parish as a whole for good, and wondered why she had
ever gone to work there in the first place. She could not
remember ever having come to a definite decision about
it—or about any other important step in her life, it occurred to her; only the unimportant ones—but decided
that she must have begun as thoughtlessly as now she
finished. And what had she accomplished, she wondered,
and what was it possible for anyone to accomplish there?
Probably nothing except perhaps your own damnation, as
Kuykendall again and again seemed to imply; but once she
had left, she was pained by the pain that she had not felt in
leaving. What could you do about Mrs. Tyree, she asked
herself, and for a time she had contemplated going to see
her again or inviting her to come to see her at Aunt
Louise's. But in the end, she had decided, there was nothing you could do but wear the pin that she had given you.
Except, as Sylvia said, it was a little horror. But there was
nothing you could do but wear it, and she took it now and
pinned it to her dress once more.

"Good luck," Sylvia said, watching her, and then as
Tripp passed near them on his way to the bar table which
Walter had set up between two of the French windows
with their hangings of heavy rose damask, she reached out

and held him by his sleeve long enough to whisper to him
not to drink too much and disgrace them all.

Above the bar was a large, ornately framed gilt mirror
in which Tripp caught sight of himself as he was putting
ice in his glass. He had had a number of cocktails at lunch
with the Mullers and several more after leaving rehearsal
to come up to Louise von Louwe's later that afternoon,
so that as a consequence he was able to look at his own
reflection now with the curious detachment that comes
with drinking—this face that was not entirely his face
staring at him from the dark, flecked glass. "And who the
Hell are you?" he asked softly with no one close enough to
overhear him. He went to the piano and setting his full
glass down on the India shawl that covered it, started to
play not loudly enough to make any of them stop to listen,
but quietly, scraps of musical comedy strung loosely together and originating more in his fingers than his mind.
He watched Anne and his mother talking side by side on
the couch, Hoye showing Kuykendall something in the
newspaper which he held out before them with an expression of concentrated distaste, Gibbs and Ed Muller,
Louise passing heavy-footed and slightly disheveled among
them with a silver bowl of ripe olives; and it was like the
last chapter of an Oz book, Tripp thought, with the most
divergent characters who had seldom if ever met all at
once before coming together at last—the Patchwork girl
and the Spider King, Jack Pumpkinhead, Glinda the
Good, and the Wizard. And I am the Wizard, he thought,
master of disguise and the ad-lib incantation.

For which of them here had seen through his deceptions, he asked himself, except at isolated moments perhaps, and one at a time? Such a moment had occurred at lunch that day with Sylvia, once Ed had left them for a meeting down-town and she had laid her hand on his arm and said: "Son, hear me a minute. You're getting married, and you're your father's son, and now I'm going to tell you the worst thing your father ever did, although maybe the worst of all was telling me about it later." It was during their court-ship, Sylvia had said, when she was spending the year with her relations in Boston and Rudy was still an undergradu-ate at Harvard. Louise von Louwe was also in Boston working as a volunteer for the Red Cross, and through her relationship to Corinne, who was on her way to being engaged to Rudy's friend Ansel Gibbs, they had all known each other. "Louise had this beau," Sylvia had gone on, "the love of her life, I guess, though heaven only knows why. He was a fat, pink boy, older than the rest of us, and everybody called him Piggy. I can't even remember his last name, but he has only a C.P.A., although of course Louise's family always had loads of money, so that couldn't have mattered less. Anyway, he joined up while the war was still on and got sent to France, and then, that winter, word came through that he'd died of pneumonia in the trenches. We all thought it was going to kill Louise be-cause it had been arranged that she was going to become Mrs. Piggy and everything as soon as he came back, and she was that crazy about him. Everybody was so sorry for her we could have died, and especially your father. He didn't have the deepest heart in the world, if you know what I mean, but it was one of the kindest. So one evening he went over to where Louise was staying to offer his condolences in person, and that's when it happened. Something borrowed, something blue," she had interrupted herself for a moment then. "Something old, and something new. Maybe that's why I'm telling you this. Something old and blue, both. And it's also something you should know, Son.

"They were all alone, just the two of them. She told him all about Piggy and how she didn't know if she could live without him. She never had much in the way of looks, Louise, but she was young in those days and she had always been lots of fun, so when she started to cry on your father's shoulder and tell him he was the only one who understood what she was going through, he didn't know what to do next. She begged him to stay with her, and he was afraid to go in case she might do something terrible if he did. So he stayed, and he ended up staying all night, and sometime before he left the next morning, he went to bed with her. He told me that himself. He made love to her that night in bed with the tears all over her face because he felt sorry for her and wanted to comfort her. Those were his own words. And you can imagine what a comfort it was. He was the handsomest boy I've ever seen to this day or ever before, and, of course, she fell in love with him. Everybody knew it, and so did he, but he didn't give a hoot for her. He kept on being sweet and kind to her after that because he never could be anything else even if he tried, but he somehow made it clear just by *being* sweet and kind that she really didn't mean anything to him and the best thing to do about the whole affair was to forget it. But I tell you Louise couldn't forget it, and I don't think she ever has."

It was clear, once she had finished her account, that she was hard put to find some reason for having given it at all. From the intensity with which she had told it, her hand tight on her son's sleeve and her face bent close to his, she had lapsed then into a kind of pensive vagueness. Tripp had half expected her to draw an analogy between this affair of his father's with Louise and his own with Anne— to warn him of possibly marrying her now out of something like pity and thus bringing misery down on them both. Or he had thought that perhaps she might use the incident in order to make some general admonition concerning the moral necessity of simply remaining faithful to Anne now that he had committed himself to her, forgoing the lusts with which, from the occasion that had resulted in his being dispatched to Kitten Dory, she felt that she was well acquainted. But she had said neither of these, and instead, unconsciously patting her gray-blonde hair in such a way as to cover the cord of her hearing-aid, she had raised her chin high, smiling, and said: "Well, there it is, Robin. I hand it over to you. You'll have to do whatever you can with it now because it's yours."

So in just that way, Tripp thought, playing the piano now in Louise's darkly hung, Victorian tent of a library, his mother had for a moment at least outwizarded him—

instinctively rather than purposely, because she had without a doubt told the tale for no more penetrating reason,
he felt, than that after seeing Louise again for the first
time in so many years, it was simply and irresistibly in her
to tell. But the result was the same. The tale became the
measure for him of many things. Just as Rudy had played
the part of comforter to Louise, so he played his parts, and
he had only to look around the room from where he sat
now to know how many and varied they were: the re-
formed satyr to Sylvia, a kind of Galahad to Kuykendall,
to Louise a flattering mountebank, to Gibbs a son. And to
Anne—he winked at her above the rim of his glass which
he raised to his lips while at the same time continuing to
strum a soft bass with his left hand—to Anne he permitted
himself to play so many parts at once that perhaps, it
struck him, it amounted to not playing a part at all.

Tripp rose from the piano without finishing the measure
that he had been playing and went over to sit on the arm
of the couch by Anne. Sylvia was still beside her, and when
she started to say something to them both, he put his
finger to his lips and then, placing his palms flat on either
side of her head, turned her gently away from them. "Run
along now," he said to her, patting her on the shoulder,
and then he leaned down to speak to Anne, his mouth close
to her ear, his eyes closed.

Louise had said that it always unnerved her to see Dr.
Kuykendall without his clerical collar—"I get a sense the
world's running amuck, the way you felt as a child when
your father came to tuck you in after too much to drink"

—and he stood slightly apart from the others now in a gray suit and dark green tie, staring down at the carpet. There was something about his face—the jutting nose and chin, the firm, ruddy skin, the look almost of terror in his eyes—that seemed to give it the brilliant focus of pebbles in an icy stream. For twenty minutes he had been listening to Porter Hoye's pontifications on the subject of New York machine politics, and, left briefly alone now, he thought back on the events of that morning. Leaving The Holy Innocents in charge of an assistant, he had gone to General Seminary, where it had been his intention to preach on the Genesis account of the call of Abraham, on the commitment of faith as it concerned the young divinity students who had crowded into the chapel in their black gowns to hear him. But, as usual, he had found himself leaving his outline so frequently that at last he had left it altogether and stood there with his hands trembling on the heavy leather Bible, his voice now almost inaudibly low, now strident, saying: "If anybody starts talking to me about religious commitment, I may listen politely, but what I'd like to answer him with is a few monosyllables that don't bear repeating here in the midst of the holy community. If you tell me Christian commitment is a thing that has happened to you once and for all like some kind of spiritual plastic surgery, I say go to, go to, you're either pulling the wool over your own eyes or trying to pull it over mine. Every morning you should wake up in your beds and ask yourself: 'Can I believe it all again today?' No, better still, don't ask it till after you've read *The New*

York Times, till after you've studied that daily record of the world's brokenness and corruption, which should always stand side by side with your Bible. Then ask yourself if you can believe in the Gospel of Jesus Christ again for that particular day. If your answer's always Yes, then you probably don't know what believing means. At least five times out of ten the answer should be No because the No is as important as the Yes, maybe more so. The No is what proves you're a man in case you should ever doubt it. And then if some morning the answer happens to be really Yes, it should be a Yes that's choked with confession and tears and . . . great laughter. Not a beatific smile, but the laughter of wonderful incredulity."

Once the service was over, instead of standing at the chapel door and shaking hands with the faculty and students as they came filing out, he had excused himself, hurried out of his robes, and taken a taxi back to East Harlem. He had been lunching on crackers and milk in his office at the church there when Honey Gruber had called to tell him about Inez Rosas. She had left her baby in its basket in the kitchen when she had gone out for an hour or so to help Honey clean up one of the Sunday-school rooms after the class there that morning. A neighbor had promised to look in on the baby from time to time while she was gone, but when Inez had returned, she had found it dead. Not fully aware of what had happened, she had run the few blocks to Honey's apartment with the child in her arms, and there Kuykendall had found them when he arrived a few minutes after Honey's call. Inez Rosas was slumped, unconscious, against the day bed. Honey was scrubbing a portion of the floor near by, and still on her knees, her plump face gray, she had explained to him what had taken place. Inez had fainted while still holding the baby, and it was only then that Honey had discovered what had caused its death. Taking it out of its wrapping of blood-soaked dishtowels, she had found its lower face and part of one arm lacerated almost beyond recognition. She had heard of such things happening before in the neighborhood, but this was the first time that she had actually seen a case of it herself. The cause of the child's death was clearly rat-bite, and it was her own vomit that she had been scrubbing up when Kuykendall had entered.

"Can I get you another drink, sir?" Gibbs asked at his elbow. "For the health of your soul?"

Kuykendall looked up at him with no recognition at first. Gibbs repeated his question, and Kuykendall was on the point of replying when Sylvia's voice rose high above the others. She was standing with her arm in her husband's at the other end of the room and raising her glass straight up in front of her, her speech slightly thick, called out: "A toast to the bride and groom! Long life and happiness to my two lambs!"

The toast was drunk by everyone, and in the little silence that followed it, Sylvia gave signs of gathering herself together to continue with some sort of speech when Ed Muller held up his hand and tried to indicate somehow —half bowing toward his stepson and Anne, laughingly putting his arm around Sylvia's shoulder and starting to draw her away—that in kindness to his wife it would be better at this point not to encourage her. Hoye was the one who, having already noticed her mounting hilarity, came to the rescue by turning away from them both and in his loud, matter-of-fact voice resuming the conversation that he had been having with Louise von Louwe. The others followed his example, and the moment passed.

"It looks like things have kind of piled up on Mammy," Ed Muller said quietly to Tripp a few minutes later, his arm still around Sylvia. "Having you leave the nest. Meeting all her old friends. And I have a feeling she's been a little edgy about me, too, maybe—not hitting it off with these folks, putting a couple of feet in my mouth or something. So I'm just going to get her out in the fresh air for a minute," he concluded, giving her shoulder a squeeze and looking down at her.

"Oh, Pappy darling," Sylvia said as he led her toward the door. "You're worth the whole pack of them put together. If you only knew what I know. But I wanted to toast Ansel, too, and you," she added to Louise von Louwe as they reached her on their way. "Here's to you, too, Mrs. Piggy."

"Who is Mrs. Piggy?" Anne asked, once the Mullers had left.

"As far as I know," Louise von Louwe said, "there never was such a person."

But the toast to Gibbs was eventually given, and in the end it was Dr. Kuykendall who gave it. An hour had passed during which Ed Muller had brought Sylvia back,

her face pale from the winter air, but obviously in posses-
sion of herself again. Louise von Louwe, although remarking that every human being gives off the heat of a
hundred-watt bulb, had nonetheless insisted upon Tripp's
lighting a fire in the little iron grate; and on the mantle in
the flickering light glistened a bowl of ivy whose leaves, at
Porter Hoye's advice, she had rubbed that morning with
mineral oil. Walter had already announced dinner, and
they were all about to leave the library to go downstairs to
it when Kuykendall turned with his back to the door and
said: "I drink this to you, Ansel, whoever you are, whoever you turn out to be. And to your involvement. It was
bound to happen. We are all involved, *mesdames, messieurs*. God have mercy on us." For one shattering moment
then, Louise von Louwe said later, she had half expected
him to raise his hand in benediction, but the uneasy quiet
was broken finally by Hoye—"Dear God, Louise, haven't
you got something for us to eat!"—and they proceeded to
the dining-room without further embarrassment.

Gibbs himself made no speech at all. He sat at dinner
with his face flushed, his glasses glittering in the candle-
light, and spoke to Anne about his trip to the ranch
several weeks before. The colt which he had seen born on
his last visit was already beginning to look like a genuine
horse, he told her, and soon she would have to come down
and take it out on a lunge-line. He had also looked over his
papers while he was there, his memoirs of the war, and for
one glorious half-hour, he said, he had contemplated
burning them. But ultimately he had decided to present

them to the Library of Congress instead, incomplete as they were, stipulating only that they be kept under lock and key until his death. "Or until I want them back," he went on, "which will simply mean that in one sense or another I'm dead already—or dead again. You cross your fingers and hold your tongue and do what you can in the time that's left. That is the only holy cause, my dear, ambivalence be damned. And *Pronto viene*," he added. "Is that how you say it?" When dessert was brought on and the champagne glasses filled, the conversation stopped for a moment as they all looked his way. He rose to his feet and said only, "No more words. It's a promise I've made," and then, standing there stiff and tall, he raised his glass to them.

A NOTE ON THE TYPE

The text of this book was set on the Monotype in Bodoni so called after Giambattista Bodoni (1740–1813), son of a printer of Piedmont. After gaining experience and fame as superintendent of the Press of the Propaganda in Rome, Bodoni became in 1766 the head of the ducal printing house at Parma, which he soon made the foremost of its kind in Europe. His Manuale Tipografico, completed by his widow in 1818, contains 279 pages of specimens of types, including alphabets of about thirty foreign languages. His editions of Greek, Latin, Italian, and French classics, especially his Homer, are celebrated for their typography. In type-designing he was an innovator, making his new faces rounder, wider, and lighter, with greater openness and delicacy.

The book was composed, printed, and bound by KINGSPORT PRESS, INC., *Kingsport, Tennessee. Paper manufactured by* S. D. WARREN COMPANY, *Boston.*

Designed by HARRY FORD.

A NOTE ON THE AUTHOR

Frederick Buechner was born in New York in 1926. He was educated at Lawrenceville School and Princeton University. Aside from spending two years in the army, he has taught at Lawrenceville and New York University, has continued his studies, and has accomplished considerable writing, including his widely acclaimed first novel, A LONG DAY'S DYING *(1950), a second novel,* THE SEASONS' DIFFERENCE *(1952), and the present book. Mr. Buechner is married and lives in New York.*